REAPER

A. Zavarelli

Boston Underworld #2

Playlist:

Lonely Day- System of a Down
Magnetic- Flyleaf
Your Guardian Angel- Red Jumpsuit Apparatus
Battlescars- Guy Sebastian
Say Something- A Great Big World
Boulevard of Broken Dreams- Green Day
Perfect- Pink
Animals- Maroon 5
If I Ever Leave This World Alive- Flogging Molly
Broken- Seether and Amy Lee
Angel- Theory of a Deadman
Love the Way You Lie- Eminem &Rihanna
Set me on Fire- Flyleaf
Jar of Hearts- Christina Perri
My Darkest Days- Perfect
Thread- Flyleaf
Stand by You- Marlisa
I Will Follow You into the Dark- Death Cab for Cutie
All or Nothing- Theory of a Deadman
All Around Me Flyleaf
My Demons- Starset
Stand by You- Rachel Platten

Prologue

Sasha

"I don't like you going out with that guy," Ma says.

I bend down to zip up my boots so she can't see the expression on my face.

"It's fine, Ma. I can handle him."

"I just don't understand, Sasha." She launches into another one of her tirades. "I raised you to be a good girl. You were always such a good girl. You had the smartest, brightest future ahead of you. A real chance to get out of this neighborhood and do something with your life. Now you're wrapped up with these guys…"

She glances at my sister Emily across the room as if the very mention of the word mafia might influence her too. The disappointment is plastered all over both their faces every time they see me with Blaine. They don't know why I do what I do. They've got no idea, but it's better that way.

Safer.

I squeeze my eyes shut and try to blink away the pressure behind them. *Five things*, my father's voice echoes inside my head. Find five things you can smell, hear, see, and touch. *Ground yourself, Sasha.*

So I do.

Nobody knows this about me. That I do this almost ten times a day. I've always been wound too tight. My Ma didn't know how to handle it, like many other things, so she left it up to dad. His voice calmed me. The humble voice of a hardworking man who loved and provided for his family. If he were here right now, he'd know exactly what I should do. Exactly how to stop me from drowning.

But he isn't here. He hasn't been since I was twelve and he died from a heart attack on Emily's birthday. Now it's just the three of us, living like a house with no foundation.

Ma falls into another coughing fit, and my stress comes back full force.

"You need to go back to the doctor," I bitch at her. "You've been hacking like that for weeks. I don't like it. You smoke too much."

She throws her hands up and curses at me in Portuguese. Although she moved from Brazil at a young age, she still uses her native tongue frequently when she gets hot headed. Which is pretty much all the time.

"I smoke too much because I'm always worried about the two of you." She reaches up and tugs on her hair. "You give me all of these gray hairs. Make me look like an old woman."

I laugh and shake my head, even though it's really not funny. I'm worried about her. But she loves to blame us for her gray hairs.

"That could have something to do with all the cigarettes," Emily chimes in.

Ma shrugs both of us off and pats my cheek with her hand.

"My beautiful daughter," she says, her eyes shining with love. "I only want the best for you."

"I know." I reach up and clasp her hand with mine.

The moment is ruined when there's a knock at the door. My gut churns, and Ma shuffles over to open it. Blaine's inky black gaze settles on her while his lips curl up into a smile. To anyone else, it would appear polite and even charming, but to me that smile belies exactly what he only wants me to see. The evil swirling just below the surface, seeking any opportunity to leak out and obliterate his grand illusion.

"Mrs. Varela." He bows his head and kisses Ma's hand. "You look more beautiful every time I see you."

Ma gives him a stiff but respectful smile, but I know Blaine can see the fear in her eyes. I see it too. He gets off on that fear. On knowing that there's nothing me or Emily or even my Ma can do. Men like him always get what they want. The problem is, it's never enough. I've been keeping his attentions occupied, but the more he comes around, the more his gaze wanders.

He's looking at Emily again right now. The ever present panic in my chest flares as his eyes rake over her. It takes all of my willpower not to let him see it bothers me. She's going to college next week. Just one more week, and then she'll be safe. One more week, and he can't hold her against me.

"Don't be too late, Sasha." Ma kisses me on the cheek, and I conjure up a smile for her.

"Stop worrying," I tell her. "And call the doctor."

She nods, and Blaine escorts me out to his car. He's whistling as he walks, and it fills me with dread.

Once he's in the driver's seat, he twists to look at me. His fingers invade my space and pinch my chin in a bruising grip. I don't recoil, but I have to work at hiding my repulsion.

"Your sister's growing up quick, hey. Anyone taken her for a ride yet?"

"She has a boyfriend," I lie.

His rough fingers trace over my cheek and down my neck, lingering on the bruise he left when he last saw me. His dark eyes admire his handiwork for a moment before shooting back to meet mine.

"You better be a good girl, Sasha," he says. "I'm growing tired of your attitude."

He leaves the rest of the words unspoken when he puts the car in drive and turns on the music. I don't need to hear his threats laid bare. I'm well aware of what he'll do.

I turn my gaze back towards the window and wish he'd never set eyes on me.

***

He's here again.

Staring at me. Always staring. Watching, considering… waiting. For what I don't know. He never says a word. Not one.

To everyone else, yes. Just not to me.

I often think he hates me for reasons I can't understand. But then he turns those mournful whiskey colored eyes on me, and I want to believe there's something else concealed in their shadows. He's the only one who sees past the fake smile on my face. Like he understands that the laughter echoing from my chest when Blaine cracks a joke is as fake as his whole persona.

False hope.

That's what I see when I look at him.

I've never believed in fairytales. There is no white knight in my story. Only me. And I'm not the girl who gets the prince. I'm the girl he bangs because he can.

Blaine isn't the first guy. They all tell me how pretty and sweet I am. When I look in the mirror, I don't see pretty. I don't see sweet. I see broken and dirty. Shame and self-loathing. The whore that Blaine uses as his own personal punching bag. The things I've had to do in this life aren't pretty or sweet, and neither am I.

I've made peace with that.

Damaged souls have their own beauty. A dark, terrifying beauty. The same type of beauty I recognize in Ronan. He isn't like those other men. The ones who tell me how much they want my body. The filthy things they want to do to me. For a girl who went from a nerd to a knockout almost overnight at the age of thirteen, I used to think those words meant something. The boys told me anything they thought I'd want to hear. And they believed a few kind words thrown my way entitled them to have me for a little while. But only for a little while.

They always throw you back in the end.

Because you're nothing to them. Just like me.

When it comes to Blaine, I'm even less.

The day that he saw me and decided I was his, my fate was carved in stone. My regret and hatred churn inside of me like a toxic poison, blackening everything that exists around me.

I no longer see good in the world. I couldn't tell you exactly when it stopped, only that it did. My heart flat lined long ago. Keeping myself locked in this void is easy. And yet the despair seeps in all too often.

But then Blaine brings me here, and I see this man with the sad brown eyes, and a sliver of sunlight breaks through my otherwise dark existence.

In his eyes, I see something different. He's deadly and quiet. Closed off and mysterious. He doesn't talk like the rest of them, just for the sake of talking. But I know who he is and what he does.

The Reaper.

That's what they call him in the MacKenna syndicate. The name speaks for itself. And yet this man- this cold-blooded killer- he can't find it within himself to speak to me. His cheeks flush pink every time I look his way, and then his jaw strains with the force of his anger.

It makes me want him in ways I shouldn't. It makes my heart stop and start every time he walks into the room. Like a rusty old engine, I'm in disrepair, and I feel like this stranger is the only mechanic for the job.

A silly notion. One for silly little girls who still believe in fairytales.

One thing I know for certain is that this killer- the Reaper- isn't my white knight. In fact, in this story, I very well suspect he may even be the villain. Because if Blaine ever finds out how I feel, it will certainly be the death of me.

Chapter One

Sasha

He's sitting in the pit tonight. Watching me as I make my way around and help Kaya with drinks. Slainte is packed this evening and the VIP room is at full capacity. It has been ever since the Irish started working on an alliance with the Russian mob. Something I'm not technically supposed to know, but everyone does.

It can't be helped when you work for them. I don't usually serve drinks, but we're understaffed tonight. The way I serve these men is by dancing for them. Putting on a show up under the glitzy lights of the stage and making them feel like I could fulfill their every fantasy.

I'm an excellent liar. A master of manipulation. I've got it down to an art now. The way I look at them and tilt my head just so. They're thinking about all the dirty things they want to do to me. I'm thinking about my dying mother back at home. About how I hate this life and everyone in it. I've got so much hate bottled up inside of me it's only a matter of time before it blows.

But I can be anything they want me to be when I'm up on that stage. A saint or a sinner. The girl next door or the one on the street corner. The only thing I can't be is myself.

Because that girl disappeared a long time ago, and I couldn't even begin to tell you who she is anymore. That's the problem with lies. Eventually they start to feel real. Eventually, you start to believe them too.

I'm one big hot fucking mess wrapped in pretty lies. The Boston Underworld set its claws on me three years ago and now it doesn't want to let me go. It's a cold and lonely place living forever in the shadow of the man that invited this chaos into my life.

I'm so over all of it. The mafia guys. The clients. The ogling and the comments and the grabby hands. While their wives are no doubt at home tending to the children they come here to ogle my tits and slap my ass. I'm exhausted and running on fumes.

I've tried to be a good girl my whole life. Just like Ma wanted me to. But now, now I'm ready to do bad. Ready to say fuck this world and everyone in it, consequences be damned. The only thing anchoring me to my sanity at this point is my mother, but once she's gone I'm all out of fucks to give.

Which reminds me that I need to get a Red Bull before it's my turn up on stage. The pill in my pocket is beckoning me. Dexedrine, my new favorite vice. They were my sister's, but now I'm using them as uppers just to stay awake.

I follow Kaya to the bar and add my drink to our order, which the bartender brings first. I don't usually drink before dancing, or even after for that matter, but lately it's the only thing getting me through my stage performances. While Kaya's attention is elsewhere, I toss the pill into my mouth and wash it down with the vodka concoction. But when I open my eyes again, she's staring at me.

"You look like shit," she notes.

"Thanks, honey."

She shrugs. "Just telling it like it is. When's the last time you actually ate something?"

I try to remember, but I can't. This morning, probably. I'm thinner than usual, I know that much. But it isn't really on my list of things to give a shit about right now. My mother is dying. Fucking cancer.

The room spins as the pill enters my bloodstream and hot wires my nervous system. My attention pings around the bar while we wait, observing the blur of laughter and noise. All these people, having a good time. Fuck them. Fuck the mafia. And fuck cancer too. I want to get out of here. Away from this life and away from the blood and gore and darkness that has enveloped every aspect of who I am.

And most importantly, away from him.

Ronan.

The biggest fucking liar of them all. Pretending like he doesn't give a shit. Pretending like he doesn't see the way I look at him. Or the way he looks at me for that matter. Like he wishes I would disappear. I'm his biggest regret.

And still, my heart beats for him.

The man who shares my secret. The man who holds my life in the palm of his hands. Sometimes, I think I could love him. But most of the time, I just hate him. For making me weak. For tempting me to stay. For wondering when he'll finally make good and kill me too.

I don't know how it's possible to have feelings that are such polar opposites. I want to slap him. I want to scream in his face and force him to acknowledge me. His cavalier attitude towards me is worse than any of the pain Blaine ever inflicted on me. I'm not even worth his attention. A moment of his time. And yet, when he walks into the room, everything else ceases to exist.

I know he's here tonight. That's why I can't focus. His dark energy hums through the building before I ever even see him. There's always this thread between us. Connecting us. Linking us. I don't know if it's the secret or something else altogether. I don't know if it can be severed. If I even want it to be. He's like a trip wire, rigged to detonate a category five hurricane of emotions inside of me. But I'm a masochist of the highest order, so I let him obliterate me. Again and again.

I doubt I'll ever learn.

When Kaya and I take the drinks and head back to the VIP lounge, that's where I find him. When I pass by his table, he glances up at me. There's already a drink in his hand. A double shot of Jameson, neat. Never anything else.

I should keep moving. Maintain the course on autopilot. Because any other option is likely to send me careening into a state I don't want to be in.

I stop anyway.

I can't help it with him. I can never help it with him. We have a silent agreement, him and I. One where we avoid each other and pretend the other doesn't exist. Only, I never really agreed to it. But I think there's also an unspoken stipulation that if I break this arrangement, he'll probably have to kill me.

I generally don't provoke him. But tonight, I'm feeling reckless. And on edge. And I want to push him. I want to send him speeding into a state of discomfort for once, just so I don't have to be alone. I want to chafe at the already raw wound festering inside of me.

My eyes move from his glass to the hands that rest atop the table. Strong. Masculine. Elegant. Those hands take life. Those hands wouldn't hesitate to take mine too. And yet, in an odd twist of fate, those very hands gave me my life back.

Sort of.

My pulse kicks into overdrive at the memory. I'm firing on all synapses. Wired and worn in his presence, fully prepared to crash and burn. The room around us is in chaos. But at its epicenter, where he and I are together, everything is still and quiet.

Like a magnet, he lures my gaze to his face. There isn't a man in this room that can rival him. Olive skin. Well-defined jaw. A strong nose and lips so sinful I want to bite them and make him bleed. Only so I can taste his darkness. Only so that I can say for certain he is human. Because sometimes, I don't know. Is he a man, or is he merely a machine? Programmed with only the burning need and desire to kill like they say.

I've seen him kill. I've tasted his rage too. Tasted it so fiercely that some of it spilled over onto me, tainting me with the mark of the animal that lives inside of him. I crave that animal. I crave everything about this man with his perfect suits and his complete lack of human emotions. Maybe, just maybe, I envy him too.

What it must be like not to feel anything. Anything at all.

I want that for myself.

My pupils are dilated, and when they sweep over him tonight, he's distorted. Even in a blurred state, he's faultless. You'll never find him in anything other than a suit. His skin is sometimes shadowed, but only one day's worth of stubble at most. His hair is shaved at the sides and worn longer on the top. He's clean cut, well-manicured and polished, and the complete opposite of the flaws that stitch me together.

Beneath his black-framed glasses, child-like brown eyes appraise me. They are fringed with thick dark lashes which he often tries to hide behind. Because he knows those eyes betray him. Those eyes fracture his cold veneer with an underlying innocence. There are times, like right now, when he can be downright benevolent. They skim over my body in a speedy appraisal and then darken. It's never hunger I find there, but madness.

Oh, I love that madness. Because madness is better than nothingness. Madness means he isn't completely immune to feelings. Madness means it isn't apathy he feels when he has to look upon me.

Fucking asshole.

"Hi, Ronan." My voice is laced with sweet venom, and I hope he hears it. "So nice to see you too. Yeah, my mom's doing great, thanks for asking. Dying, but you know, that's life. Oh and Em's great too, in case you're wondering."

He blinks at me, and for a second I almost think I'm hallucinating. Because I could have sworn a frisson of guilt flashed through those brown irises. But it quickly turns cold under his stare, and I feel the sudden urge to hug myself.

I don't know why I'm being such a bitch to him. But he's irritated with me and I want to irritate him too. These pills make me act crazy, but it's either that or collapse from exhaustion. I want to pick a fight with someone, and right now that someone happens to be him. He doesn't respond though. He never responds.

He adjusts his collar and glances towards the door, mentally seeking an escape. In his eyes, he counts the steps to the door. He always does that. He doesn't think I notice. But I do. The numbers are there in my head, and I'm counting right along with him.

I make him uncomfortable. It isn't hard to guess why. I'm sure he often contemplates ridding the one loose end that could unravel him. I have no doubts whatsoever he regrets the thing that happened two years ago. To hammer that thought home, he dismisses me by dragging his phone from his pocket.

One of the clients snaps his fingers, and it breaks me from my reverie. The moment I leave the table, Ronan is up and out of the door.

***

When I stumble into the run-down apartment in Dorchester that I call home, I can barely keep my eyes open.

The place isn't much to look at. It's the same apartment I've spent my whole life in, with a mother who worked hard to keep the water-stained roof over our heads. There are two bedrooms, a parlor, a kitchen, and the most basic of furniture.

We never had nice things. After my father died, Ma spent her money keeping me and Emily fed and clothed and healthy, and that was pretty much the extent of it. But the place was always neat and tidy, and it always felt like home.

Now there is dust collecting on the furniture, and a musty smell that I can't seem to rid no matter how much I air the place out. My clothes from work are scattered around the apartment, along with the various pill bottles and medical equipment mom needs.

Emily's in California, on a scholarship to UCSD, so most of her stuff is gone. Without all of her pink girly things around, everything is washed out in gray. It's the same place I've always lived. But looking at it now, it doesn't feel like home anymore.

I plod into the kitchen and find Amy sitting at the table, flipping through a magazine.

When Ma got too sick, I had to hire a home nurse for when I couldn't be here. Amy was the woman for the job. She's sweet and kind and very good at what she does, and she makes Ma as comfortable as she can these days. Plus, she makes me food, so basically she's the only one keeping me alive at this point.

"How is she?" I ask.

"She's actually awake right now," Amy answers. "And pretty lucid, if you want to go see her."

I toss my bags onto the kitchen table and seize the opportunity with gusto. There aren't very many of these moments anymore, so I take them as they come.

"Thank you, honey."

"No problem," she says. "I'm going to head out for the night. Supper's in the fridge."

"Okay, drive safe. I'll see you tomorrow."

Amy slips out the front door and I throw on a sweatshirt before heading into Ma's room. I don't want to smell like perfume and liquor when I visit with her. She knows what I do for a living, but it doesn't mean I have to throw it in her face. I try not to if I can help it.

My mother had high hopes for me. As a child, she affectionately deemed me her 'little calculator'. I worked hard in school and made the honor roll every year. But when it came to math, it was always my worst subject. I'd failed so many homework assignments that the teacher finally pushed Ma to hire a tutor for me. And when the tutor came to help me, I learned I wasn't bad at math at all. In fact, I could do any calculation she threw at me, so long as it wasn't on paper. Before long, I was doing calculus and university level math equations.

It was a shock to everyone, but especially my mother. When they asked me how I did the calculations, I couldn't explain it. It was just one of those weird things that came naturally to me, and my mother was convinced I would go places with it. So you can imagine her disappointment when I took my talents down to the local strip club instead.

But I can't be sorry for it, because it means she's here with me in her final months. And math didn't do that, but dancing did. It's the only way I can look my mother in the eyes right now and believe that I'm doing the right thing. Because if I wasn't dancing, she wouldn't be here. In her own home. I wouldn't be able to take care of her the way she deserves. The way that she's taken care of me my whole life.

My eyes land on her tiny frame in the bed. She occupies barely any space now. It doesn't matter how many times I see her like this, the sight still hits me like a ton of bricks every time. A painful lump takes shape in my throat and my eyes fill with pressure, but I choke it back as I move towards her.

"Hey, mama." I lean down and kiss her on the cheek. "How are you feeling today?"

She coughs and stares up at me through cloudy gray eyes. Those eyes that used to crinkle when she laughed no longer hold any light inside of them. Only pain. Her lips are dry and cracked, but she doesn't even try to budge them. She's too weak to talk right now. These days have been getting more and more frequent lately, and I know what it means.

She's near the end. There's nothing else we can do for her now except to manage her pain. Most of the day, she's in and out of consciousness. On the days when she can speak, much of it is incoherent.

It's the most awful way to watch someone you love go. Every night when I come home and see her like this, I feel as though I'm crawling across a bed of nails. But as horrific as it is, I know she's grateful. Because she's here in her home, where everything is familiar and peaceful. I wouldn't let her go to a hospice. It takes most of my income to pay the home nurse and keep up on the rent, but it's worth every cent. At least in the end, I can say she died where she was most comfortable. Where she was most happy.

It will be the only good thing I've ever really done in my life. The only thing I can be proud of. Ma would try to tell me otherwise, but she's not a very good liar. She still thinks I'm a good girl. That I'm her angel. But she's wrong.

I used to be good. I went to church. I volunteered. I worked hard in school. I did all of the things that my Ma told me were important, even when I really didn't feel like it. I've been good my whole life, and where has it gotten me? A piece of shit wise guy and a mother with cancer. That's where.

She's leaving me soon, and I don't want her to go. I tell her as much through the tears because I can't help myself. She squeezes my hand, and it sends me into another one of my outbursts.

"I'm not your angel, Ma," I tell her. "I'm nothing without you. I don't want to try anymore. Look at me. Look at you. This isn't frigging fair."

Ma understands my craziness. She blinks up at me and a tear rolls down her cheek. I wipe it away as my own eyes blur. She knows where I just came from. She hates that I'm trapped in this world and that I can't get out. I know she worries about me. That's always been her biggest concern, that I would get out before she goes. But we both know that isn't going to happen.

Getting away from the MacKenna Syndicate isn't going to be easy. I know too much. Have seen too much. If I were to leave, I know who it'd be to hunt me down. I don't want him to be the one to kill me. I could deal if it was anyone else. But not him. I can't look into his eyes as I take my last breath. That would be even worse than death itself. It would be the most painful way to go. Because this time, after everything that's happened… this time, I know he wouldn't stop.

So for now, I just have to put it out of my mind and focus on what's important. One day at a time, taking care of Ma. That's all I can do.

I walk into the bathroom to grab a cool cloth. She likes this, and it makes her feel better. The one small comfort I can give her. I place it over her forehead and watch her watching me. Her eldest daughter. Her pride and joy.

"Do you know what, Ma?" I whisper. "You don't have to worry about me. Because I'm going to get out. And I'm going to move to California. Near Em. Maybe I can help her with her school work, who knows. I could be like her math tutor or something."

Her lips twitch, and I can almost see her smiling the way she used to. The smile that lit up an entire room. She was always so beautiful, and now, she's just an empty shell.

"She says the weather is nice there year round," I continue. "And I have a friend from high school there too. You remember Sarah, right?"

She blinks, but her gaze is fixed on my face, enrapt. Sarah still lives in Dorchester, and she works in a dive bar and has four kids, but Ma doesn't need to know that. The hardest part of all of this has been for her to worry about what will happen to me and Em. And I don't want her to worry. I want her to be at peace. I still feel guilty for my emotional outburst earlier, so I keep going.

"She's an actress," I tell her. "Says she can get me some work. Nothing fancy, of course. Just some extra stuff. You know the people that sit in cafes in the background or whatever?"

She blinks to signal that she wants me to keep going.

"I'm going to find me a nice boring guy, too. You know, like an accountant or something. He'll probably drive a Prius and run marathons on the weekend, when he's not donating to charity or whatever."

Ma's lips are twitching again. She either knows I'm full of shit, or she's buying what I'm selling hard. It's difficult to tell anymore, but she seems happy. I resolve to tell her this every day until she goes. And then, and only then, will I allow myself to break down and accept reality.

The chances of the Irish letting me leave are grim. But I have to try. Even if it means I don't make it. At least I can say I tried. Because behind all the makeup and the stilettos and the glitter and hairspray that girl up on stage is done. Done being a pawn in everyone else's games. Done with men who use and take and do whatever the fuck they want without any consequence.

The best day of my life will be when I never have to see any of their faces again.

Chapter Two

Ronan

Obey.
Be prepared to sacrifice yourself for the benefit of the greater good.
Never surrender. Always resist.
Do not hesitate in eliminating any threat.
Exercise self-control.
Always be well polished and clean.
Continually strive to strengthen body and mind.
Live cleanly. Do not drink, smoke, or partake in sugary substances.
Do not associate with outsiders.
Never question orders.
Always be striving towards the goal of a free nation.
For as long as Ireland is in chains, so too shall you be.

"*C*rack on with it," Farrell says.

Glass digs into the skin beneath my knees as I struggle to repeat the core values one more time. I'm thirsty and my tongue is dry so it's sticking to the roof of my mouth. Farrell's patience is wearing thin, and if I don't speak soon, the punishment will be worse.

I stumble over the words and forget which number I'm on halfway through. My eyes are heavy, and I don't know how many days have passed since I slept. I'm starting to see things. Things that aren't real, I think.

My arms are stretched above my head, but I can no longer feel them. My legs are keen for the reprieve from standing, even it if it is only to kneel in broken glass. In the two years since my training *began, I've come to know that life is simply trading one pain for another.*

There is never comfort. Not even for one moment. Because operatives are not made in beds of roses. That's what Farrell told me when they took me from the only four walls I'd ever known. One house, four beds, four other lads. Lads I'm not supposed to speak to.

I think I was eight at the time. They always start training at eight, Farrell said.

I'm ten now. Ten.

I don't feel ten.

Farrell glances down at me in shame, and it burns through me. I cast my eyes to the floor and wait for the punishment. My shoulders sag and I bow my head in defeat. My eyelids are growing too heavy, and I'm afraid of falling asleep. Every bone aches. My skin burns, and I tremble with each movement.

Without another word, Farrell releases the cuffs holding my wrists in place. The resulting fall smacks my face against the concrete. I can't move. My cheek burns and I reckon it's bleeding. The sound of Farrell's boots echo off the floor as he moves around behind me.

He pulls my trousers up from around my ankles and I try to jerk away from him. Coyne presses his boot into the flat of my back, keeping me pinned to the floor. And then I hear the buzzing of the cattle prod.

I find a dark spot on the wall to stare at before he jabs at the soles of my feet. But it doesn't help. Nothing ever helps. There's only pain.

Pain. Blackness. Pain. Blackness.

I like the blackness.

Water splashes on my face, and I startle awake. Farrell is standing over me, shouting out orders again.

"Get up."

"I can't," I tell him.

It's not a lie.

He nods at Coyne and they both heave me up by my arms. I'm naked now. They've taken my clothes again, so I know what follows. They stuff my hands back through the cuffs that stretch my arms overhead and it requires me to stand on the balls of my feet to maintain the position. The burns are so bad I feel on the verge of passing out again. But I know I can't.

Coyne appears with the hose. He sprays me with cold water for a long time. My body is shivering, but I try to focus on sucking some of it into my mouth. I'm so thirsty.

The hose shuts off, and Coyne looks to me and then back at Farrell.

"He's fading."

Farrell nods and then retrieves another pill from his pocket. I don't like the pills. Anything but the pills. I squeeze my lips together, but he forces it inside my mouth anyway. It tastes bitter on my tongue, and there's no choice but to swallow it.

My heart beats too fast, and my eyes feel like they are going to pop out of my skull. Farrell walks around behind me and pulls the noose around my neck again. It's tied to the wall behind me, with just enough give that I have to stand completely straight.

He slaps me on the cheek and they walk towards the door. The one that leads to places I've never seen before. The one I sometimes think about when they aren't looking at me.

"Don't fall asleep, little fella," he says. "Or you'll never wake up again."

***

Unfastening the buttons of my suit, I hang the black jacket over the usual hook on the wall. Everything in this room is precisely the way I fancy it. Clean and organized, a workspace suited for my needs. I have a ritual when I walk into this room. And even with the anticipation thrumming through my veins at the moment, I ensure that I perform to my exact standards.

Every object has its place. Every step must be taken carefully and deliberately.

My watch comes off, followed by my undershirt. Two buttons on the remote, and Bach's Cello Suites flow through the speakers. Always sixty-two decibels, the perfect volume. I'm not particularly keen on music, or noises of any sort for that matter, but this doesn't bother me so much. When I was still a young lad, Crow's mammy taught me that this music could help me to concentrate. Which is precisely what I could do with at the moment.

Chapter Three

Ronan

"What does it eat?" I ask.

Conor points at a bag of dog food, and I grab it without looking at the label.

"It's got a pink collar," Conor observes. "And it looks like there might have been a tag on there at some point."

"So?"

"So it probably belongs to somebody," he says. "I don't see Donny buying a dog a pink collar. Or even taking care of one for that matter. There weren't any dog toys or even food in the house. Maybe it's one of his whores."

The lad does have a point, but it makes little difference now.

"I could take it to the pound," he offers. "Someone might adopt it."

I imagine the place he's speaking of, and all I see are four cement walls and nothing but darkness. I don't like his suggestion. I ignore him and grab a few other things off the shelves before I walk to the checkout.

When we get back to my house, I hand Conor the key and pop the boot on the beamer.

"Feed it for me, will ye? I have business with Crow."

"You know you can't just leave it for days at a time, right?" Conor asks. "You'll have to come home every few hours and let it out. Make sure it has food and water. You know, actually keep it alive."

"That's what I have you for," I tell him.

He grunts and shuts the door, and I wait until he's inside before I drive back to the club. Once inside, I head straight to the bar and order two glasses of Jameson neat. Crow won't be here for another thirty minutes, so I've got time to kill. I walk towards the rear of the building, slipping into the VIP room unnoticed. Or so I'd hoped. Within two minutes of entering, Kaya slinks in my direction.

"Hey, Ronan," she greets me. "Want some company tonight?"

"No," I answer tersely.

The same answer I always give her.

She rolls her eyes and follows my gaze to the stage. It's no secret I'm here every night that I'm able. When Sasha works. She doesn't know that, but Kaya does. She found me back here in the shadows one night and has taken it upon herself to bother me ever since.

Lately that hasn't been as frequent on account of me having to babysit Crow's troublemaker Mack. She came into the club and turned everything on its arse with her lies and her agenda. But regardless of that fact, Crow was mad for the girl and I was saddled with guard duty until he sussed out her motives. That, I reason, is how Donny must have been getting to Sasha. Coming here when I was preoccupied so he could put his filthy hands on her.

"You know," Kaya's voice breaks through the silence, and I blink up at her. I don't know why she's still standing here. "I think we might have a problem on our hands, Ronan. And I'm really not sure who to talk to about it."

She's making a whole production with her lips. Pushing them out like she's pouting. I tilt my head and try to work out what it is she wants from me.

"What sort of problem?" I ask.

"Sasha's been popping an awful lot of pills lately," she says. "I think maybe she's turning into a junkie or something."

My response is hasty and uncontrollable. Before I can cop onto myself, I've got a hold of her by the arms, glaring down into her terrified face.

"Do ye like working here at Slainte?" I ask her.

"Y-y-yes," she stutters.

"And do ye like waking up every morning?"

She nods her head spastically, but no words come out this time. It's just as well, because I don't know what I'm doing. Only that I can't control myself where Sasha is concerned. Which is why I stay far away from her.

"Do not ever so much as mention Sasha's name again," I tell Kaya. "In any form, or conversation of the sort. Do ye get me?"

dosage so she can rest. But it means she'll be out of it. You should call Emily and tell her to come now."

I nod and a tear escapes my eye, falling down my cheek and splashing against the table. The table where we all used to eat as a family. I have the sudden urge to break it. To see it piled up like matchsticks. Instead, I settle for scratching my nail against the wood, marring it.

Amy stands up to leave, but gives my shoulder a gentle squeeze before she goes.

"I'll see you tomorrow."

"Thank you."

The front door closes, and the only sound in the apartment is the machine from the other room. But I can't go in there. Not tonight. I can't see her so close, but so far away.

So I walk to the closet and rifle through the jackets until I find what I'm looking for. The black suit jacket hidden in the back is yanked off the hanger and brought to my face. His scent has long since faded, but I like to pretend it's there. This pathetic little ritual of mine is one of the only comforts I have left in this life. It's amazing how when your world is so dark and unsettled how you can find comfort in the smallest of things. This material comforts me. But it has nothing to do with the jacket itself and everything to do with the memory it invokes.

My dark prince. The reaper. The man who spilled blood for me without pause. For that reason alone he'll always be on a pedestal that no other can reach. He'll always be the memory I revisit in my darkest of times.

I sneak out the front door and walk down the hall of our building, opening the door to the stairwell. Every step I take towards the top burns my legs after a full night of dancing, but I forge on. When I reach the rooftop door, my arms are so weak I can barely open it. But I do.

And with each step that echoes off the cracked cement, I feel better. The air that fills my lungs is cool and crisp. Clean and unsullied. That's why I love it up here. The fact that I can see the entire city doesn't hurt either. I like to count the streets leading out of it. Imagining myself on one of those roads, going somewhere. Anywhere but here.

I find my usual spot up against the brick wall and sit down, curling my knees into my chest and wrapping Ronan's coat tighter around me. My head falls back against the cool brick and I glance up at the stars, trying to piece together constellations in the night sky. But just like my life, they are nothing but a jumbled up map of dots that don't connect, and they only leave more unexplained questions.

I don't know how long I sit there for. After a while, my body grows numb from the cold. My shoulders and eyes are both heavy with exhaustion, and I know I should go back inside. But I can't find the energy to move. To care about anything. So I let my eyelids drift shut for just a moment to rest and sleep swiftly carries me to another place and time.

***

"Apologize," Blaine orders. "And I'll forgive you."

"I'm sorry," I tell him robotically.

This is one of his favorite games. Humiliation is just one of the many weapons in his arsenal of torture. And there is never forgiveness to be had, no matter how small the slight, or in most cases- how imaginary.

His dark irises are completely overshadowed by the blackness of his pupils, and that's how I know he's on the verge of another rage. He always gets agitated, restless, and his eyes go black. I can see these events coming now. Others look at him and think he's just in a bad mood. But I know different. I know that bad mood will build and build inside of him until there's nothing but pure rage, and that eventually, it's going to explode on me.

I glance up at him, waiting for the next poisonous arrow he will fling my way. I'm so tired. Physically and emotionally exhausted. I'm living my life from one breath to the next. My body and mind have shut down, but there's no escaping this hell.

I invited chaos into my life the moment I agreed to his relentless requests for a date. He was obsessed with me the moment he saw me. Back then, I was young enough to be flattered by it. I keep thinking that maybe if I hadn't accepted, things could be different. That he would have moved on. But somehow, I know that isn't true.

What Blaine wants, Blaine gets. By any means necessary.

I don't know what he sees in me. But it's something he needs to have. It doesn't mean he loves me. It doesn't even mean he's exclusive to me. Blaine fucks whoever he wants wherever he wants...

but still he demands that he owns every part of me. It's never enough though. There will never be enough of me to satisfy him.

I used to be one of those people who couldn't understand how women could get themselves into a relationship like this. Or how they would stay. But it isn't that simple. It's never been simple with Blaine.

Fighting with him is like fighting with a child. Only, one who is prone to violent outbursts. He keeps me in check by holding Emily and my mother over my head. I know what he'll do to them. There isn't a scrap of doubt in my mind about that. I'm trapped in his clutches, and I may as well have signed my own death warrant. There is no escaping him. There is no escaping the mafia.

These are the hard facts. The only facts I know. There isn't a court order in existence that can shield me from him.

"Get down on your knees and beg me," he orders. "Tell me how sorry you are."

My brain keeps playing the same thought on repeat. I want it to be over. I just need it to be over. I want to hesitate. To cause him anger. To push him until he hurts me to the point of no return. That would be the easiest thing to do. This is the solution I keep coming back to. No matter how many times I recalculate this problem, there's only one solution. Only one way to solve it. And that's to take myself out of the equation entirely.

But my brain and my body aren't on the same page. I'm doing as he asks, even though my mind is still fighting it. I'm falling to my knees before him. It isn't about submission or even fear. These things don't resonate with me anymore. There is no pride or morals or even strength at this point. He's siphoned all of those things right out of me. Right now, the only thing I have left is my self-preservation. It's a natural response. A biological need to protect oneself. Bowing to his whims is the only way I can ensure he doesn't carry through on his threats towards my family.

Still, I question it. If I'm dead, he wouldn't need to hurt them. Because then it won't matter. It's the only thing keeping me here. You can't outrun the mafia. You can't hide from a man like Blaine. But Emily's safe in California now. It's just my Ma. And she'll be safer if I sever the one tie that could hurt her. And that's me.

I look up at him. This man I once thought somewhat handsome. And charming. There's nothing when I look at him now. Nothing but emptiness and a black pit of insanity in the shape of a man. I've never wanted to hurt someone. My Ma raised me to be good. Do good. I've never wished anything bad upon anyone. But I wish it on him. That he would step outside and get hit by a bus. Or when he goes out with his crew he will be the one who doesn't come back.

It's awful feeling this way. Wishing those things on another person. This is what I've become. This is all that's left of me since he set his sights on me two years ago.

"Tell me how sorry you are," Blaine repeats.

"I'm sorry that I looked at him."

"Do ye like looking at that freak?" he asks. "Because he's always fucking staring at you."

I don't respond. Because I do like looking at him. The man with the troubled brown eyes. He has a way of captivating me like no one else can. The one who is quiet and mysterious. The only one who I think notices that something might be wrong with Blaine. All the rest of them, they don't see it. They don't want to see it. He acts so funny. The clown who hides his evil behind the laughter. They all think that I'm his by choice.

"I asked you a fucking question!" Blaine spits in my face and then grabs me by the hair, ripping strands of it out as he shoves my face onto the floor and rubs it into the filthy carpet. I don't fight him. I can't even muster up tears anymore. There's just... nothing.

I'm only grateful that the club has shut down for the evening and everyone is gone. I don't want anyone to see. That's the worst part of it. Thinking how humiliated I would be if someone caught him doing this to me. But then they would know. Would they help me? Would they even care?

He would. I know he would. That man with the brown eyes. Or maybe that's only what I want to believe. Because it's easier to believe that someone would care than to face reality.

"Answer me," Blaine growls. "Do you have a thing for the retard?"

I just want it to be over.

He's staring down at me expectantly, waiting for me to lie to him. To tell him there's no other but him.

"He's nice to me," I whisper.

"Nice to you?" he bellows. "He's never said a fucking word to you. How the fuck can he be nice to you?"

He moves to unzip his pants. "Suck me off and I'll be happy again."

A sound of disgust rips from my lungs before I can tamp it down. And like a switch, Blaine flips. There isn't even time to ponder the consequences of what I've done before he's heaved me into the wall. The impact disorients me, and all I can make out is his blurry shape charging towards me again. He pins me to the ground and slaps me over and over, harder with every blow. It doesn't even hurt anymore. I don't feel anything when he hits me. My body has found a way to separate itself from the trauma.

Maybe that's why I'm so tempted to defy him all the time. I should give him what he wants. The crying and the begging and confrontation he so desperately craves. But I just don't have it in me anymore. He sees that. He can always read me, and he knows. He's looking right into my eyes, dissecting what I'm too weak to hide right now. The emptiness. The numbness. The hatred.

And it only makes him angrier.

His hands wrap around my throat and squeeze. "What the hell is wrong with you?" he snarls. "You stupid fucking bitch. You worthless whore."

"I never wanted you," I croak.

I can feel my lips curling into a smile, and Blaine's entire body shakes with the force of his anger. Tighter and tighter he squeezes. And I know this is it. It's all going to be over soon.

This is the moment I'm going to die. His hand constricts arounds my throat, and he slams my head back into the floor. The air is slipping away, blackness seeping in around my eyes. I close them and think of my mother. I hope she'll be okay. I hope she won't hate me for giving up. And Emily too. She already does hate me. She thinks I'm weak. But she doesn't know.

Breath.

I take a breath, and the oxygen comes into my lungs freely. Blaine's weight is gone, and I don't know why. When I open my eyes, I find my salvation, in the form of the man who has never spoken to me. The one with the coffee colored eyes. The one I have secretly watched and fantasized about since the moment I first saw him.

He's on top of Blaine, his own body shaking with anger. His fist is driving into Blaine's face. Over and over and over again. Blaine is fighting back, but it's futile.

Ronan's stronger. Harder. Fiercer.

My protector.

I've never witnessed so much wrath in one man. The force of his hits, the expression on his face. The man on top of Blaine appears every bit the soldier in combat with only one mission. Maim. Kill. Destroy.

His neck is corded, his veins and muscles throbbing with the need for blood. He gets it. Spattered across his suit. I don't know how long it goes on for. Only that at some point Blaine's face is unrecognizable, and I know he's gone. But the man keeps striking out at him. Like it isn't enough. Like it ended too soon, and he regrets that he didn't get to make him suffer.

So even when the beating is over, he takes Blaine by the hair and snaps his neck with a sharp twist. The seconds tick by and turn into minutes as Ronan and I both stare at the mutilated face of the man who has tormented me for so long. I want to crawl to him. To check and make sure it's real. But I don't move.

Dark eyes find mine, and horror washes over me as his breathing changes yet again. The realization and shock of what he's just done washes over his face, and that's when it hits me too. He's going to kill me. He's killed one of his own. And now he's going to kill me too. Because that isn't supposed to happen. Not for me. Not for anyone.

I scramble backwards on my hands and knees, trying desperately to escape. Ronan catches me by the ankle before I even make it five feet. And then he's on top of me, flipping me over. I squeeze my eyes shut and wait. I don't know why this man scares me more than the rest of them. It's his silence. He's a killer. He's one of them. And he just committed the ultimate sin because of me.

His hands touch my face, and it's so gentle, a sob bursts from my lungs. The tears that I couldn't find ten minutes ago are leaking from my eyes, and I'm shaking with fear and confusion. I thought I wanted to die, but now I'm scared.

"Shhhh...." he whispers.

That's it. Nothing more. But it's enough to make me open my eyes. I stare up into his. The rage is gone, and there's something else in its place.

"You don't need to hurt me," I tell him. "I won't say a word. I swear it. I won't tell anybody."

He doesn't respond. His eyes are moving over my face, taking in every detail. He's still breathing hard, and his body is so close to mine. Warm and solid and strong. He smells of malt liquor and roasted pine nuts. I don't know where it comes from, but it's the only way to describe it. The scent is unique and incredible.

His grip on me is rough, but I realize as the seconds tick by it isn't because of the need to kill. It's something else in his eyes. Something I know must be reflected in my own. I cling to his biceps and pull him closer against me. I don't know why. Only that I want to.

"Ronan," I murmur against him. "Ronan."

I don't know why I'm saying his name. If it's a plea or something else.

A sound rips from his throat, and he buries his face in my neck and inhales my skin as he grinds against me. He's hard. And it's completely insane, but all of the tension snaps between us. All the boundaries that ever existed dissolve under the proximity of our bodies. When his hands roam over me, it stirs a long dormant need inside of me. Feelings I haven't felt before. Feelings I'll probably never have again.

I reach down and yank his pelvis against mine while my other hand strokes through his hair. His hands are everywhere on me, touching me anywhere he can reach. We're like two wild animals, going at each other in a fight to the death.

Somewhere in the chaos, he unzips his pants. I pull up my skirt and tug my panties aside. There's a moment of hesitation on his part. And I know it's so wrong. My boyfriend is lying dead on the other side of the room. Where Ronan just killed him. He's still covered in his blood. And now we're trying to fuck right here in the aftermath. I'm so broken. So fucked up to want this. I don't feel anything over the loss of Blaine, but I know that I want this. That I might die if I don't have it right now.

I reach down and touch him. He's thick and hot, and I want him inside of me. Ronan makes another agonized sound as I guide him there. I wrap my legs around him and he sinks all the way in. He fucks me in a jerky and uncoordinated rhythm. But when I reach up to touch his face, he pauses.

"Don't," I tell him.

He can't stop now. I won't let him.

The feelings I have for this man at times are unexplainable. I'm drawn to him. I always have been. But this is something else *altogether. This is pure physics. He's the lightning, and I am simply a conductor. We were always bound to converge.*

When he moves again, he's looking down at me with uncertainty even as he thrusts inside of me. I don't care. I can't think straight. About anything. He pushes, and I give way. My body melts into the floor, yielding to him completely. I barely touch myself, and I explode around him.

The resulting tremors that move through me cause Ronan's entire body to jerk as he collapses forward and comes inside of me. The whole event couldn't have lasted more than five minutes, but I can't recall a time in my life where anything ever felt so good.

Until he pulls away like I'm toxic, threatening to pollute him too. His eyes move towards the door, then back to me. And then he says the first and only word he's ever spoken to me. A bullet to my heart at point blank range.

"Leave."

***

I wake up in a cold sweat, tangled up inside of my bedsheets. Confusion takes over when I sit up and glance around the room. I'm still wearing my yoga pants and a sweatshirt, but Ronan's jacket is hung on the back of my bedroom door. I don't remember putting it there. I don't remember coming inside at all.

The faintest hint of malt liquor lingers on my sweatshirt and I bring it to my nose and inhale. It's fresh. I scrub the sleep from my eyes and shake my head as I glance at the clock. It's only six am. I haven't had nearly enough sleep. But I get up anyway and pad down the hall to mom's room. I just want to be near her now. And forget everything else.

Chapter Five

Sasha

It's my day off, and even though I resolved that I wasn't going to take the pills unless I was working, I'm too tired to function. I can't get to sleep anymore. It doesn't come, no matter how exhausted I am.

When my head hits the pillow, I just lay there and think about my Ma. About what my life is going to be like when she's gone. I had to call Emily and tell her it was time to come home. It's only made everything that much more real.

That's what my excuse is when I reach into my purse to pull out the pill bottle. I've been full of excuses lately. But I don't really give a shit either. I'm doing the best that I can to get through the situation.

Only when I pull the bottle from my purse, I stare at it in confusion. Because it's empty. The lid is screwed on tight, and the pills are gone. It doesn't make any sense. But my suspicion only grows. Instinctively, my eyes dart to the jacket hanging over my doorknob. The same one I was wearing last night up on the roof. I know I didn't walk back down here by myself. And I know that Ronan's scent didn't just magically appear on my sweatshirt.

And lastly, I know these frigging pills didn't just get rid of themselves.

But none of it makes any sense. Why would he be here? And an even better question is, how did he know about the pills? No matter which way I spin it, none of it makes a bit of sense.

These questions are all left unanswered when a knock sounds at the front door. I quickly scoop up the empty container and throw it in the garbage before doing a quick once over in the hall mirror.

I'm not expecting anybody, but on occasion the neighbors drop in to see how Ma's doing. That's who I assume it is. So when I open my door and find Lachlan Crow standing there, words fail me. He's technically my boss, and soon to be the new underboss of the MacKenna Syndicate, if the gossip around the club is correct.

But he's never paid me a house visit before, so when I find him standing here now, I have to admit it makes me a little nervous. I don't know him that well, but his girlfriend Mack is totally cuckoo for this guy. He's always been respectful towards me, but it doesn't change who he is. He's a mafia guy, through and through. For that reason alone, I try to avoid him.

But I adore Mack. And after recent events with Donovan, I owe her a lot.

When Blaine died, I thought that I was free. But I quickly learned that in this life, you only trade in one form of chains for another. Donovan soon took on the role of Blaine and filled his shoes easily. He wasn't as violent, but his threats were as real. He just wanted to get off. And I was right back where I started. I did what I had to in order to keep my secret. In order to protect Ronan too. He killed Blaine because of me, and there was no way I was ever going to rat him out to the syndicate.

But my loyalty didn't make it any easier to accept what was being doled out to me. So when Mack came along, she took me by surprise. Most of the other dancers at the club hated me.

I had been on my own for so long that I forgot what it was like to have friends. Even though Emily and I used to be close, we drifted apart during the time I was with Blaine. Mack was the first real friend I'd had in so long. She reminded me so much of the girl that I used to be. Before Blaine, and before cancer, and Donny and every hard ball that life threw at me.

I used to be strong like her. I used to feel like I could take on the world. But I certainly wasn't strong when I met her. Every person has their limits, and I had finally reached mine. I was at my breaking point, and Mack could see that. She kept Donny away from me when I couldn't take it anymore. And then she almost got killed because of him.

Mack only came into this world because she was searching for her missing friend. I don't think it was ever her intention to stay. But then she fell in love with Lachlan, and things got a little crazy after that. It turned out that not only was Donny betraying the syndicate, but so was one of the other dancers. She ended up taking

Mack for a little joyride with a gun to her head and divulged some hard truths about the friend she'd been looking for.

I know it hasn't been an easy road for her, and I want to return the kindness that she showed to me when I needed it the most. But she hasn't answered any of my texts, and I haven't seen her at Slainte in a while either. Which is why I'm guessing Lachlan is now standing at my door, looking a little lost himself.

The guy that I never would have guessed had a softer side apparently does. And it only comes out when he's around Mack.

"Is everything okay?" I ask Lachlan. "Is Mack alright?"

"That's why I'm here," he says. "Mind if I come in?"

I nod and gesture him inside. It's weird having him in my apartment. None of the guys have ever been here except Blaine.

"Mack's still having a bit of a rough time," he says. "Dealing with everything. I was hoping ye might come visit her. I know your mother is sick…"

"It's okay," I tell him. "I'd love to come see her, if she's up for it."

"Grand," he says. "I'll have Ronan pick ye up this evening."

"Okay."

There's a weird expression on Lachlan's face. Like he wants to tell me something else. But he doesn't. So I show him to the door, and then spend the entire day in Ma's room, hoping for a lucid moment. It never comes.

***

Ronan arrives at my door to pick me up just after six. He doesn't say a word when I open it, but just stands there looking as stiff and uncomfortable around me as usual. Ronan always does whatever Lachlan tells him to, but I'm a little surprised he agreed to drive me tonight. He usually goes out of his way to avoid me, and I somewhat expected Rory or Conor to be the ones to show up in his place.

"Hi, Ronan." I smile weakly.

He doesn't respond. We walk to his car and he opens the door for me and then drives me in silence. I hate it. I don't know why he doesn't speak to me. He talks to everyone else. Even Mack. And as much as I hate to admit it that bothers the hell out of me.

I alternate between staring at him and trying to keep my attention focused elsewhere. I know he feels me watching him. His hands twitch, but it's the only obvious sign. He's always edgy around me. And I've always been too much of a scaredy cat to call him out on it. My methods of dealing with his perpetual silence usually swing between acting completely irrational or avoiding it altogether.

But today made me realize that I really don't know the first thing about this situation. And I could just pretend it never happened, like we seem to do with everything else, but I don't want to. The words bounce around my brain as I try to think about the best way to go about asking it. How does someone accuse another of stalking without sounding like a narcissistic asshole, exactly? I don't know. So I decide to just go for it and blurt it out.

"Have you been following me?"

Ronan's grip tightens on the wheel and his eyes are suddenly laser focused on the road. But there's a flush creeping down his neck. This big, strong killer gets embarrassed when I talk to him. I've never understood it. He's not like this with anybody else.

He's blunt and short and tells things like they are. With everyone but me. He can't even seem to look at me most of the time. Like right now. I just asked him if he was following me and his only response is to drive faster.

And yet I can't help feeling like he's silently judging me. Like I need to explain myself. So I make the situation even more uncomfortable and awkward by doing exactly that.

"I'm not a junkie," I tell him. "I only took ten of those pills. And only on days I worked. I've been tired, and stressed, and…"

The words sound even lamer when I say them out loud. There is no excuse for taking them. My head drops into my hands and I groan. I don't know what the hell I'm doing anymore honestly. But it's time to pick myself up and reel it back in.

The car is silent and fraught with tension as we continue to drive. I have no more confessions or accusations to level at him, so I keep my mouth shut.

When we pull up to Lachlan's house, I have to admit I'm a little surprised. I've only ever been here once too, and that was when Ronan had to drop Mack off. Not many people know where Lachlan lives, so the fact that I'm one of them is just another reason for me to be nervous. Another reminder that the likelihood of them letting me go anywhere is not good.

Ronan turns off the car and moves to get out, but I grab his arm and halt him.

He looks at me, but doesn't say a word.

"Thank you," I whisper. "For looking out for me."

His eyes soften, and then he gets out, walking around to open my door for me. He unlocks Lachlan's front door and gestures me inside. I know he won't be following, so I give him a little smile and then slip on through, leaving him behind in the cold.

Conor is on the sofa, reading through a magazine, but glances up when I shut the door.

"She's in the bedroom," he says.

I nod and walk down the hall to find Mack nestled into Lachlan's bed, staring up at the ceiling.

"Hey." I smile at her from the doorway. "Mind if I come in?"

"Hey, Sash." She gives me a weak smile. "Sure, I could use the company."

I sit down on the edge of the bed, and Mack leans back against the headboard. She still has a few bruises from her ordeal with Mandy and Donovan, but otherwise she appears healthy. She's a beautiful girl. Petite and fiery. With dark hair and blue eyes like my own. The defeat weighs heavy in those eyes though. Her friend is gone, and Mack thinks she failed her. I would tell her that isn't true, but the thing I know about guilt is that nothing anyone else says will alleviate it for you. She'll have to come to that conclusion on her own.

"How are you holding up?" I ask her.

"Nuh-uh." She shakes her head. "I don't want to talk about me. Tell me about you. How's your mom?"

I glance down at the bedspread, and Mack sighs. "I'm sorry, Sash. Things seem to suck for everyone right now."

I nod in silent agreement.

"Well," Mack says. "On the bright side, I guess you'll never have to worry about Donny bothering you again."

I swallow the lump in my throat at the image of Ronan in that room with him. I knew what he did in that basement. Blaine used to tell me that he was missing a few screws. That he was all sorts of fucked up in the head and that he liked to kill people. I didn't want to believe it. I still don't. But that's what being a part of this life entails.

Following the orders that come down the food chain. It doesn't matter why or how. When the boss wants someone dead, they're dead.

I can't feel sorry for the loss of Donovan. He could have screwed me and Ronan both with the information he held over us. And if he was actually loyal to the syndicate, he would have. But instead, he chose to exploit my loyalty. He knew somehow that I would protect Ronan. That I wouldn't let Donny give him up and make him pay the price for his actions. Because Ronan killed Blaine for me. And Donovan being the opportunist that he was, chose to abuse that from every possible angle. Holding it over me and threatening me constantly to get what he wanted.

But I never gave him my body. My mouth and my hand, but never my body. I think that's the thing that pissed him off the most. In any case, I won't miss seeing his face lurking around the club and waiting for his moments to strike.

"I'm glad he's gone," I tell Mack.

"Lach said that Ronan really made him suffer for what he did to you."

I blink up at her, and a million questions drift through my mind. But I can't voice any of them out loud. Thinking about Ronan's motives only gives me a splitting headache and an aching chest. Instead, I choose this moment to seize an opportunity of my own selfish desires.

"Mack, I know things aren't very good for you right now," I begin. "And I know you've done a lot for me already…"

"What is it Sash?" she asks. "Tell me. I'm feeling about as useless as a sack of potatoes right now, so if there's something I can do to help…"

"Well…" I hesitate. "It's just that you have some obvious sway with Lachlan. And I was thinking maybe you could run something by him."

"Like what?"

I look up at her and clear my throat. I'm nervous as hell, and I feel like a coward for asking this of her. But I worry that if I go to him directly he will just turn me down straight out of the gate.

"He's been good to me," I preface my request. "And I want to do right by him. I'm really grateful for everything…"

"Sash," Mack interrupts. "Just spit it out, will you? It's me. You can tell me anything."

I wring my hands together.

"Look, my mother isn't going to make it much longer. And when she goes, I'll have nothing left here. I was sort of thinking about maybe leaving town. Going somewhere else, you know. Start fresh. I'd never say a word about anything."

Mack nods in understanding and gives me a weak smile. "I want to tell you that I won't ask him. But only because I'm going to miss having you around. You're the only one of the dancers who doesn't hate my guts."

We both laugh, and it feels good.

"So you will then?"

"I will," Mack agrees. "But I can't make you any promises, Sash. Lach will probably have some stipulations."

"I know," I tell her.

I have a feeling Mack won't be going anywhere either after the things she's seen. But she doesn't seem to mind so much. Her and Lachlan have something special. I almost envy her in that way as strange as it sounds. All I've ever wanted was to get out. But when I see the way Lachlan looks at her, I understand why she wants to stay.

Mack tosses me a knowing glance and follows it up with a sigh. "How did a sweet girl like you get wrapped up in this world to begin with, Sash?"

"I'm not sweet," I deny. "And I thought I told you I dated one of these guys."

"Yeah." Mack shrugs. "But you never talk about him. In fact, you kinda get all weird whenever I ask you about it."

I stare down at the quilt and try to steady my voice. I hate lying to her. But I have to. To protect Ronan.

"His name was Blaine," I tell her. "He was five years older than me, and I met him when I was nineteen. At the time, I was working in a diner that Niall's sister owns. I didn't know that it was mafia affiliated."

"I didn't know you worked for Niall's sister," Mack says. "Lach has mentioned that place, but he's never taken me there."

"They mostly only go there for breakfast," I explain. "Late at night, when they've had a rough night or whatever. I was working there part time while I took night classes. I worked the day shift, so it was only by chance that I ever even saw them. I was filling in for one of the other waitresses."

"What luck, huh?" Mack teases.

"Wrong place, wrong time," I reply. "The typical bullshit. That was the first time I saw Niall. He sat at the head of the table, and the way people looked at him, I knew then. His sister introduced me and had me help with drinks and food. I noticed Blaine staring at me, but I had my eye on someone else."

Mack smiles. "Let me guess. Brown eyes. Tall. Broody as hell?"

"That would be the one," I laugh. "He didn't talk to me, so I figured he wasn't interested. And in all honesty, I knew I should stay far away from guys like that anyway."

"Our stories are starting to sound eerily similar," Mack notes.

"Yeah, well, Blaine noticed me. And he didn't like taking no for an answer. He kept coming back to the diner after that. He was so persistent that I couldn't help being a little flattered. He brought me these crazy over the top gifts that cost more than our entire month's rent. I didn't really know what was happening. But eventually, I agreed to go out with him."

"That sounds sort of sweet," Mack says. "But I've got a feeling it wasn't."

"No, it wasn't," I tell her. "It was just supposed to be one date. A harmless dinner. But Blaine kept pushing me for more. I knew right away he wasn't what I was looking for. I tried to let him down easy."

Silence falls over the room, and I can't find the energy to relay the rest of the story. The guilt and the manipulation. The threats and the games. I never want to think about it again.

"I think I can guess the rest of it," Mack says gently.

"He got bored of me eventually and left town," I lie. "And I thought I could get my life back. But then my Ma got sick. And we didn't have insurance. I had no idea how to make the kind of money that I needed to take care of her. One night, Niall was in the diner. His sister had mentioned what was going on with me, thinking he might be able to help. And he offered for me to come and work at the club. He said he would help me out until Blaine came back. But obviously, he never did. And so now, here I am."

"Wow, Sash." Mack groans. "That really didn't help at all."

"How's that?" I ask.

"Your story is just as depressing as mine."

We both laugh again, and then a few tears leak out of my eyes. I can't tell if they are happy or sad, but I'm glad that Mack is here with me.

"I'll talk to Lachlan," she says. "And I give you my word, I'll do everything in my power to convince him."

Chapter Six

Ronan

"*One more minute.*" *Farrell glances at his watch.*

I grip the edges of the tub and count the seconds in my head. Every muscle in my body burns from the cold.

"*Again," Coyne repeats.*

I rattle off the ingredients for the bombs they taught us how to make. These parts come easily to me. The lists. Remembering things. I can do that. When the lady in the room used to teach us things, she always said I had good attention to detail.

Farrell nods in approval and then points at the weapon hanging over his shoulder. I list off the steps to assemble it and then repeat them in reverse.

"*Time's up," he calls out.*

I jolt out of the ice bath and nearly collapse.

"*Keep moving," Coyne says.*

My movements are clumsy and awkward. But I keep at it.

"*Ye did well," Farrell says. "Now to the pit."*

I freeze in place and shake my head.

"*And for that ye can enjoy an extra day's accommodation in there."*

His words force me into action again.

I walk with Coyne in front of me and Farrell follows behind. They open up the door to the pit, and though my body wants to hesitate, my mind is already following orders. Before I climb down inside they give me another pill. And then they lock me in, sacrificing me to the blackness.

It isn't the dark that I'm not keen on. I've grown accustomed to living in the darkness. It's the uncertainty of what will come with it this time. Every month, I progress to a new stage of training. A new phase of uncertainty. And every visit to the pit can only end one way.

They'll send another man down. Another man I have to kill. I can't see them, and they can't see me. But we both have only one option. Kill or be killed. I always do the killing.

And then they leave them with me. Sometimes for days. The rats come out. And the bugs. And the smell. But that isn't even the worst of it. It's the sound I don't like. The ones I always hear.

The speakers come on, and I cover my ears before it begins. But it makes no difference. I still hear it anyway.

The screaming. An endless soundtrack of wailing. Tortured sobs. Crying babies. My heart is beating too hard. Too fast. It's going to explode. And then it turns to ringing.

***

I wake to the sound of my phone and something wet against my cheek. When I open my eyes, I'm met with big brown ones. The dog I still haven't worked out what to do with.

"What are ye after?" I grunt.

She head-butts my cheek and then barks. I shove it away and reach for my phone, only to have it barge in from the other side. She wiggles her arse and hops back and forth before flopping onto her back and flashing her belly at me.

The phone rings again and I groan as I bring it to my ear.

"Aye?"

"Fitzy," Crow chirps from the other end of the line. "Did I wake ye?"

"You did."

The dog barks again and I try to quiet her.

"What the hell is that?" Crow asks.

"It's a bleeding dog," I tell him. "What does it sound like?"

"When did you get a dog?"

"Did ye have a reason for this call?" I grumble. "Or did ye just ring to give me an inquisition?"

"Open your front door," is his reply.

The line goes dead and I tug on a pair of track pants and a tee shirt. The dog follows me to the door and starts to have a go at Crow when he steps inside.

"What sort of dog is that?" he tilts his head to the side to examine her. "Is there something wrong with its wee legs?"

"Conor thinks it's a Corgi," I tell him. "Google said their legs are supposed to be wee. I looked it up."

"What the hell are ye doing with it?" he asks.

"It was at Donny's flat."

"So ye decided to keep it? Do you even know what to do with a bloody dog?"

"I haven't a clue," I admit. "That's why Conor feeds it."

"Well it looks like it's hungry now," Crow points out.

"Is that why she's carrying on like that?"

He shrugs. "What the hell do I know about dogs?"

I walk to the kitchen and grab the bag of dog food off the counter, scanning the label on the back. "It doesn't say how much to give her."

"Ah Jaysus, Fitz." Crow laughs. "I don't know how ye manage to keep yourself alive let alone a bloody animal."

He grabs the bag and fills the dish on the floor and then makes himself comfortable at my kitchen table. I don't have much in the way of furniture, but it serves a purpose. I mainly only use the place to sleep if I'm lucky. Though I've been spending most of the last couple of months on Crow's sofa while I watched over Mack.

"I spoke to Niall this morning," Crow says, getting straight down to business. He knows I've got no patience for small talk.

"Aye, and what did he say?"

"I reckon we came up with a solution for this whole mess. One that will get me out of hot water and save Mack from his wrath."

I'm not fond of the tone of his voice. I've known Crow long enough to know when he wants something from me. And I've already worked out that this is one of those times. He got himself into this hot water by allowing Mack into the club. I told him the girl was up to no good from the get go. And now his promotion within the syndicate is at risk.

"You should throw her to the wolves, far as I'm concerned," I tell him.

"You don't mean that." Crow stares at me in disappointment. He isn't the only one. I'm used to disappointing others. But I hate it when they look at me like that. "You can understand why she did what she did."

He has a point, but I don't let onto it. She put him in danger. She put all of us in danger with her lies. I have no time for liars.

"Look," Crow says. "There's still a chance that Niall might promote me. He said it isn't off the table."

"Ye're the best man for the job," I tell him. And I mean it. I don't lie.

Crow taps his fingers against his leg, a sure sign he's nervous. I can always tell. He's like a brother to me. Or at least that's what he says. I don't know what having a brother is like, but I imagine if I did, it would be like this.

"I can't do this without you, Ronan," he says. "If I'm to be promoted, you'd have to take on more responsibility as well. Are ye following me?"

I nod, but don't reply.

He wants me to be his second in command. His left hand. I don't mind, I've been doing it all along anyhow. But with him moving up the food chain that means I would too. Things wouldn't be the same as they are now. He knows I'm not keen on things changing, generally. Only, this time I don't mind so much.

"I've been giving that some thought," I tell him.

"Have ye?"

"I had it in my head that maybe…" I clear my throat. "Maybe I could do some other things. Things besides just sorting out the clients in the basement."

I stare at the table and don't look at Crow. The room is quiet for a pause, and I know he's thinking over what I said. Trying to work out my motives. I don't really understand them myself. I've only ever wanted to follow his orders. That's what I'm good at. But lately, I've been thinking that maybe if I take on some more responsibility, that it would help. That I could be worthy of something. Or someone.

"All ye ever had to do was say so," Crow says finally. "If ye want more responsibility, I'm happy to give it to you. You've earned it, Fitz. But I just have to ask if ye're sure that ye're ready for such a thing."

"I'll still have your back," I assure him. "That isn't going to change, no matter the title."

"I know, Fitz," he says. "And I have a big ask for ye right now."

"I had a feeling."

"Niall's worked out an offer with the Russians. They want three of our lads to take a fall at the fights."

"You can't be serious."

That's worse than death. Taking a beat down like that. All for a woman. I've never seen Crow do any such thing for anyone other than his mates. And now I know, he's definitely gone completely mad.

"I am serious," Crow answers. "Rory and myself have already agreed. I just need one more."

I look up at him and wonder for the thousandth time in the last two months if Mack's still going to ruin him in the end. After everything he's done for her. Sacrificed for her. I've never seen him so out of sorts. He's putting everything on the line for that woman. It's completely fecking stupid and also a little too relatable.

"You want me to take a fall for Mack?" I clarify.

"For me," Crow answers.

He's not doing himself any favors by using that on me. He knows I owe him everything. But he's never chosen to throw it in my face before.

"You can say no," he says quietly. "I'd understand."

"No, ye wouldn't."

"I don't want ye to do it out of guilt," he replies. "I know how ye are with these things. They have to be on your terms. I don't want to put ye in a situation that's going to bring up bad feelings for you, Ronan. If you say no, I'll understand."

Silence falls between us, and I try to work out my feelings about this whole situation. It isn't an easy task for me. I understand risk and loyalty. I understand doing something mad for someone. Crow doesn't think I can, but I do. He isn't clued in on what I did for Sasha. What I would do again even if it meant getting caught.

Now he's here, asking me for a favor. My best mate. There's no way I could refuse him, even if I had reason to. Which I don't.

"Just tell me when to show up," I say. "Ye know I'll be there."

Crow grins and relief passes over his face. He wouldn't let on to it, but this means a great deal to him.

"Are ye certain you'll be able to handle it?" he asks again. "I can't have ye going nuts and killing one of the pricks in the middle of the fight."

"I can handle it," I tell him with certainty. "The pain never bothers me."

Crow frowns and gets up to leave, but pauses at the door. When he glances back at me, his face is solemn.

"I can't tell you what this means to me, Ronan. Thank you."

Chapter Seven

Sasha

I'm sitting on mom's bed, watching her favorite true crime shows. I narrate them for her since she isn't really able to see them for herself. I don't know if she can even hear me, but I like to tell her who I think did it and add my own reasons to their motive.

Just like we used to do.

Those days are never going to happen again. She still hasn't woken. It's been two days. Her skin is growing more pallid by the hour, and I know the end is coming soon.

I'm angry with her. I'm angry that she decided to give up, even though that isn't fair. I want her to fight. I want to be selfish and demand that she stay a little longer. I didn't even get to say goodbye. The medication she's on makes her sleep all the time, and I worry that she'll go before I get a chance to say anything at all. Emily's flying back home in two days. It's all becoming too real.

Amy said she would taper off the dosage of her medication before she progresses to the point of no return. It still doesn't comfort me. Because getting that chance doesn't change the words that won't come. What am I going to say to her? How do you tell someone you love so much goodbye?

My phone beeps from the dresser beside me, and I consider ignoring it. Nobody ever texts me unless it's work. One of the other dancers probably called in sick. I don't feel like working tonight. But I don't feel like sitting in this house and watching my mother die either. I'm not spoiled for choices, so I pick up the phone.

I'm surprised to see it's Mack. After one glance at her message, I'm up and out the door before I can even give it any thought. I don't know where I'm going. The only thing I know is that I need to get to him.

***

By the time Rory and Conor's cars pull up to Lachlan's house, I've nearly worn a hole in the pavement from my pacing.

Mack jumps out of one car, barking out instructions as Michael and Rory carry Lachlan up the stairs.

"Where is he?" I demand.

"Conor's helping him," Mack says, pointing at the other car.

I rush over to help, and the sight of Ronan lying in the backseat with his face beaten makes me irrationally angry.

"How could you let him do this?" I yell at Conor. "He needs to see a doctor."

"The doctor cleared him to come home," Conor answers. "And there's another on the way. And for the record, I don't have any say over what Ronan or Lachlan does."

Rory appears at my side a moment later, giving me a gentle squeeze on the shoulder. "Hey, Sash. He's going to be just fine, okay? Now step aside so we can get him in the house."

I do as he says, watching as they lift his limp body up into their arms. I feel like I should be doing something. Helping somehow. Ronan's always been so strong, I never imagined seeing him like this. I never imagined anything could ever actually hurt him. That he'd ever let anyone close enough to.

The guys carry him inside and I'm hot on their heels.

They heave Ronan onto the sofa and then Rory gives Conor some instructions while I walk into the kitchen and grab a wet cloth. When I come back out Rory is gone and only Conor is sitting in the parlor.

I kneel down beside Ronan and wipe away the blood on his face when Conor hovers over me with a nervous expression.

"I'm not so sure you should be doing that," Conor says. "He went sort of nuts at the fight and they had to sedate him after. He said not to let anyone touch him. He was very, very clear about that."

"Well I'm not anyone," I argue. "And I don't care what the stubborn bastard said. I'm cleaning him up."

Conor remains quiet while I continue to do just that, but it's obvious he doesn't like it. There isn't a single part of me that cares what he thinks. I know Ronan is his superior. He gives out instructions, and Conor has to follow them. That's the way it works in the mob. But I'm not one of their lackeys, and I'm sure as hell not going to follow a ridiculous order at a time like this.

Ronan was there for me when I needed him. And as distant and strained as our relations are right now that's not going to stop me from being there for him too.

He has a cut just above his eyebrow that's been packed with some sort of salve, but there's still blood trickling out of the wound. I wipe away what I can and then check his head and neck.

"The doctor will be here soon," Conor offers in another effort to get me to stop.

I ignore him and sit down beside Ronan on the sofa while we wait, watching his chest rise and fall in an even and steady rhythm. It reassures me, at least a little, that he's going to be okay. When the doctor finally does come, he tends to Lachlan first, which only serves to irritate me further.

By the time he comes out to check on Ronan, it's been over an hour since they brought him here. An hour of putting his health on the line, and for what? Another surge of anger moves through me, and I only have one place to direct it. I wait to see what the doctor does with Ronan, which isn't much, but he does manage to rouse him for a few moments. Just hearing his voice, no matter how briefly, calms me. He's going to be okay, the doc says. He's going to be just fine.

But that's not true. Because how can anyone be just fine when they've been beaten to a pulp like that. I'm pissed off. And all I can think about is how this happened. Why this happened. Once the doctor's done and out the front door, I walk down the hall to Lachlan's room to find Mack sitting on the bed. He's passed out too, and in about as good of shape as Ronan.

Mack looks up at me, and there are tears in her eyes. I don't care.

"What the hell is wrong with you?" I demand.

She blinks at me in confusion. I've never yelled at her before. I like Mack. I respect her. And I'm grateful for what she's done for me. But that doesn't stop me from being angry at her right now too.

"I'm sorry," she says quietly. "I didn't know they were going to do it until it was happening."

"But you let it happen anyway, didn't you?"

"I couldn't stop it," she says. "I'm sorry, Sash."

Her voice is sincere. She's genuinely as sick as I am over what happened, but right now I don't care. I want to lash out at her. And it isn't until the words are out of my mouth that I even understand why.

"He did this for you," I snarl. "Ronan did this for you."

Mack stands up and reaches out towards me tentatively. "That isn't true, Sash. He did it for Lachlan."

"No," I argue. "He talks to you. Why? Why can he talk to you, but not me?"

Again, Mack stares at me in confusion. "He doesn't talk to you?"

"No," I bite out. "He never says one fucking word to me. But you come in here, and he has no problem talking to you. Or fighting for you…"

My words drift off as Mack pulls me in for an unexpected hug. I know she doesn't like to hug. But she's hugging me now. And it turns out to be the thing I needed because I break down in her arms.

I don't know why. I'm just emotional with everything that's happening. With my mom and Ronan and all of the unknown changes I'm facing in the future. That's what I tell myself.

"You should just try to talk to him, Sasha," Mack says as she pulls away. "Believe me when I say Ronan never talks to me by choice. I usually just annoy the hell out of him until I get him to talk."

I smile through bleary eyes and wipe my tears away. "I'm sorry. I didn't mean to yell at you."

"It's okay," she says. "I would yell at me too."

"I should go sit with him."

She nods, but then gives my arm a little squeeze. "Hey, Sash, for what it's worth, I talked to Lachlan."

"Oh." I swallow. "And?"

"And he said you can go. He'd even help you out if you need him to. He just wants to talk to you about it first."

I should be happy with that. But I'm not and I can't figure out why. So I just give Mack a weak smile and a nod. "Thank you."

Chapter Eight

Sasha

When I walk back out into the parlor, Conor is passed out in the recliner, so I sit down on the sofa beside Ronan. He's sleeping, and at peace right now, even with his bruised and beaten face.

His glasses are missing, and he's wearing a tee shirt. I didn't notice it before, but I am now. I've never seen him in a tee shirt. It makes him look younger. More like his age. At twenty-nine, he's only six years older than me. But he doesn't carry himself that way.

He's an old soul trapped in a young man's body. But then there are moments when I glance at him, like right now, when he seems so young too.

I quietly squeeze my body into the gap between him and the back of the sofa and use the opportunity to soak in his handsome features. We're so close right now I could touch him if I wanted to. Conor's words still linger on my mind and I wonder why Ronan told him not to let anyone touch him.

In the three years I've been hanging around the club, I've never seen him touch any woman. Or vice versa. Which is a good thing because I don't think I'd like that at all. He's so quiet and guarded that I doubt he lets anyone touch him.

But he did let me once. I was high on him, but I still managed to notice how unsure of himself he was. He never even kissed me. I have so many questions about him. Almost everything about this man is a mystery. And against my better judgment, I want to know him.

I reach down and drape his arm over my hip. And then I touch his face. I can't help it. It's been so long since I've felt him. I want to feel him right now. My fingertips ghost over his cheeks and his jaw line. He shaved this morning, so his skin is smooth. I want to kiss every inch of it. My thumb drags across his lips, and they part a little for me. And then he moans. Afraid that I'm hurting him, I let my hand fall away and lean closer to give him a gentle kiss on the forehead.

I don't know when it is exactly that he woke during my exploration, but I can feel it now. His eyes are still closed, but his breathing has changed, and his hand has tightened reflexively on my waist. He doesn't move, or say a word. So I nuzzle closer and drape my own arm across his stomach, falling asleep enveloped in his warmth.

It's the best sleep I've had in three years.

***

With the arrival of dawn, so comes something else.

It takes me a moment to understand what it is. The words are muffled, but Ronan is thrashing beside me as he repeats them over and over again.

"Will not speak," he murmurs. "Will not question. Protect your brethren… free the chains. The chains. The chains."

His voice grows more strained with every word. More agonized. And I don't know what to do. I've always heard that you aren't supposed to wake someone during a night terror, but it seems cruel to let him suffer through it.

"Ronan." I give him a gentle shake, and he still doesn't wake. So I clasp his face in my hands and try to soothe him with a calm voice.

Before I can even make sense of what's happening, he's got me flipped onto my back with his hands wrapped around my throat. I can't breathe. I can't even fight him. The man is a goddamn machine. He's crushing every part of me with his body, and the only defense I have is to claw at his hands with my own. But it doesn't even faze him. I've never felt strength like this before.

He just keeps repeating the same garbled words under his breath.

Free the chains.

I try to choke out his name. But it's too quiet. He isn't hearing me. Blackness is seeping in around my eyes again, and the irony is too painful to consider. This is how I was dying when he saved me. And now he's going to kill me the same way.

I shove at his chest, but he's like a brick wall, and I'm too weak.

"Ronan!"

Someone else is shouting now. Through my hazy vision I can barely make out Conor, trying to pry Ronan off of me.

"Ronan!" he screams again.

He manages to loosen Ronan's grip enough that I can take a breath, and in the next instant, Lachlan is charging down the hall with Mack trailing behind him. He tackles Ronan to the floor, and I gasp for air as Lachlan holds him down and repeats a bunch of stuff I don't understand.

"Ye're not there," Lachlan says. "Ronan. Ye're okay. You are in Boston now. With me, Lachlan. It's okay."

Ronan's breathing hard and fast, his eyes fully dilated as they dart around the room. He's a cornered animal right now. Unrecognizable. But those eyes. They remind me of a small boy. One who has no idea what he's just done. And when they land on me curled up on the couch with Mack trying to calm me, they fill with horror.

"I told you not to touch him," Conor whispers.

"I didn't know," I croak.

My voice is hoarse. I can barely speak. And I have no doubt I'll have bruises around my neck when I look in the mirror. But Conor is right. I should have listened. But I couldn't have known. My eyes find Ronan's again, and he looks away.

Lachlan takes over, shouting out directions.

"Conor, take Sasha home."

I try to argue, but I can't even speak. Mack gives me a worried look and then pulls Lachlan across the room where they start to argue. But it doesn't matter. One look at Ronan, and I know he doesn't want me here. I never should have come here.

I stand up on shaky legs and nod at Conor. He helps me across the room, and Mack runs over to meet us at the door.

"I'm so sorry, Sash," she says. "They gave him something to knock him out. It must have done something. I don't know. But it'll be okay, I promise."

I give her a nod because I can do nothing else.

It's the lie we all want to believe. That it will be okay.

The problem is that it never really is.

Chapter Nine

Ronan

From my bed, I listen to the deep voice by the door. The man is big and strong and has brown eyes like me. The lady who looks after us said he is my father. But I do not know him. I know nothing but these four walls. And these three other lads beside me.

And this lady. The nice lady who looks after us, but tells us not to speak.

I do not even know her name. But she's all I've ever known. This lady and these four walls. She is not my mammy. I do not know who my mammy is. But this man, she says, is my da.

He comes to the bed where I am and sits beside me. I curl my knees up and look at him, wondering if he's come to take me home. This place is all I've ever known, but these other lads, they say that they came from other homes. They say I must have a home too, somewhere.

"You are a good lad," the man says. "I've heard many reports about you, my son."

"Am I coming to live with you now?" I ask him.

"No," he says. "You will continue to live here until you finish training. This is the way soldiers are made."

They always tell me the same words, but I don't understand them.

"I have something very important I need ye to do for me today, son."

"What is it?" I ask.

He holds out his hand, and I stare it.

"Come with me," he says.

"To where?"

"Today marks a special day. Today you are eight years old. And today your training will begin."

He takes my hand in his. It's warm and big and it feels strange. I don't think I ever remember someone touching me before. The lady who feeds us never touches us. She says it is not allowed.

My da opens the door, and I freeze.

"I am not allowed to go out the door," I tell him.

He smiles at me. "Today you are, son."

I don't want to go out there. But he pulls me through and shuts the door behind us. The air is warm, and it smells strange. Everything feels strange. My eyes try to adjust to the darkness as I'm pulled along.

When we turn the corner, there is a large fire blazing. And people. A lot of people. I've never seen them before, but they are all staring at me.

My father kneels down in front of me and meets my eyes. "Do ye remember everything the lady has been teaching you in that room, son?"

I nod. I always listen carefully so I don't miss anything she says.

"So ye remember then that we must make sacrifices to prepare for a better future. And today, Ronan, you will become known by another name. You will become a man. A future soldier. And after tonight, you will not see me again until you finish training."

"But I only just met you," I argue.

"This is the way soldiers are made," he says.

His eyes are wet and it makes me nervous.

"I know that you will do me proud, Ronan."

He musses the top of my hair and then leads me towards the people. They are split into two groups, and between them is a large pit. A beam lies across the center like a bridge, only it's very narrow.

"You stand here," my da says. "And I'm going to walk to the other side. And when I tell ye to, you must walk across that beam towards me, Ronan. And ye must only look at me as you do it. No matter what anyone says or does. You only look at me. And you cross the beam. Do ye follow?"

I nod, even though I really don't.

He lets me go and walks around the pit, and the people are starting to yell things at me. They are all watching me. I try not to *listen and do as my father says. When he tells me to, I steady my feet and move onto the beam.*

When I look down below me, I get scared. It's a long way down, and I don't want to fall. My father directs me to move, and I try to remember everything the lady has taught us. That we must always do as we are told straight away without any hesitation.

I look at my da, and he's holding out his hands. I move slowly and carefully towards him one tiny step at a time. But the people are talking louder now. Chanting. The rules that the lady has been teaching us. They are chanting them over and over as I cross the beam.

And then something hits me in the arm. It hurts and surprises me. But I don't take my attention off my da. It happens again on my leg, and this time I notice it's a small stone. The people are throwing them at me.

I don't understand. But the chanting is getting louder, and my hands are sticky. I'm halfway across the beam. And then something wet hits me in the face. It smells like fruit, only rotten. I try to wipe it from my eyes, but something hits me in the leg as I do. And that's when I lose my balance.

The last thing that I see before I fall into the pit below is the disappointed expression on my da's face. And he was right. Because even when the men come and carry me back to the room and tell me that my leg is broken, I never see him again.

***

Conor tries to accompany me to my house, but I tell him to stay put. I just want to be alone. He apologizes again, and I disregard him entirely.

The drive home is short and quiet. Not many people know I live on the same street as Crow. I've followed him all my life. Ever since he found me in that bloody massacre of a church so many years ago. The memories are blurry at times, but occasionally sharp too.

I walk up the steps to my door and am greeted by the dog. When I collapse onto the sofa, she jumps into my lap and whines as she nudges me. I don't know what she wants. I wish she would leave me alone, but I can't bring myself to push her away.

"I suppose ye're hungry again," I tell her.

She whines in agreement and then curls up on my lap. It's odd that it doesn't bother me. I've never been around an animal before. But I know she'd never try to hurt me. So it doesn't bother me.

My head falls back against the chair and I think of Sasha. The horrific thing that I've done which I'll never be able to wash away.

The blood of others has never troubled me. I kill to protect the syndicate. Crow, Conor, Niall. The men who have been loyal to me. My brethren. But I've never hurt a woman.

I never wanted to hurt Sasha.

She didn't come to me. She didn't trust me enough to protect her from Donovan. Or to tell me that he knew our secret. I've been out of sorts since I learned the truth. I wanted to fault her for it. Shake her and demand that she tell me why. She was supposed to trust me. To understand that I would take care of her.

But now I know. I know exactly why.

She'll never trust me again.

Two days come and go with calls unanswered before Crow comes knocking at my door. He lets himself in and sits down across from me.

The dog is in my lap, and he looks at her and then to me with a stupid grin on his face.

"I'm not keeping her," I tell him.

"Ah sure," he agrees. "She's awfully fond of you though."

I set her down on the floor and tell her to go away. She sits down and rests her head on my foot instead.

"Ye're needed back at the club," Crow says. "We have a shipment tonight, in case you forgot."

"I haven't forgot," I tell him.

"Could have fooled me," he says. "Being as I haven't heard from ye in two days."

"I've been busy."

Silence falls between us, and I can't look at him. Crow knows me better than anyone. He doesn't judge me. Or blame me. He's always let me be who I am and never asked me to change. But I'm still ashamed for what I've done.

"She's fine, if ye're wondering," he says. "Mack's checked up on her twice, as have I."

I don't reply, but his words make the tension in my muscles dissolve just a bit. Even if they shouldn't.

"Do ye believe it would be the end of the world if you just talked to her, Fitz?"

"And what exactly would I have to say?" I reply.

"The truth. She could understand it if you gave her a chance to."

"I still don't understand it myself," I tell him. "How can ye expect me to explain it to her."

"Or that's what ye like to say anyway," Crow says. "Suit yourself."

He stands and walks towards the door.

"Six tonight," he says. "Don't be late."

I nod, and he pauses with his palm on the handle. "I guess it also won't interest ye to know that Sasha wants to leave when her mom passes."

I look up at him, trying to process his words. The tension that dissolved only moments ago returns with a new sort of pressure, and my head swirls with the frustration of trying to sort out this unfamiliar emotion.

"But as ye said, no point in talking about it," Crow continues. "Just in case ye did care to know though, I told her yes."

Chapter Ten

Sasha

I'm halfway between sleep and consciousness when I feel the weight of the bed dip. At first, I wonder if I'm dreaming. Because in my sleep addled brain that's the only possibility I want to accept.

But when I catch the shadow of a man hovering over me, followed by his gloved hand sliding over my mouth, I try to scream. The hand clamps down tighter over my mouth, and all I can taste is the leather of his glove while I thrash beneath him.

He climbs on top of me and pins me with his weight, and tears leak out of my eyes unbidden. But when he leans forward, his scent lingers between us. Malt liquor and roasted pine nuts. And it has the immediate effect of calming me.

"Ronan?"

The question is muffled behind his glove, but when he senses me calming, he smooths my tangled hair away from my face. I can make out his eyes now in the dim light, wild with rare emotion. He isn't wearing his glasses. And his suit jacket is missing, leaving only a crisp white button up stretched across his chest. His neck is corded, his breathing harsh. He's angry. But I'm not afraid.

I reach up and pry his hand away from my mouth so I can talk freely.

"What are you doing here?" I ask. "How did you even get in?"

Those are the two most logical questions to ask in this situation, rather than why he's sneaking into my room, scaring me half to death. Ronan always goes about things in odd ways, and it's almost comical that I've come to expect this sort of behavior from him. He doesn't answer me though, as usual, so I continue to push him.

"Talk to me," I insist. "Tell me what's wrong."

I don't actually expect him to answer. He never answers me. So this time when he does, it shocks the ever living hell out of me.

"You didn't tell me," he says.

His voice is accusing, tinged with hurt and anger.

"I didn't tell you what?"

"About Donovan."

Shame wells up inside of me, and I blink back tears as I shake my head. I don't want to talk about that. I don't want to try to explain my logic. It will never make sense to him. These guys, they all think the same. He would be offended if I told him I was trying to protect him. But the alternative is even worse.

"I knew what you would do to him if I told you," I whisper. "I don't think you would be able to help yourself. Just like with Blaine."

He's quiet and still, studying me with his eyes. Those eyes make me feel exposed. Like I can't hide from him. But right now, I don't want to.

"Am I right, Ronan?"

Silence. I hate his silence. I don't understand why he can't just talk to me. Why it's so hard for him to talk to me, but not everyone else.

"I knew what the consequences would be if you killed him," I say. "And I couldn't let that happen. I couldn't let anything happen to you because of me. Because of what you did for me."

He doesn't blink. Or move. Or show any sort of a response to my confession whatsoever, except for an overwhelming sadness in his eyes. It makes me feel like I betrayed him. He can't understand. He could never understand.

"I know what you must think of me," I attempt to justify. "But I never gave him my body. I did things I'm not proud of to keep him quiet. But I just wanted him to keep his mouth shut. I just wanted…"

A sob bursts from my lips, and Ronan lowers his body over mine, swallowing me up completely. He's got me pinned, the heat of his body soaking into mine. He expels a deep breath. And then another. He's wrestling with himself. Eye fucking me while he tries to talk himself out of it at the same time. But it's too late. We both know it.

He's on me then. His hands are on my body, groping me. They feel huge against me. Rough and calloused. The hard to my soft. His face is buried in my hair, wrecking it as his nose drags along my neck. He's breathing me in. Taking another hit of me like it's the thing he's been jonesing for all this time. His cock jams against my hip bone when he grinds into me.

He nudges my legs apart and pushes his palm between my legs like he owns that part of me. Who am I to argue? He does fucking own me. He's polluted my mind so that I can only ever think of him. Only ever want him.

My hands slide up his back as I wrap my legs around him and pull him closer. My breath is hot against his ear, murmuring his name. Any shame or confusion has dissipated into a haze of manic craving. I will never understand what it is about this quiet, enigmatic man that renders me completely senseless.

Ronan feels it too. This explosive link between us. All I have to do is enter his orbit, and I'm a slave to his power. I suspect that's why he's always avoiding me. He doesn't want to give in to the same force.

But right now, in the darkness of my bedroom, he's already surrendered. He's fumbling with his belt buckle, even as he pleads with me to put an end to the madness.

"Tell me to stop," he chokes out. "Tell me not to touch you."

I don't. Instead, I drag my fingers through his hair and watch him shudder.

"Take off your clothes," I counter. "Let me feel you, Ronan."

He ignores me, too far gone to hear or make sense of my words. He yanks my panties aside roughly and plows into me in one hard thrust. A strangled sound of shock and pleasure bleeds up from my throat, and he freezes to look down at me.

"Keep going," I beg.

He couldn't stop if he tried though. He's fucking me like he's drunk. He's manic and out of control. Banging into me so hard it's going to leave bruises. His eyes keep falling shut, but he's trying to keep them open. Watching me.

He's searching my face, but for what I can't tell. I feel like he needs my reassurance. That he hasn't killed me in his insanity. That he's doing this right. I don't know why, but there's vulnerability in his eyes.

I stroke my fingers down the base of his neck and pull him closer. I want to kiss him. He's never let me kiss him. I can't even imagine how good it's going to feel, but I know once I have a taste I'll be ruined forever.

It takes him a moment to understand what it is I want. And when I brush my lips against his, he hesitates. But it only lasts a second. A visible shudder moves through him when my breath mingles with his, and it triggers something inside of him. His fingers grip my face roughly, holding me in place as he tastes me too. It's not soft. It's not sweet. It's something wild and three long years in the making. A kiss that purges the memory of all other kisses before him.

Ronan devours me with his mouth and with his body. His thrusts are erratic and out of control. I think he's trying to be gentle, but he can't rein himself in. His hands are cupping the back of my head, our tongues and teeth clashing with the force of our want for each other. He looks like he's in agony. Drugged, so high on me I can't bring myself to look away for even a second. This man's strength is unrivaled in anyone else I've ever known, but right now he's a slave to me.

It isn't one sided. Every part of my body responds to him. To his taste and his touch. It's chaotic and hot, the way our hips bump against each other and we can't seem to find a comfortable medium. We're caught up in the madness, and I've never been more turned on in my entire life. He's fucking me like I'm his prize. His trophy.

And then he's not fucking me at all. His head falls back and his entire body shakes as he lets out an agonized groan. Warmth fills me, and it surprises me. I'm not the only one.

There's a beat of silence before Ronan pulls away awkwardly, searching my eyes again for something he doesn't want to see. Even if it isn't there, he's seeking out anything he can latch onto. A reason to leave. I grab his face and pull it back to mine, mauling him with my lips.

It works. Because whatever was on his mind only a moment ago is soon forgotten as he grows inside of me again. The longer we kiss and touch and feel each other, the harder he gets. And then he's thrusting into me, again. I kiss my way down his throat, tasting his skin and his scent. I'm moaning against him, and every time I do, a sound of relief and pleasure echoes from his own chest.

My hands find his ass and I try to pull him deeper inside of me, but he pushes my palms up to his back. I don't question it. Ronan is different. I don't know if something awful happened to him. I don't know why he won't take off his clothes or what his unspoken rules are. And I don't want to push him past his comfort zones.

But it doesn't stop me from testing them. When I slip my hands beneath the fabric of his shirt to feel his skin, he sighs out his pleasure. His movements are still jarring. Hard, brute thrusts that he can barely control. His body is powerful and solid in my hands. But he's unsure of himself.

When he yanks down my chemise and my breasts bounce free, he becomes distracted and stops moving altogether as he pauses to stare at them. His eyes are heavy with hunger when he dips his head to taste me. He pins me down and licks at my nipples. And then he's sucking me into his mouth, groaning against my skin.

He's a mixture of brutal and sensual. Sweet and hard. Rough and thoughtful.

Everything about him is so fucking male. His hands, his mouth… they dwarf every part of me. In his arms, I'm small and fragile. Completely at his mercy. His cock inside of me stretches me to the point of pleasure and pain.

He starts moving again, and I can't do anything but lay here and take it. His perfect hair mussed from my hands, his pants hanging just off his hips as he fucks me into the bed. I never want it to end. But the pressure I so desperately need to escape is building inside of me, and I can't hold back any longer.

My head jerks back against the pillow and I dig my fingers into his back as I come hard and clamp down around his cock. Guttural and unfamiliar sounds vibrate from my throat against Ronan's chest as he echoes me with his own. Warm spurts of his come fill me as he tips his head back and closes his eyes.

I wrap my arms around him and squeeze, terrified that he's going to go away now. Like he always does. That he'll leave and pretend this never happened for another two years. I'm not ready for that. I can't handle that.

I don't want to stop touching him. I don't want to stop feeling this way. The way I do when I'm with him. Maybe it makes me weak, to want someone so much. But if he were to say the word right now, I would be his. I'd do anything he asked of me in this moment.

But just as I feared, when his breathing has calmed, he pulls away. He won't even look at me as he fastens his belt buckle and zips up his pants before smoothing his hair back into place.

"Ronan?"

There's no response. He just ignores me as if I'm nothing. And I can take that treatment from everyone else in my life, but not him. So when he gets up to leave, I lash out at him the only way I can.

"When can I expect you back?" I yell at his retreating form. "Another two years from now? You just gonna' come in here and fuck me as you please like every other man in your outfit tries to? Well next time, make sure you bring a condom because I'm not on the fucking pill!"

His shoulders draw together as he reaches for the door, and I know I've hit a nerve with him. I shouldn't have said it, but it's the truth. He doesn't have to worry about these things as he goes on his merry way, but I do.

Just like the last time.

I saw the way he watched me after it happened. For months, he kept glancing at my stomach. Wondering. Fearing. Worrying. I could see it in his eyes. He was afraid he'd gotten me pregnant.

That only makes it hurt worse.

And if I had needed any confirmation that leaving this place is the best thing for me, this is it. But when he slams the door behind him, it doesn't make it any easier to accept.

Chapter Eleven

Ronan

*T*ime in this black space does not exist.

I haven't any clue how long it's been since I've seen another human. Not even Farrell or Coyne. The closest I come is when the door opens and a small sliver of light spills in for a moment as they toss me a mesh bag with my rations for the day.

The bread is always moldy and stale, but I eat it nonetheless. I miss the lady in the room. The one who cared for us. But they told me I will never see her again. I'm a man now, they say. It's time to forget all else apart from my training and my purpose.

The racket never ceases. Every day, it's loud music. And then crying babies. Tortured screams. An endless reel of noise. I've become immune to it. Learned to sleep with it. But the bugs and the rats, I cannot. They are always crawling on me, and I can't see them.

I feel as though I'm going mad. I think that's what they want. Then I question if the bugs are even real. If perhaps I only imagine them in my head.

I don't know the day or even the year when they come for me again. Coyne and Farrell. They look different. They have beards now, and when the cool air hits my skin, I realize the season has changed too. They speak to me as we walk, but the words don't register.

My mind has drowned everything out. Even them. They lead me to a big building I've never been in before. And then to a kitchen, with a metal door. Farrell opens it and shoves me inside. He points at the corner, where there's a bucket and a blanket. His lips move, but there's only the screaming. Wailing. Loud music.

And then they leave.

It's cold. Even colder than the cellar where they kept me before. It's a freezer, I realize. Soon, Coyne and Farrell come back with another lad. I've seen him during parts of my training. Alex. They shove him inside and point to the other bucket and blanket.

He tries to speak to me too. I sit down and wrap the blanket around my shoulders and question how old I am now. Twelve, I think. Maybe even older. I haven't a clue. Only the darkness exists, even out here in the light.

The air becomes colder with each passing minute, and soon my eyes grow heavy. I fall asleep, and it feels nice. I'm warm. And comfortable. But then someone's kicking me with his boot. I look up to see Alex, and the ringing in my ears has finally stopped. I can hear him now though it's still distorted.

"You have to keep moving," he says.

I kick him away with my foot and try to go back to sleep. But he persists.

"If you go back to sleep, you will die. You have to keep moving to stay warm. It's a test. When you get really cold, you feel like you want to go to sleep. But if you do, you'll never wake up again."

I blink up at him and process his words. I don't know if he's right or not, but maybe he is. Maybe that's why I feel so warm. Why I feel like I don't want to move.

When I finally do, my body is stiff, and I can't feel my fingers when I press them to my lips.

"We have to keep moving," Alex says. "It's the only way to stay alive. We have to do it together. Keep each other awake."

I stand up and wait for Alex's lead. I don't know how he knows so much, only that he was brought here a lot later than I was. He speaks of the places outside of the compound. Of school and the things he learned there. I know none of these things, but when he speaks, I believe him.

He paces the length of the freezer, and I follow suit. And then he tells me more about the places. He talks about a church. A big white church where him and his mammy used to go every Sunday. He never tells me what happened to her, but his voice is sad when he says her name. He tells me a lot of things about her, but never what happened.

I don't have a mammy. Or a da. Only Coyne and Farrell. And now Alex too.

We aren't supposed to speak to each other. But he always speaks to me. And we always seem to be in the same phases of training together too.

Throughout the next hour, he tells me all sorts of things. But we're both slowing down. My eyes will barely stay open, and Alex is slurring his words.

When Coyne finally comes back for us, I am relieved. But that relief never lasts long. He doesn't take me back to the pit. Instead, he takes us to the pond where Farrell is already waiting.

We stand in line with some of the other lads, and they bind our hands and feet. And then one by one, they shove us into the water.

Ten of us go in. Only seven ever come out.

***

As I'm heading off from Sasha's, Crow rings me. As always, his timing is impeccable.

"Aye," I answer. "What is it?"

"Niall's received word from the Russians that Andrei is back in town," he says. "They want you to take care of it."

"Where?"

"It's a house," he replies. "I'll text you the address."

"Fine."

"Just scope it out first," Crow tells me. "They don't know if he's there alone."

Silence falls, and I think of Sasha upstairs. How I've made an arse of myself with her again. How I haven't a clue what I'm doing with her or how to pleasure a woman. When she touches me, I have no control over my reactions. It feels too good. And I know I'm going to embarrass myself. Just like I did tonight.

I could ask Crow about it. But the notion of that is even worse. At this stage in my life, I should have worked these things out by now. But I haven't.

I've only ever been good at one thing. And it isn't this.

"Fitz?" Crow breaks the silence. "All good?"

"It's all in hand," I tell him. "I'll sort out Andrei."

"They want it done clean," Crow says. "OD or suicide would be preferable. Anyone he's been working with needs to know he's dead."

"I'll take care of it," I reassure him.

"I'm sure I don't need to remind ye how you mentioned you wanted more responsibility," Crow says. "This job is an important one, Fitz."

I don't reply. He doesn't need to spell it out for me. He wants me to prove my worth. To the syndicate. To him.

To Sasha.

I had a notion that taking on more responsibility might make me worthy of her. But as it stands I'm clearly not, and I doubt I'll ever be the sort of man she needs. My weakness tonight only further proved that. It wouldn't do to be cocking it up every time I'm around her. It's the reason I've kept my distance.

"Are ye sure everything's alright?" Crow asks again.

"Aye. Everything's just grand."

***

When I reach the address that Crow texted me, the familiar pressure and rage has coiled so tightly inside of me I can scarcely contain it.

This is why I'm the Reaper.

None of the other lads in the syndicate are keen on this job. They don't have rage like I do. Or bloodlust like I do. They don't feel this pressure inside them. They kill when necessary. But it's a switch they can turn on and off. Mine never turns off. There's always this rage, simmering below the surface. I only have to choose a memory, a thought... and it's there.

I disengage. These lives I take are insignificant to me. They mean nothing. These men have done wrong. The unredeemable. My only job is to send them to meet their maker. It's never bothered me much before. Only now, I see Sasha's face. The way she looked at me in the basement at Slainte. I wonder what she thought of me, in that moment. I wonder what she thinks of me right now.

It makes no difference, I suppose.

I pull the duffle bag from the car and gather what I need. The house has too many lights on, which tells me that Andrei isn't alone.

Most people don't leave so many lights on when they are alone. Unless they are afraid. And Andrei isn't afraid.

He's a butcher, like me. But unlike me, he does it for pleasure. Women, mostly. Prostitutes. He's been carving them up and leaving a trail of gore in every city he visits. He was an associate of the Russians, but he betrayed them. It doesn't surprise me. I doubt the man has ever met a moral he didn't scoff at.

Crow wanted this done cleanly. If I go in there now that isn't going to happen. His expectations of me swirl around in my head, combining with the bitterness of this evening. Of Sasha.

I embarrassed myself in front of her.

The rage resurfaces, and washes away everything else. I screw the silencer onto my weapon and walk around to the back of the house. There's a window at ground level. I kick it in and then move to the back door, waiting quietly as voices erupt inside the house.

Footsteps sound on the stairs into the basement, and someone yells out in Russian to check the back yard.

The first man barely has the door cracked before I put a bullet in his head. He falls to the floor and I walk over his body and straight towards the spray of gunfire that's now aimed at me.

From the adjoining wall, I manage to take out another shooter.

The remaining two voices speak in muffled Russian before coming to an agreement. There's still a man in the basement. And two in the kitchen. I haven't worked out which one of them is Andrei. I won't until I see him.

The front door shuts, and I have no choice. I go in blind. A bullet whizzes past my ear and then another hits me in the shoulder.

The man who fired it receives a bullet between the eyes in return. His friend is edging towards the door. It isn't Andrei. I suspect that being the coward he is, he's the one who slipped out the front door and ran. This one's only a young lad. He's holding a gun, but I have a notion by the hopeless look on his face that it's empty.

His eyes are wide and filled with fear. It isn't an expression I'm unaccustomed to. Most people fear death. It's only natural. But this lad, he looks like someone else I once knew. That boy from the compound. The one who died under Farrell's hands. The one who set into motion all of the events that made me into the man I am.

And looking at this lad now, I both pity and loathe him.

But I can't find it in me to raise my weapon.

He's already had a clear look at my face. It would be unwise to let him go. But that's exactly what I do. And to make matters worse, when he slips out the door, I sign my own death warrant.

"Tell Andrei that the Reaper sends his regards. We'll meet another day."

Chapter Twelve

Sasha

There's a dull thump coming from the front door.

At first, I'm certain that I'm dreaming it, but the sound continues until it dwindles down to a light tapping.

I slip out of bed and throw on a tee shirt and some yoga pants. I didn't even bother to get dressed or shower after Ronan left. Because I still wanted to smell like him. Pathetic, much?

By the time I get to the front door, the sound has stopped. And when I look out the peephole, I don't see anything either.

It's starting to feel like a horror movie, but I keep the chain on and crack the door open. And then I find Ronan, slumped against my door, with blood all over his shirt. I have to cover my mouth to keep from screaming.

I unlock the chain and open the door, and he looks up at me with those frigging sad brown eyes of his.

"Ronan?"

"No doctors."

It's the only thing he says before his head lolls to the side. And I'm officially freaking out. I kneel down to inspect him. He's bleeding from a wound in his shoulder and it looks like he's already lost a lot.

I clasp his face in my hands and give him a little shake.

"Ronan, I need you to stay awake, okay? And I need your help getting inside the apartment. Can you do that for me?"

He doesn't reply, but he does move. He tries to stand up, and I wrap my arm around his back. But he's too large, and I can't support him.

We make it just inside the door before he collapses again. I can't stop looking at the blood. Too much blood. And I'm close to panic. I know Lachlan will kill me if I call an ambulance, but I really think he needs one this time.

I make him as comfortable as I can on the floor, unbuttoning his coat so I have access to the wound. I whip off my tee shirt and press it over the bullet hole and then reach for his hand. His eyes are barely open, and he's so weak. I feel him slipping away, and I can't have that.

"I have to get you a doctor."

"No doctors," he croaks.

"Jesus, Ronan. I don't have a choice."

"No doctors," he says again.

I press his hand over the tee shirt and hold it firmly in place. "You stay right there. I'm going to call Lachlan, okay?"

He nods, and his eyes close.

I run to my bedroom and fumble around the nightstand for my cell phone. When I find it, something else occurs to me. It's going to take Lachlan a while to get here. And even longer to find someone who can help him. But I know someone who can, and she's on standby, waiting for me to call anytime I need her.

I know it's wrong, and they'll probably just as likely kill me for this, but I scroll through my contacts and dial Amy's number. She answers on the third ring, her voice sleepy.

"Sasha, is everything okay?" she asks.

"No," I squeak out. "I need you to come over please. Right away."

"Okay," she says. "I'll be there."

"Please hurry."

I hang up the phone and dial Lachlan as I move back towards Ronan. He's barely conscious, but he's still breathing. I hold pressure over the wound and give Lachlan a quick explanation of what's happened. He tells me he's on his way, so I hang up and wait.

Minutes come and pass, and I keep Ronan's head in my lap, tracing over the lines of his face and stroking my fingers through his hair. Occasionally he finds the strength to look up at me.

"I'm going to take these off," I tell him as I remove his glasses. "Okay? I want you to be comfortable."

He doesn't reply. He's just watching me, calm as ever, like it's no big deal. I want to ask him what happened. I want to ask him why he came to me. I have so many questions for him, but I know he needs to save his energy. So instead, I just sit beside him and stroke his face.

"You have kind hands," he murmurs.

His eyes close again, and he starts to slip into unconsciousness.

"Ronan, you've got to stay with me."

I watch his chest, and it's still moving, but it's hard to tell because my eyes are blurred with tears. The door opens and Amy nearly trips over both of us.

"Oh my God," she says. "Have you called an ambulance?"

"No," I tell her. "He doesn't want a doctor. Please, you have to help him."

"I... I can't," she sputters. "I don't have the tools, my license..."

"Amy, please," I beg. "He's going to die if you don't do something. Just help him until Lachlan can get a doctor here."

She hesitates for another moment and then seems to come to some sort of a decision.

"I'll help him get stabilized," she says. "But he needs to go to the hospital when I'm done."

She kneels down beside me, and starts listing off things that she needs.

I run around the house like a lunatic trying to gather everything and get them to her as fast as I can. She cuts his shirt off, and for the first time I see his chest. And I'm shocked by the amount of scars that litter his body.

Amy is too.

"Who is this guy?" she asks.

"He's my..." I pause. "My friend. A really good friend."

The door opens again, and this time it's Lachlan. His face is white, and when his eyes land on Ronan, it's obvious how much he really does care about this man. I've never felt like Lachlan and I would be able to relate on anything. But as it turns out, Ronan is our common ground. He's staring back at me too, searching my eyes for answers before he can even ask them.

And then his gaze snaps to Amy, who is poking at Ronan's wound.

"Who is she?" Lachlan asks.

"My mother's home nurse."

I leave out the part about me calling her.

"Can you help him?" Lachlan asks her.

Amy shakes her head in serious refusal. "He needs to go to the hospital. The bullet is still in there, and…"

"Sasha." Lachlan interrupts. "Is there a bed where we can move him?"

"My room," I tell him.

"Good, go get it ready. I need a moment to speak to Amy."

I hesitate for the slightest of seconds and the guilt burns through me. He's probably going to threaten her. Or maybe offer her money. Either way, I don't care. The only thing I care about right now is Ronan and making sure he is okay.

So I do as Lachlan asks, and I walk down the hall and pull back the covers and move everything out of the way.

A moment later, Lachlan is behind me, lingering in the doorway.

"I need you to help me move him in here," he says. "I've called some of the other lads, but I don't want to wait. Amy's going to help him, okay Sash?"

I nod and scurry after him. It takes all three of us to get him into the bed. And then Amy brings in her medical bag, and she starts setting up an IV line.

"What are you going to do?" I ask her.

"She's giving him something to keep him calm," Lachlan explains. "If he wakes up and someone he doesn't know is touching him…"

He leaves the rest lingering, and I nod.

But Ronan does wake up. As Amy's trying to set up the IV. And he goes completely ballistic. For a moment I'm too horrified by what I'm seeing to really understand it. He's always been so strong, so calm and sure. The only time I've ever seen him lose it was with Blaine. But right now, he's like a caged animal, thrashing around in the bed as Lachlan tries to hold him down. His wild and panicked eyes find mine, and my heart splinters. I crawl up on the bed beside him and grab his face.

"Shhh, Ronan," I whisper. "It's okay. Just look at me. Only me."

To everyone's surprise, my words seem to soothe him. So I keep repeating them, stroking his face beneath my fingers. He never takes his eyes off me.

"Do you trust me?" I ask him.

He nods.

"Okay, good," I whisper. "Because I would never let anyone hurt you. Do you know that?"

He blinks and his breathing slows a little as his eyes search mine. Those deep brown eyes look so much like a small boy's in this moment and not the man I know him to be. Right now he isn't a violent predator. He's my sweet, handsome Ronan. And behind the fringe of dark lashes and the armor he's worn for so long, there is trust. For me. And I have a feeling that later, when I reflect on that, I will finally understand the gravity of what that means. Because I doubt Ronan trusts anybody. Even his best friend, Lachlan, who he's known all his life is considered an enemy right now.

But not me. And I won't ever take that trust for granted.

I thread my fingers through his and squeeze.

"I trust Amy," I tell him. "And she's trying to help you, Ronan. Okay? I won't let her hurt you."

He doesn't reply, but he doesn't need to. Everyone can see that he's calmed and Amy seizes the opportunity to get the line set up. Ronan watches me the entire time. But once the line is in, his eyes drift shut. I lean down and kiss him on the forehead, and when I look up through tear soaked eyes, Lachlan is staring at me.

"You calmed him." His voice is tinged with disbelief. "I've never seen anything like that before."

"Oh," I choke out.

The room goes silent, and Amy gets to work. I'm grateful when she asks for my help and I don't have to feel the weight of Lachlan's questioning gaze on me. Throughout the procedure, I act as her assistant. She tells me what she needs from me, and not a word more. She isn't meeting my gaze, and I have a feeling she's really hating me right now for putting her in this situation.

When she's removed the bullet and stitched him up, she washes her hands and packs up her medical bag. Her gaze moves to Lachlan as she lingers in the bedroom doorway.

"Is that all you need from me?"

Her voice is flat and cold. And I don't like it. Because Amy's always been good to me, and I feel horrible for involving her in this.

"Aye," he tells her. "It is."

"Amy," I call out.

She glances at me, and I hug my arms across my body, unsure of what I should even say at this point.

"Um, thank you."

She nods and leaves.

The front door closes, and then it's just Lachlan and I, left to the silence of the room. It's strange, being here with him. I don't know what to say or do. I've never known what to make of this guy. Sometimes he can seem so cold. But seeing him with Mack, I know he's human too. My way of dealing with him has always been to avoid him, but right here and now I can't.

So I sit down beside Ronan on the bed, and Lachlan takes the chair across the room.

"You aren't going to hurt Amy," I blurt. "Right?"

He shakes his head with a grunt. "No, Sasha. I'm not going to hurt Amy. She was paid well for her time here tonight, and I don't think there's even reason for it to be spoken of again."

I nod and brush my fingers over Ronan's hand and arm.

"Tell me what happened to him," I whisper.

"It's not my story to tell," Lachlan answers.

I look up at him, and my eyes are filled with tears. "I just… I want to understand him. I don't know how to understand what he needs, or wants."

Lachlan sighs and leans back in his chair. His eyes dart to Ronan a few more times and then back to me.

"Then ye understand how he feels perfectly."

"Huh?" I stare at him in confusion.

"If you feel like you can't make sense of your own thoughts or emotions, then ye know exactly what Ronan's going through. Only he feels that all the time."

"Oh."

"Come with me," Lachlan says.

"But, what if he wakes…"

"He won't," he says. "He needs to rest."

I stroke Ronan's face one more time before I follow Lachlan down the hall and into the kitchen. He makes himself at home, going through the cupboards until he finds a bottle of wine. He opens it up and pours me a glass. And even though I'm exhausted and the last thing I need to do is drink, I take it. Because I need to know what Lachlan has to say.

"I can't tell you Ronan's story," he says. "Because even I don't know the half of it. I met him when I was thirteen. I won't tell you the where or the how. I don't even know where he came from.

Only that he was raised in a paramilitary training camp run by a political fringe group. They were well known for bombings, copper killings, things of that nature. Their ideologies were radical, and Ronan had been spoon fed them since he was only a wee lad. He had no say in the matter. About any of it. He was born and reared to do one thing alone."

I close my eyes because I can't stand to hear him say it. That Ronan's nothing more than a killer.

"He's a good man," I tell him.

"Aye, he is," Lachlan agrees. "But he's still recovering from the things he went through. Truth be told, I don't know if he'll ever fully recover."

"What do you mean?"

Lachlan scrubs a hand over his face and takes a seat across from me. "I don't know how to say this in a way that you can understand, Sasha. But Ronan doesn't know what to do with himself if he isn't being told. Thinking freely does not come naturally to him. His days are completely regimented. If he isn't working, he's at home. He works out. He eats at a certain time, and only from a small selection of foods. He reads. He works. And he takes orders as they come. Anything else, he doesn't know how to handle it. He comes to things in his own time. And on his own terms."

"But he came to me on his own," I say. "Why?"

"How long do ye think it took him to come to terms with that decision?" Lachlan asks.

I stare down at the table, knowing he's right. It took Ronan two years to come back to me.

"I just want ye to know what ye're getting yourself into here Sasha," Lachlan says. "Ronan needs stability in his life. And if ye're planning on leaving like you say, then the best thing you can do for him is to leave him be. For him to open up to you and then have ye walk away, I fear it will do him more harm than good. And I won't stand for that."

I blink back my tears as I process his words. He's right. I didn't plan on staying. I still don't. So I should stay far away from Ronan, and hope that he can overcome these issues on his own. But the thought of that causes a deep well of despair to spring up inside of me.

"I just want to lay beside him," I tell Lachlan. "For the night. Until he's better."

He nods and then makes a gesture with his hand. "Well go on then," he says. "I'll be here if ye need me."

"You're going to stay here?" I ask.

"Aye." He nods. "He's my brother. I'll be here until I know he's okay."

I give him a small smile and pad down the hall. Ronan's still asleep, my blankets folded over the lower half of his body. I crawl into bed beside him and curl up against his chest, breathing him in. And even though I know what Lachlan said is true, and it's the right thing to do, I don't want to let him go.

And yet when I wake up the next morning, only to find the space beside me empty and every trace of him gone, I'm not in the least surprised.

Chapter Thirteen

Ronan

"**H**ave ye any idea how bad you've fucked this, Fitz?" Crow asks again.

I focus my attention on the dog in my lap, the one staring at me with the big brown eyes.

"I don't know where the bleeding hell your head's at lately," he continues. "Are ye trying to get yourself killed?"

I don't answer.

Mack walks down the hallway and sits down on the sofa beside me. She hasn't let Crow out of her sight since that night he fought for her. I still don't particularly care for her, but I do believe she's proved to be loyal to Crow now.

"It's a nice place you got here, Ronan," she says. "Although, it could do with a woman's touch."

The dog in my lap barks in agreement, and Mack smiles.

"I didn't take you for a dog person," she says.

"I'm not," I tell her.

Crow is staring at the two of us, shaking his head.

"Do ye have any other pressing concerns to discuss?" he asks. "How about the shade of your curtains? I don't think it suits the goddamn sofa."

Mack laughs. "Cut him some slack, Lach," she says. "Ronan looks like he's having a bad day."

"This is why women don't attend business meetings," Crow says in response.

"I wanted to see where he lived," she argues. "I didn't realize it was just down the street."

"You'd do well to forget it," I tell her. "Nobody else needs to know it."

Crow glares at me.

"C'mon, Mack. Let's go."

"I think I'll stay here for a bit," she says. "With my old buddy Ronan. I don't feel like going to the club just yet."

Crow glances at me, and I shrug. I don't want her here, but I've learned to pick my battles with this one.

"You'll bring her along after?" he asks.

"Aye."

"Have Rory come too," Crow says. "I don't want you going out alone until we find Andrei."

"I don't need a bleeding escort," I reply.

"It wasn't a request," Crow answers.

Mack walks him to the door where they participate in another display of shite I have no need to see. So I busy myself in the kitchen feeding the dog until he's gone. But if I was hoping for a respite from Mack, she isn't giving me one.

"Whatcha doing?" she asks as she sits down at the table.

"Feeding the dog."

"Obviously." She laughs. "So what's the deal with you and Sash?"

I blink at her, wondering what she knows. All of the things Sasha could have told her filter through my head, and it makes me angry. She's laughing at me. Because I embarrassed myself.

"Relax, Ronan," Mack says. "It's just that I've noticed you've both been more screwy than usual lately. I mean I know she has a reason, with her mom and all. But what's the deal?"

"I don't know."

I haven't any idea why I'm even indulging her with this line of questioning. But there is a part of me, a small part of me, that wants to ask her some things. I take the box of donuts from the cupboard and set them on the table. When Mack spots them, she grins and it makes me uncomfortable.

"Did you know I was coming?" she asks.

"Crow told me."

"And you bought me donuts," she coos. "Aw, Ronan, you're the best."

She springs up on her feet and tries to hug me. I bat her away.

"I sent Conor out for them this morning. Go hug him."

The next minute, she's sitting at the table shoveling a donut into her mouth.

"Look," she says between mouthfuls. "You can talk to me, Ronan, you know? You don't even have to bribe me with donuts although it certainly does help."

I sit down across from her and fold my hands. I don't even know where to begin. Or what to say.

"Just one sentence," Mack insists. "The first thing that comes to your mind. And go."

"I don't know what she wants," I tell her.

"Well that's easy." She shrugs. "She wants you silly."

I look up at her and scrub my face.

"What I mean is," I clear my throat. "I don't know what she likes."

Mack stops chewing and stares at me. Shame washes over me and I look away.

"Ronan," she says in a voice that's too high. "You're blushing!"

I don't reply. I think she's going to laugh at me, but she doesn't.

"Have you tried asking her?" Mack continues.

"No."

"Right," she snorts. "Because you're... well, you."

"Ye're a girl..." I tell her.

"A woman," she corrects. "But yes. I am of the female variety."

"What do people like you want?" I ask.

"You mean women?" she smiles. "That's a timeless question, Ronan. And one that you'll never have the answer to. It changes every five minutes, and if you try to figure it out, you'll just go mad."

I nod because I suspected as much.

"Ronan, I was joking," she laughs. "Sheesh, you're so serious all the time. Just relax, will you?"

Silence falls between us, and I find myself wishing she'd gone with Crow. This is pointless.

"Look," Mack says. "I can't tell you what Sasha likes, because everyone is different. And even so, I think you kind of have to figure it out together. You know, it takes... like practice."

She makes a face as she says it, and my cheeks burn.

"Do you know what I love about Lachlan?" she asks.

"What?"

"He just takes charge. He does what he wants. And he does it unapologetically. He doesn't ask for permission to kiss me. He just does. If you're so wrapped up in wondering if every little thing you do is wrong or right, then it's not going to be enjoyable for either of you."

"But what if she doesn't fancy it?"

"Then she'll tell you. And you fix it. Simple. It's all about communication, Ronan, which I know isn't your strong suit. But you can't expect to figure all this shit out telepathically. You've got to put yourself out there a bit."

The dog jumps into my lap again, and Mack reaches for another donut.

"But I will tell you one thing though, Fitz. If you want to make a play for Sash, you better do it soon. Girlfriend's getting ready to pack her bags and get outta dodge, and I can't say I blame her."

"I have no idea what any of that means," I tell her.

Mack groans and brushes the crumbs from her hands. "We have a lot of work to do, Ronan."

Chapter Fourteen

Sasha

Emily flew in last night, and she hasn't left Ma's side. She's taking it hard, and in a way I feel guilty that I got more time with her. But this is how Ma wanted it.

"She looks so different," Em whispers. "I didn't want to remember her this way."

"So don't," I tell her. "She wouldn't want you to, Em."

"I'm going up to the roof," she says. "I need some air."

I nod and let her go. Emily is strong. And smart. And I know she's going to do great things in her life. But this is going to leave a gaping hole in her heart. She's too young to have lost both parents. She reminds me a little of Mack in that way. I see similarities between them. The tough fronts they put up for the world. Em's always been like that.

With Amy fixing the dosage of Ma's medicine, she's managed to have a few lucid moments throughout the day. And I'm surprised when Emily leaves, she opens her eyes again.

I lay down beside her and try not to cry. When I look into her eyes tonight, I know it's going to be the last time. She's in too much pain to wake any more. And it isn't fair to her.

So this has to be goodbye.

I hold her hand and talk to her. Anything that comes to my mind, I just blurt it out. I'm telling her about things that will never happen. A house I'll probably never have. The names of my future children. Anything to keep my mind off what's coming.

Ma watches me talk, but doesn't respond. I don't expect her to. She's weak and tired. But I still want to hear her voice. Just one last time.

I promised myself I'd be strong for her. But I can't. I'm too emotional. So eventually, I break down and just cry. She holds me, the way that mothers do.

"Tell me it's going to be okay, Ma," I whisper. "Because I don't feel like it will. I don't know what I'm going to do without you."

I don't expect her to say anything. But she does.

Her voice is faint and scratchy. But she speaks. For me.

"He says," she forces out, "he will protect you."

"What?" I blink at her, desperate for more.

But she doesn't speak again. She smiles and pulls my face down so that she can kiss me on the forehead. And then she closes her eyes and falls back into unconsciousness.

***

Amy is still in the kitchen when I finally emerge, and I'm grateful for her presence. She's made dinner, which isn't part of her job requirement. Neither is staying this late when she isn't even getting paid for it. She hasn't said a word about what happened with Ronan. And I appreciate that too. I know she's not over it, but whatever Lachlan said to her has kept her from bringing it up.

I give her a shaky smile as I sit down and she hands me a dish of spaghetti.

"Thank you, Amy."

"How was she?" she asks as she makes herself a dish.

"She seemed very coherent," I tell her. "But she said something strange. I couldn't really make sense of it."

"It happens," Amy says softly. "Sometimes their thoughts only make sense to them. The medication can do that."

I nod, deciding that's probably the best possible explanation. But even as I tell myself that, I can't stop thinking that isn't it. That Ma knew exactly who she was talking about. And he goes by the name of Ronan.

***

The next morning, Mack shows up at my door with Dunkies.

I'm surprised to see her, but it seems like everyone has decided to start paying me regular visits. Amy told me this would probably happen. People don't really know what to do in these situations, so they try to be helpful. They make casseroles and bring cards and flowers. I don't mind. It keeps the apartment from being so quiet. Even with Amy and Em here round the clock now, it still feels empty. We're all just walking around like zombies, waiting for the end to come.

"Hey, Mack," I greet her. "C'mon in."

She makes herself at home on the sofa and pulls out an impressive spread of donuts. The girl is a certified sugar addict. Although right now, nothing sounds better than some sugar and caffeine.

"How is she?" Mack asks.

"Amy says it probably won't be long now," I tell her.

Mack gives me a gentle smile and then gets down to business. "Well, my reasons for being here are twofold. I came to see if you needed anything and to tell you that Lach wants you to take as much time off as you need."

She drops a stack of cash onto the coffee table, and I swallow the lump of emotion in my throat.

"Thank you," I whisper. "Please tell him I said thank you."

Mack nods, and we eat our donuts in silence for the next few minutes.

"There is something else," she says. "It might not be the right time to bring it up. But then again it might help take your mind off things. I'm not really sure."

I look at her, and she has a blush on her cheeks. I've never once seen Mack blush.

"What is it?"

"Uh… well Ronan and I sort of had… like a birds and bees talk the other day."

I nearly choke on the coffee I just drank.

"There were donuts involved," she says nervously. "And a lot of awkwardness."

"He talked to you about this?" I ask.

Mack stares down at her feet, and I realize why she's being so weird about it. She thinks I'm going to be upset with her.

"I'm not mad," I tell her. "If that's what you think."

Her shoulders sag in relief and she nods. "I don't know how to do this whole thing. I mean, I'm sort of friends with Ronan, but not really. I think he just feels comfortable talking to me about you because he has no one else, ya know? I couldn't even imagine him talking to the guys about it."

I focus on my coffee cup and bite my tongue to keep from asking her a million questions like a teenager with a stupid crush. But Mack must sense my curiosity because she explains on her own.

"The whole conversation was pretty vague, but I get the gist that he isn't very experienced. He's nervous, and he wants to talk to you, but I honestly just don't think he knows how, Sash."

"Tell me about it," I sigh.

"I don't know what's up with him. Lach is really weird about it. Like oddly protective of him. More so than the rest. He doesn't let people touch him. And once, I saw him threaten Michael when he laughed at Ronan at the club. Like he wanted to tear off Michael's head for laughing at him."

I'm somewhat surprised by the fact that Lachlan seems to have told me more about Ronan than even Mack knows, and I have to think it's for a reason. But then I remember what he said and try to tell myself that this is for the best. That I need to let Ronan go and concentrate on my future.

"I don't get it either," I reply. "I know next to nothing about him. And it doesn't matter anyway at this point."

"Doesn't it?" Mack asks softly.

"No," I say firmly, still feeling the tug in my chest at the way he left the other morning. "I meant what I said, Mack. When Ma is gone, I can't stay here anymore. I just can't. It's time for me to get out of this vacuum."

"Okay, Sash," she says. "If that's what you want, then I respect that. And I fully back you up on whatever you choose to do."

Chapter Fifteen

Sasha

I'm lying in bed, staring up at the ceiling when I hear him come in.

He isn't loud. In fact, he's so quiet it only serves to remind me who he is and what he does. I don't even know how he's getting into the apartment. Or when this habit of his started. Any normal person would be upset. Freaked out, probably.

But when I feel the bed dip and the leather from his gloved hand as he reaches out to touch me, I'm enveloped by a sense of calm. Relief. I feel safe with him, this killer. This man with the somber brown eyes who I don't understand, but want to more than anything.

"Ronan."

My bedside lamp turns on, and he blinks down at me. "Ye're awake."

"I am. How's your shoulder?"

"Almost good as new," he answers. And for some reason, I think he actually believes that.

He has a cheap plastic shopping bag next to him. It looks out of place resting beside this sharp dressed man with the flawless hair and suit. On the outside, he's so perfect it's hard to believe I could ever measure up to him.

I'm sullied. Tarnished. Unclean.

And yet he's looking at me right now like he's never seen anything more angelic in his life. His eyes are unguarded and open. It doesn't happen often. And I'm honestly surprised he's here at all after what happened the last time.

He comes and goes as he pleases. When things get uncomfortable, he runs. But somehow he always knows when I need him. And tonight, I do need him.

"What do you have there?" I gesture towards the bag.

His cheeks flush as he dumps the contents onto the bed. There's an entire armory of condoms, lube, foams, and other over the counter birth control methods.

"I didn't know which ones you like," he says.

His eyes are avoiding mine, and I'm grateful. Because I'm smiling. He's overwhelmed and uncomfortable. I don't know why he gets like that. But I'm curious as hell the more I get to know about him. I want to know how many others he's been with. I want to know why he's so keyed up about something that is second nature to the majority of the men he spends time with.

But I also know that those subjects will likely push him away, so I don't ask.

I grab a box and open it, handing him the foil packet.

"We only need one to start with," I offer.

The room is quiet while Ronan stares down at the packet in his hands. After a pause, he tries to tear it open. It doesn't work. He's fumbling with it because he's being too rough, and there's a red flush creeping up his neck.

I place a hand on his shoulder and he startles. "Do you want some help?"

"No," he clips out.

I bite my lip and wait, and eventually he gets it open. When he pulls out the condom, he stares at it again. I can't see his expression, but he keeps tugging at his collar and the vein in his neck is now throbbing.

It's only when he gets up to leave that it occurs to me he doesn't know what to do with it. I jump out of bed and chase after him, catching him around the arm. He's staring down the hallway, desperate to get away. His skin is on fire beneath my palm, and I know he's counting the steps to the door.

He's frustrated. And I don't know what to do in this situation. Because he won't tell me what's wrong. So I take a chance, and leaning up on my tiptoes, pull his gaze down to mine.

"Come back," I whisper. "I don't want you to go."

His gaze dips to me, and he studies me like I confuse him. Like he doesn't know what keeps bringing him back here. To me. But he isn't trying to leave. He isn't saying no. So I reach down and link our hands together and pull him along behind me. When we get to the bed, I gently push him down on the mattress. I shove all of the products he bought save for one condom into the nightstand drawer so he doesn't have to think about it. And then I crawl up and kneel beside him.

I have his undivided attention. And I'm fully aware that one wrong move on my part will make him bolt. He's here, but he's already halfway out the door. I need him to relax. I need him to feel comfortable with me.

So I start out gradually. My hand grazes his thigh, waiting for his approval or rejection of my touch. He doesn't flinch away, so I take it as a sign to continue.

I drag my fingers up his muscular thigh and over the heated bulge in his trousers. He makes a strangled noise in his throat and closes his eyes as I rub him several times over. His trousers are stretched to their limit here, straining against his swollen erection beneath.

His eyes are losing the battle raging inside of him, growing sleepy with lust. He's so hard against my palm it must be painful for him, but he's waiting to see what I do next. I find the tab of his zipper and pull it down. His belt comes next, and I unwrap his trousers and then grasp him through the cotton of his briefs. My hand slides over the soft cotton, jacking him off through the material. Ronan's hips jerk with every pass, and I know I've eased him back from the edge a little.

I take a chance with my next question, my hand never leaving his shaft. I don't want him to think about it too much.

"Can I take off your pants?"

He blinks up at me, but doesn't answer. The confliction is distracting him. He's uncertain, and I don't want to push him.

"We can leave them on," I amend. "It's not a big deal."

I pull them out of the way as best I can, and he watches as I tear open a new condom wrapper. When I tug down his briefs and his cock springs free, his breathing stops completely. Mine does too. I'm staring at his erection, plump and heavy against his thigh.

Jesus.

He's huge. I knew that, but seeing it is something else entirely. But I'm afraid that if I stare too long, he's going to misinterpret that. So I reach forward with a shaky hand and roll on the condom. Ronan isn't breathing. But he's watching the whole process carefully, like he's memorizing it for next time.

It doesn't make sense. The man is fucking gorgeous. And twenty-nine years old now. It's been two years since he claimed me after killing Blaine, but surely there would have had to be women before that. Right?

As much as I want to ask, it's still too soon. It's going to be one battle at a time with Ronan. And right now, I just want to make him feel good. I want to give him another dose of the drug he craves. I want him to keep coming back to me.

We're oil and water. We don't mix. I'm bad for him. And he's no good for me either, probably. But I'm his, regardless. He needs to know that.

So I remove my chemise and then straddle his hips.

"Is this alright?"

He's staring at my breasts. He's probably seen them a thousand times up on stage, but you wouldn't know it by the way he's ogling them right now.

"Aye," he replies in a husky voice.

I lean forward and take his face in my hands, rubbing my body against his. His hands find the back of my head, and he kisses me hard and rough. Then his head falls back against the pillow, and he just watches.

I give him what he wants. What I've imagined myself doing to him every time I'm up on the stage at Slainte. I grind against his body, and his hands find my ass cheeks, splaying me apart roughly and without finesse. His hips thrust upward, seeking out my warmth.

I let him in, but I don't let him rush it. His hands are still on my ass, trying to pull me down onto his cock when I lean back and take control. I use my hips to guide him inside of me inch by inch. His eyes are glued to the place where we are connected, a contented sigh escaping his lips once he's fully rooted inside.

I roll my hips and use his thighs for leverage, sliding my body up and down over his. He watches himself disappear inside of me with a heavy gaze, like he's doped out of his mind. I know because I feel the same. By all outward appearances, this would look like nothing but a quick fuck to anyone else. His clothes are still on, our skin isn't even touching, but it's the most intimate feeling in the world having him inside of me. His eyes fall shut, and I worry I'm going to lose him. Lose this connection.

"Tell me what you like, Ronan," I whisper.

His eyes open and meet mine. Soft and sweet and content.

"All of it," he answers in a rough voice. "I like all of it."

I want so desperately to know him, even though I shouldn't. I can't get any more attached to this man than I already am. But looking at him here, now, in my bed and underneath me, starving for my touch, I can't help it.

"Do you ever think about this?" I ask. "Do you ever think about me like this?"

"Aye," he answers.

"Tell me what you think about. Tell me what you want me to do."

He doesn't reply, but he's trying to. His eyes are still heavy. He's struggling to keep them open. Every time I rock down against him, he shudders. He groans and grabs my hips to still me, but I keep going, pushing him towards the edge.

He lets out an agonized growl and jerks inside of me as he comes.

His hands tighten around my hips. Whatever progress I think we've made falls to the wayside when he shuts me out again. He's locked inside of his own head, and he's going to bolt at any moment if I don't stop him.

"Ronan, look at me."

He does. And I crack wide open under the weight of those soft brown eyes.

"We have all night," I tell him.

I didn't think they would, but my words relax him a little, so I keep going. My fingers ghost up his neck and over his shoulders, massaging him lightly as he watches me.

"Do you want to know what I think about?" I ask him.

He doesn't answer. I reach for his hand that's still resting on my hip and slide it down between us. I press his fingers over my clit and show him what I like.

He watches me carefully. Taking mental notes of every breath, every reflex, and before long he's doing all the work himself. My hand falls away, and he takes over. He jerks my body forward, shoving my breast into his mouth.

Now it's me who's out of control. Thrashing all over his body, whining at his every touch.

"This is what I think about," I tell him. "I think about you touching me. Just touching me like this. Any way that you want. Hard or soft. I just want you to touch me."

His eyes are dark and warm as they appraise me. He likes what he's doing to me. This is what he wanted.

"Anywhere, Ronan," I repeat. "Just keep your hands on my body. I want to feel you."

My voice is desperate. Frantic. I'm betraying all of the emotion I've bottled up inside of me for the last two years. I'm just blurting out whatever I like now. There is no filter.

"Always you. Only you, Ronan."

He's hard inside of me again. His breathing is harsh, and he's not even moving inside of me. All he has to do is look at me like this and it makes him lose control. That thought is what sends me over the edge. I've barely finished coming around him when he's got me flipped over onto my back. He pulls out long enough to tear off the condom, and then he's thrusting back inside of me.

I cling to his back and suck his throat while he fucks me hard and fast. It isn't like before. There isn't a part of him that's unsure or hesitant now. He's driven purely by his urges. By his instincts.

"I want you to do the things you think about," I tell him. "I want you to fuck me the way that you like."

Ronan groans and fucks me harder. I like to watch him. The way he moves inside of me. The way his arms flex and he loses control.

"Sasha," he grunts between thrusts. "I can't stop."

"Don't," is my reply. "Do whatever you want with me."

The next thing I know, he's heaving me up into his arms and carting me across the room. I don't have time to question it when he pins me up against the wall and starts to fuck me there.

His pants clatter to the ground from the force of his thrusts. I wrap my legs around his waist and he cups my ass in his hand. His other hand is in my hair, wrecking it as he kisses me again.

"Is this what you think of?" I ask when he moves his lips to my throat again. "Fucking me against the wall?"

"Aye," he grunts. "At the club. I want them all to see."

"See what?"

I'm desperate for information, anything he will give me, I want to know.

"I want them to see that ye're mine," he roars as he explodes inside of me again, filling my womb with his warmth.

He buries his face in my neck, the next words out of his mouth coming unbidden.

"I think about ye all the time."

I reach up and stroke his hair, and for a few blissful moments, we just remain there. Our bodies locked together, holding each other. When he finally lets me down, his come leaks down my thigh.

I look down, and so does he.

He didn't use a condom the second time.

Again.

That same panicked expression washes over his face. I want to reassure him, even if it is false.

"It's okay, Ronan."

But he's already buckling his pants up, preparing to flee again. And I can't take this. Indulging these encounters with Ronan is like playing Russian Roulette with my heart. He keeps pulling the trigger. At some point, the wound is bound to prove fatal.

"Don't go," I try again.

He smooths his hair back into place. His face is blank. There's nothing there now. The guard is back up, blocking me out.

He walks towards the front door, and I follow after him. His palm pauses on the handle, and I tell him one more time.

"Don't leave."

But he turns the handle.

And this time when he walks through the doorway, I let my anger chase him.

I grab the door behind him and call after him. He turns around to look at me, and I tell him what I know is best for me.

"What I meant was, don't come back."

Chapter Sixteen

Ronan

"**I**'ve got a lead on Andrei," Crow says.

I nod and toss back the whiskey before standing and shrugging on my coat.

"Rory already checked it out." Crow interrupts me. "So there's no need to rush off anywhere."

"Why?" I ask.

"Ye haven't been yourself lately, Ronan. I don't know what's going on with ye, but we need to tread carefully here. You need to tread carefully here. I need this handled in the proper fashion. Do ye follow me?"

"So I fecked up once, and now ye have no faith in me, is that it?"

"Ah, Fitzy, quit being so bleeding contrary," Crow grunts. "The job is still yours. I just want to be sure everything is in line this time."

I move to leave, and Crow grabs me by the arm. I shake him off.

"Fitz, I need ye to be careful. He's got men scouring the city for you."

"I'm not fussed about it," I tell him. "Let them come. I'd gladly welcome them to try."

"Goddammit, Ronan." Crow slams his fist down on the bar. "Ye're being a gobshite."

"Ah well," I answer him. "That's what I'm good at. Isn't it?"

I try to leave again when he stops me. He's staring at me the way he always does. Like he's trying to work me out. Get inside my head. I don't like that. I don't like people looking at me like that. He knows it too.

"I've got one in the basement for ye," he says. "One of his lads. I doubt you'll get anything else from him, but ye're welcome to try."

***

The music from upstairs vibrates down through the floor as I assemble my tools. There isn't much left of the lad at this stage.

My methods of torture are effective. I know, because I learned from personal experience. So I also know by now this man has nothing else to tell me. He would have given it up if he had.

Most men would like to believe they could withstand anything through sheer will alone. But it isn't true. They all give something up in the end. I don't like what I have to do to them any more than they like getting it.

But it's part of life. The job. The endless stream of days that blur together. Usually, it doesn't bother me so much. I don't like the loud noises. The screams. So I always gag them for this part.

I can't stand the screams. That's the thing I've no stomach for, out of all of it. Loud noises. They grate on me. Make me uptight. Even so, it doesn't usually last too long.

But tonight it's different. Long after I've cleaned up the body and my work area, they are still ringing through my head. It isn't just his screams. The nameless, faceless man that graced my table tonight. I don't remember their faces. Or their names. Only the way their blood looks when it paints the floor.

It always creates a different pattern. Each one is unique.

But tonight, I saw something familiar in this one. It looked like Farrell's blood. And now I can't stop hearing the screams. All the screams. They swirl around me, suffocating me in their intensity.

I stagger back and collapse against the wall, covering my ears. But even when I close my eyes, I still see their faces. Alex. Farrell. The other lads who didn't make it through training. But worst of all is the noise. They were only young, but when they screamed like that, I wanted to kill them.

"Ronan?"

I blink and see Crow standing in the doorway. Only he's distorted, and I don't know why. There's water on my face. He comes to kneel beside me and reaches out to touch me before he changes his mind and withdraws his hand.

"You've been down here for hours, mate," he says.

"I don't like kids," I try to explain. "Because they'll scream. And then... I can't handle the noise. And I'm not good with kids. I'm not good with people."

Crow stares at me, trying to work me out again. "I'm not sure I follow ye," he says.

"I can't ever be around kids," I say. "Because they scream."

Silence falls around us, and Crow just sits beside me for a while. He's good at that. He doesn't judge me. Or laugh at the broken bits of thoughts that I manage to get out. He's usually pretty good at working them out too. Just like he does tonight.

"Ye know, Fitz." He scratches at his stubble. "I don't really think that's true."

"I can't ever find out."

"Ye know that dog ye have at your house," he says. "That dog makes noises, doesn't she?"

I think about his words for a moment before I nod. "Aye, I suppose she does."

"And those noises don't bother ye."

"That's not the same."

Crow is silent for a while again.

"Well, what about Michael's kid? Katie. Remember when he had to leave her at the club with ye that time?"

I do remember. But I'd never thought of it before.

"She was a baby."

"Aye," Crow replies. "And babies cry. And scream sometimes. But ye held her anyway. I think ye even calmed her if I remember correctly."

I stare at the wall ahead of me. I know he's trying to make me feel better. That's what Crow does. But I just keep thinking how I fucked up with Sasha. How she might fall pregnant, and I can't be the man that she needs.

I can kill for her. Fight for her. Do anything for her. Anything for her but that. I can't be a father. I don't know how. Just as I don't know how to be a boyfriend, or a husband, or even carry on a proper conversation.

"Ye know what, Fitz," Crow says. "I haven't told ye before. But I've got this picture in my head, of how I want it to be."

"How's that?" I ask him.

"I'm going to marry Mack," he tells me proudly. "She's going to be my wife."

I stare at him, and he grins.

"I know ye like her, deep down inside. I know ye do. You can quit pretending you don't. Anyway, back to the picture I have in my head. I want to have a family with her. Kids. And part of that picture involves you, Fitz."

"I don't think I follow," I tell him.

He looks at me, and he's got that serious expression on his face. He doesn't get it very often, but I know when he does that what he's about to say is important.

"Ye're a brother to me," he says. "And I want my kids to know and love ye like I do. The way Mack does too. I want my kids to know their uncle Ronan. And I have no doubts in my mind that you will protect them the way ye do me. The way ye do all of your family here in the syndicate. Am I right?"

"Aye." I nod. "I will."

"Ye didn't even have to think about it, Fitz," he says. "And that's how I know you'll be just fine around kids. So whatever's got you tied up in knots, ye need to let it go."

He gets up and I follow him to the door. But before he goes, he stops to look back at me again.

"Ye know, Fitz. Sometimes people think they can't change. But I remember that day I met you so many years ago. And if anyone ever tried to tell me you haven't changed, I think you'd know exactly what I'd have to say on the matter."

Chapter Seventeen

Sasha

It happened this morning.

She slipped away in her sleep somewhere in the middle of the night when the house was dark and quiet. Amy has been and gone as have the medical personnel. I watched them carry her away, and now it's just me and Emily, sitting on the sofa, silence stretching between us.

It hasn't really hit me yet. I think I've been preparing for it so long that I'm not really even sure how I should feel. Right now, I feel nothing. Just... nothing.

"So what now?" Em's voice finally breaks the silence, somewhere in the late evening hours.

We haven't eaten all day. Or moved. Or even spoken. But now she wants to talk. I knew it would come. She wants to get back to her life in California and pretend this didn't happen. That's Em's way of dealing with things. Mine is to let her go and pretend I don't need her. Because that's what big sisters do. I've always looked out for her. Protected her. Sacrificed for her.

Sometimes I wonder if she knows how much I've sacrificed for her. To keep her life the way she wants it to be. So she can be young and go to school and have all those experiences I never got to. When I see her right now, looking at me like she doesn't want to be here, I wonder if she even knows. If she even cares.

"What do you mean?" I ask her, even though I know what she's trying to do.

She's been spoiling for a fight ever since she got here. Because fighting makes it easier to leave. Easier to lash out at someone when you're hurting. She's been lashing out at me ever since Blaine came into my life. And every bruise, every stilted conversation has driven us further and further apart.

She talked to me like I was so stupid. Like I was just one of those women who didn't know any better. The truth is, she's the one who doesn't know any better. She doesn't know what it's like to have to choose. Sometimes I resent her for that. Like right now when she's acting like she's too good to be here anymore. In this apartment and in my presence.

"What are you going to do now, Sash?" she asks. "Keep working at the strip club until you're old and gray? I thought you said you had a plan."

"I do have a plan," I tell her.

"Really?" she mocks me with accusing eyes. "Because I saw that guy sneaking out the other morning. That mafia guy."

I blink at her and she laughs. "You just can't fucking help yourself, can you?" she says. "You just won't stop until you self-destruct."

"Now you listen to me, kid," I yell at her as I jump off the sofa and stare at her in disbelief. "You don't know anything about the way the real world works. And for good reason. Ma and I always protected you. Sheltered you. So that you never had to deal with these kind of realities. You have no idea the sacrifices I've made to keep you safe. So that you could go to college and have a shot at a normal life."

"Oh I know," she says condescendingly. "I know all about your sacrifices, Sash. Spreading your legs and taking your clothes off up on stage. Is that how you sheltered me?"

There have been moments in my life when I felt like nothing. Thought I was nothing. But to have my own sister say it, my own flesh and blood... it feels like I've just been knifed in the stomach.

I know she regrets the words the moment they are out of her mouth. She's grieving, and she's angry and she needs someone to take it out on. But I'm so fucking sick of being everyone's punching bag.

"Get out," I tell her as I walk towards the kitchen to grab my keys. "Get your shit and fly back to California tonight. I want you gone."

"Sasha..." Her voice breaks, but I can't look at her. Because there are tears running down my face and I'm embarrassed.

"Go back to your life, Em," I tell her. "Just go back and be... happy."

***

Slainte isn't as busy tonight as it has been, but it's probably the late hour.

It's almost one am by the time I arrive. And I don't know what I'm doing, only that it's familiar to me. These faces. This environment. But I'm really only searching for one face.

I find him in the back of the VIP lounge sitting next to Conor and Rory. And I don't know why, but it pisses me the fuck off. Kaya passes me and I grab two of the drinks off her tray.

"Hey, watch it," she snarls. "Those are for the guys."

I shove a hundred-dollar bill at her and she shuts up. "Keep them coming."

And she does. Over the next twenty minutes, I sit in the back and watch him. He hasn't looked at the stage once. He's locked inside his head again. I want to know what he thinks about. I want to make sense of this man that infuriates me.

And right now, in my inebriated state, I want to feel him.

I move towards him, and I can barely walk straight. Turns out, a lot of alcohol and no food isn't a great combination. All three of the guys look up at me in surprise when I stumble into their line of sight, but I only have eyes for Ronan.

Those sad brown eyes land on me, and my entire world comes into focus. It has a way of doing that when I'm in his sights.

I move closer and sit right down in his lap. His entire body goes stiff, and he's got that wild look in his eyes again. Like I'm a potential threat. It only serves to provoke me. I smile and catch his face in my hands and then lean in to whisper in his ear.

"Do you like watching the other girls dance?" I ask him.

"I'm not," he answers.

I kiss the shell of his ear and then drag my lips down his neck, tasting him. "I know."

His breathing grows harsh and his hands move to my thighs. He holds them there as if he isn't sure whether he wants to push me away or pull me closer. I make the decision for him by grabbing the back of his head and crushing my lips against his.

For a second, he loses himself in the kiss, groaning into my mouth. He's hard as hell beneath me, and I grind down on top of him. And that's when he rears back and glances around the room. Everybody is watching us. I don't care. But Ronan does. His cheeks are flushed and he's embarrassed by my very public display of drunken affection.

I knew it was a recipe for disaster, but I wanted to push him. I wanted to make him uncomfortable and provoke a reaction. Maybe Emily was right. Maybe I won't stop until I self-destruct. He grabs my wrists roughly in his grasp and pulls my hands away from him.

"I don't like you like this," he says.

"Like what?" I challenge him.

"Like a whore," he clips out.

I yank my hand back and slap him. It's an instinctive reaction. One that only fuels my anger and makes him stare at me with that lost puppy look.

"Don't you look at me like that!" I scream. "Don't you look at me like I hurt you when you hurt me."

I want to slap him again, but Conor is yanking me away. Ronan's just staring at me in shock, unmoving as he presses his hand to his cheek.

"You're all fucking pigs!" I scream to the room. "Every last one of you! I hate you all!"

Lachlan appears in the doorway, and I know I've fucked up. He glares in my direction and makes a gesture. Rory and Conor drag me down the hall to his office and drop me into one of the leather chairs opposite his desk.

I curl my knees up and release a sob, and all three of them look to each other in confusion. Lachlan tells them to get out, and they do. And then it's just the two of us.

"Sasha, what the bleeding hell are you doing?" he asks. "You hit Ronan?"

I press my forehead into my knees and cry. Lachlan doesn't pressure me to talk, he just waits for me to get my shit together.

"It's not an excuse," I tell him between sobs. "But my mother died this morning. I just wanted…"

I look up at him, and his face is kind. And filled with understanding. And for some reason it only makes me cry harder.

"I just wanted to…"

"I know, Sasha," he says softly. "I know what you wanted. But you can't ever hit Ronan like that, do ye understand?"

I nod, because I know the code these guys live by, and I'm sure that's what he's talking about. I could be killed for a lot less than what I did tonight.

Lachlan helps me over to the sofa and grabs a jacket off the door and covers me over with it. He pauses to look down at me, and there's a forlorn expression on his face.

"He can handle it from anyone else, Sasha. But never you."

More tears come at the sound of disappointment in his voice, and it only makes me feel worse. But then he's on his phone, whispering into the speaker while I close my eyes. It isn't long before I drift off into unconsciousness.

When I wake again, Mack is beside me, stroking my hair and smiling down at me.

"Why are you smiling?" I croak.

"Because," she says. "You did me proud tonight, Sash. I mean, I can't be the only crazy one around this place."

I laugh, and it feels good. But then the tears come soon after again.

"Sorry," I mutter as I swipe at the hot mess that is my face.

"Don't be sorry, doll," she insists. "There's nothing a good bout of ugly crying can't fix."

"I'm going to have to take your word for it," I reply.

"C'mon," she says. "Rory and I are going to take you home."

"Okay."

Chapter Eighteen

Sasha

I'm sitting up on the rooftop, shivering in the cold as I stare up at the sky. When a shadow passes over me, I don't have to look to know it's him. The shame inside of me won't allow me to, so instead, I continue to stare at the stars, waiting for him to say something. Anything.

He doesn't.

"How did you know I was up here?" I ask through a scratchy voice.

He still doesn't answer, and when I finally get the courage to look at him, he's uncomfortable with my question. I've often wondered if Ronan watches me. So many times, I could have sworn I felt eyes on me when nobody was there. But if he does watch me, he doesn't want me to know it.

He surprises me by bending down and lifting my limp body into his arms. My head lolls against his strong chest and I close my eyes and let his warmth envelop me as he carries me back down the stairs and into my apartment. When I open them again, he's pulling back the covers and laying me into bed. I'm so scared he's going to leave me again, leave me alone to let my grief swallow me whole.

So when the bed dips and he climbs in behind me, I almost sob with relief. I hold my breath, wondering what he's going to do. After tonight, I'm sure he thinks I'm more unhinged than he is. But that's one of the things about Ronan. He'll never throw it in your face. He'll never say a word about it. And he's here right now, because he knows what I need. He tugs me against his body and holds me.

"I'm sorry I hurt you," I whisper.

He holds me tighter and nuzzles into my neck like I'm his source of comfort and not the other way around.

"I'm sorry about what I called you," he replies. "I didn't mean it."

"Ronan?"

"Aye?"

"Please don't let me go," I tell him. "Or at least stay until I fall asleep."

And he does.

***

The next morning, I wake to find a pair of brown eyes gazing down at me. They are warm, like melted chocolate. Open and soft. He's leaning against the headboard, still completely dressed save for his suit jacket. You'd never know he just woke up.

"You're still here," I say.

"Would you prefer me to leave?" he asks.

I reach out and touch his hand with mine, and he lets me. "No."

"I'm not the only one," he tells me. "Mack and Crow are on the sofa in the lounge room."

"Oh."

"I'm sorry about your mammy," he says.

"Thank you."

"I don't know what to say in these situations."

"You don't need to say anything," I tell him. "Thank you for staying with me last night."

He nods, and something else pops into my mind. Something that I shouldn't ask because it's only going to make it harder to do what I need to do.

"Did you talk to my mother?" I ask him.

He doesn't reply, but I know that I'm right. He clears his throat, and it takes him a minute to find the words.

"I wanted her to know you'd be alright," he says.

His eyes find mine, and they've never looked more serious. "And I will protect you."

"Oh," I murmur. "Well... thank you for telling her that."

"I meant it," he says. "I haven't done a good enough job of it in the past. But I will keep you safe."

"You have kept me safe, Ronan," I reply. "Probably more times than I even really know. But you can't protect me forever. I'll be leaving soon, anyway."

He looks away. And I can't tell what he's thinking. I want to ask him if he cares. If it bothers him at all. But that would be stupid. Because none of that matters. I need to leave. To get away from this life before I lose the few marbles I have left.

He climbs to his feet without any sort of response.

"Are you going?"

"Aye." He still won't look at me. "I have to go feed the dog."

"Dog?"

"Let me know if ye need anything, Sasha."

And with that, he disappears down the hall.

I wait until the front door shuts and then move to the bathroom to get cleaned up. The woman staring back at me in the mirror looks like shit. And I feel like it too. No matter how much I tell myself it's the right thing, I can't bring myself to get excited about leaving.

But it is the right thing. That's what I need to believe. And there's no better time than the present to talk to Lachlan about it. But when I walk out into the parlor, the only one still here is Mack.

"Good morning," she says from the kitchen. "I had Conor buy donuts. I tell ya girl, I'm really getting used to this. Did you know I can send them out for me any time I want? Seriously considering changing my name to the Queen."

I laugh and sit down at the kitchen table, grateful for the coffee she shoves in my direction. I cup it in my hands and let the warmth spread into my skin.

"Are you with me for the day?" I ask Mack.

She nods. "You aren't getting rid of me that easily."

"Then I hope you don't mind running errands with me, your highness," I tell her. "I've got to go to the funeral home. Pick out a casket. I have a ton of phone calls to make…"

"Sasha." Mack reaches across the table and grabs my arm to stop me. "It's all been taken care of."

"What?"

She smiles at me softly. "It's been paid for. Everything is taken care of, you don't have to do a thing but show up."

"By who?" I ask.

"I highly suspect you already know that."

There's pressure behind my eyes again and I push it away. "God, I'm such an awful person."

"Why because you slapped him last night?" Mack asks. "Don't worry about it, they need to be put in their places every now and again."

"It was a really nice thing to do," I say.

"It was," Mack agrees. "Just when you think he's another bastard, he has to go and do something nice like that."

I nod, because I know Mack is all too aware of how I'm feeling right now. But I can't let it sway me. I can't let this world suck me back in, and especially when I don't even know how Ronan really feels about me.

"There is something else I have to do," I tell her. "I think that I should talk to Lachlan. The sooner the better."

"Okay," Mack agrees. "But I have a big favor to ask you, Sash."

"What?"

"Lachlan and I are getting married. Next week."

I'm dumbfounded, and my face shows it. Though it shouldn't come as a surprise, but she seems happy.

"Stay until after the wedding," she begs. "I can't get married without you there. You're the only one I've really got, besides Scarlett, and it would mean a lot to me if you were there."

"Of course." I give her a weak smile. "I wouldn't dream of missing it."

Chapter Nineteen

Ronan

When I walk into Crow's office, I notice straight away that something is off. He's sitting at his desk, staring at a manila envelope when he gestures to the chair across from him.

"What is it?" I ask.

"Someone delivered this to the diner," he says. "Asked Niall's sister to give it to him."

"And?"

"And Jaysus, Ronan." He throws a stack of grainy photos across the desk. "Did ye really fucking kill Blaine?"

Tension springs up inside me, and all I can think of as I sort through the photos is Sasha. Wondering if there is anything in here that will implicate her in any way. I need to be sure that doesn't happen.

"Aye," I admit. "I did."

He stares at me and sighs. He's getting married next week, and this is the last thing he wants to sort out.

"I'll take whatever punishment you see fit," I tell him. "Whatever the cost."

"Care to tell me why?" he says. "Or is that all I'm going to get?"

"He was hurting her," I say. "So I stopped him."

"For good, apparently," Crow replies dryly. "Niall knew something about that wasn't right. He's suspected it, Fitz. He wants answers. Whoever sent this is likely to have more copies."

"Probably," I agree.

"Are ye even aware of the fact that he could have you killed for this?" Crow asks. "Or do ye really just not give a shite about any of it?"

"I do," I answer. "I told you I'm prepared for whatever punishment you see fit. So long as none of it falls on Sasha."

Crow leans back in his chair and appraises me. "So that's what this is all about."

"She had nothing to do with it. I won't stand to see her harmed in any way."

Despite the seriousness of the situation, Crow grins. "Now who's gone mad?"

"I'd have done the same for any woman in the same situation."

"Ah, sure," Crow replies. "Of course."

I don't like his tone, but I'm in no position to argue at the moment.

"You let Donovan of all people see you," he says. "I can't even fathom how that occurred."

"I was distracted."

"By?" Crow presses.

I clear my throat and look away. I don't want to tell him about this. But perhaps it will make him understand.

"I fucked Sasha after."

His brows raise and he's holding back a grin. He covers his mouth with his hand to keep from laughing.

"Ye're kidding me."

"I wish I was. I took her on the floor next to her dead boyfriend."

"That's quite a way to lose your cherry, Fitz."

My cheeks burn, and I ball my fists up. I feel like he's laughing at me, and I don't like it.

"I understand now," Crow says. "Ye don't have to say anymore."

"I had no intentions to."

"Leave it with me," he says. "I'll find the best way to bring it up with Niall. In the meantime, I suggest you start shaking some of Donovan's trees and see what kind of vermin falls out."

"I'll handle it."

"And, Fitz, I'll still need to speak with Sasha."

My eyes snap up to his, and he holds up his hand before I can argue. "I just need to know I can trust her," he says. "She won't be harmed. But Ronan, you need to be aware that with this kind of evidence floating around out there and her as a potential witness, ye could do far worse than being killed at the hands of the syndicate. You could be looking at prison."

"You can trust Sasha," I tell him.

"We'll see."

"If you threaten her…"

Crow narrows his eyes at me and cuts me off.

"What, Ronan? What are you going to do if I threaten her?"

"Don't," I warn him. "I fecking mean it. If you even so much as scare her, you'll have me to contend with."

The air between us thins as we stare at each other across the desk. Crow and I have never had a problem. But things with Sasha are different. And I need him to understand that she isn't like anyone else that he can say whatever he wants to. In my mind, she already belongs to me, even if I can never really have her. And I will protect her, no matter the cost.

"I have to admit, Fitz," he says. "You've jacked this whole thing arseways. But if there's anyone who can understand, it's me. So out of respect for you, I will not threaten her. But I just hope your loyalties don't prove to be wrong."

Chapter Twenty

Sasha

The burial is a small affair. My Ma didn't want a big production, and I respected her wishes. The flowers and the casket and everything Ronan picked out is perfect. And I have to admit I'm surprised when all of the guys show up in their nicest suits. Even Ronan himself.

"Thank you for coming," I whisper to Mack as she stands at my side.

"I've got your back, Sash. You're just another fruit in this big fucked up family of ours. And that's what family does."

Her words make me smile, even though it feels wrong. I've always told myself these guys were never on my side. But she's right. It is like one big fucked up family. Sometimes it takes being at your lowest point to see who's really there for you. And they're all standing right beside me now.

The service is short and done at the burial site. Mack remains beside me the entire time, and when it's over, she insists I ride with them.

We end up at the diner that Niall's sister runs. The same one I used to work at. The place where it all began. When Sally sees me, she kisses me and gives me a hug that's entirely too tight. Despite the family business, I really do think she has a heart of gold.

She feeds us and allows us to sit and drink and talk until the late hours of the evening. And when it's time to go, Lachlan offers to drive me.

"I'm heading back to the house," Mack says. "But just call me if you need anything, Sash. Anything at all."

"Okay." I nod. "Thank you again, for everything."

Ronan turns to escort her to his car, and I reach for his arm. "And thank you too."

He nods and then hesitates. I hope he will say something. Anything.

But he doesn't.

***

The drive with Lachlan is quiet.

I know he plans to talk to me, so when he follows me up to my apartment, I don't argue. I set down my keys and bag and then gesture to the kitchen.

"Would you like a drink?"

"No, Sasha," he says. "Thank you. Why don't ye just have a seat so we can chat for a few moments."

I nod and take a seat, wringing my hands together. I know Lachlan fairly well. I've never known him to be hot-headed or unreasonable, but I also know he will squash anything he perceives as a threat without batting an eye. He does it for his brothers. For the syndicate. And with the obvious tension in his shoulders and voice, I can't help but thinking he views me as a threat somehow too. He clears his throat, and I look up at him.

"I understand why ye want to leave," he says. "But I'm sure you can understand there are a few things we need to go over first."

"Of course." I give him a shaky smile.

"All the same rules would apply as if you were still working for us, Sasha. No speaking to the cops. Ever. And I do mean ever."

"I won't," I assure him. "You have my word."

"You'll be given some new ID's, and you'll need to use them for your safety and ours. As far as the club is concerned, you never worked there. Do ye follow?"

"Of course."

"And the MacKenna family?" he asks.

"I don't know who they are."

"That's good," he says. "Very good, Sasha."

He stands up, and I think he's going to leave. But instead, he paces towards the window and looks down onto the street, his back turned towards me.

"There's just one more thing," he says.

"Okay."

"I need ye to tell me what happened to Blaine."

All of the blood drains from my face, and I pray that he won't turn around and see it. Because I've been hiding this secret for the last two years, but not from someone like Lachlan. Not when asked directly.

When everything went down before, Ronan took care of it. I didn't have to do a thing. I don't know how he did it, but they were convinced that Blaine had left town. When they questioned me about it, I told them exactly what Ronan told me to. He told me he was going home for a visit and I didn't know when to expect him back. And that was it. They didn't question it further. Blaine was always a bit flaky, and they thought he'd come back, but he never did.

And I had sort of just hoped that it meant he'd fallen off their radar. But apparently that isn't so.

Lachlan turns around and pins me with his gaze. He sees right through me. "I know he didn't leave town," he says. "I need ye to tell me what really happened, Sasha. That's all you have to do. And then you are free. You can leave. Do whatever it is you please."

My chest is heaving like there's a giant cement block resting on top of it. It's getting harder to breathe. My eyes dart around the room seeking out objects to ground myself. I can't lie to him. He's going to know. But I can't give up Ronan. Correction. I won't give up Ronan. He did what he did for me. And he's carried that secret for these last two years knowing that I could be a threat to him.

He could have killed me at any time, but he didn't. Because he trusts me. And I trust him. And I won't betray that trust, no matter what. Lachlan is his brother, but Lachlan is also loyal to the syndicate and all of the rules that come with it. I don't know what he'd do in this situation, and I'm really not willing to find out.

"I'm sorry to disappoint you." My voice comes out shaky. "But I don't know what happened to Blaine. I already told you…"

"What you told me was a lie," he says. "We checked flight records. Blaine never went back to Ireland."

"Well, then I don't know," I say quickly. "Maybe he went somewhere else. Maybe he's still in the states. I don't know what he's doing."

Lachlan narrows his gaze and stalks closer, kneeling down until he's on my level. He's a lot scarier when he's this close. And I know he senses my nerves. I'm all over the goddamn place. I'm shaking. My eyes are watering. And I think he really might kill me now.

But I won't give up Ronan. I wouldn't even be alive if it wasn't for him.

"Sasha," Lachlan says, his voice softening. "If somebody hurt him, and it wasn't you, you have nothing to be concerned about. All ye have to do is tell me. And I will take care of it. Hell, I'll even give you some extra cash to disappear with."

My bottom lip trembles, and I bite it to keep from telling him to go fuck himself. Because that's all I really want to do. He's pushing me, and I don't know why. But I can't handle it. Not right now.

"Look, I don't know anything!" I yell at him. "You're barking up the wrong fucking tree, okay? I don't know what you want me to say. Blaine is gone. I haven't seen him. Haven't heard from him. That's all there is to it. Nothing you do or say is going to change that."

Lachlan rocks back on his heels and rises up to his full height. And then he just nods and walks toward the door. I'm left completely stunned when he pauses with his hand on the knob and turns around.

"I have to admit, Sasha," he says. "I really thought you might break. Ronan was right about you."

"What?" I whisper in confusion. "He told you?"

"Aye," he says. "Because he had no other choice. And you'd do well to stick to the same story whenever anyone asks about it."

He leaves, and I fall back against the sofa in a state of disbelief. Ronan told him. And didn't even warn me. He just let him come here and test me, and there probably would have been a very different outcome had I told the truth tonight. He could have killed me.

It pisses me off. But worse than that, it hurts. I can't believe Ronan did that to me. I pull out my phone and debate calling him when I realize there's no point. This is the way it is.

So instead, I pull up my calendar and count the days to Mack's wedding. Five more days. And then I'm gone. For good.

Chapter Twenty-One

Sasha

It's the day before Mack's wedding, and I've spent the entire week packing up the apartment and helping her with wedding things.

It's not going to be a big event. Mack says she doesn't see the point in going overboard on everything. That's just part of the reason why I love the girl. I haven't spoken to Ronan or Lachlan since the day of Ma's burial. And that's honestly the way I prefer it.

So when Lachlan's name flashes across the caller ID of my phone, I debate on ignoring it. But then I think maybe they need me to help with something else for the wedding, and my guilt gets the better of me. So I answer it.

"Sasha," Lachlan's voice filters through the phone. "Are you there?"

"Yes."

"Look, Kaya twisted her ankle. She's going to be out for a couple of weeks. I know ye're leaving on Monday, but we have a special event booked on Sunday and I really can't do without another dancer."

"I don't know." I bite my lip and glance around the apartment, looking for any excuse to keep me from going back to the club. I don't want to see Ronan again. I don't want to get sucked back in, and I'm afraid that's exactly what will happen if I go.

After a minute of hesitation on my part, Lachlan sighs on the other end of the line. "I know ye have a lot going on right now," he says. "But I'm getting married tomorrow, and I just need everything to go smoothly."

"Ugh," I groan. "You just had to play that card, didn't you?"

He laughs, and it eases some of the tension between us from our last visit.

"Okay, fine alright," I agree. "One last shift. That's it though, I mean it. Come Monday morning, no matter what, I'm out of there."

"Absolutely," he says. "Ye're a lifesaver, Sasha, truly. Mack and I will both be eternally grateful."

He hangs up the phone and I flop down onto the sofa, staring at the barren apartment. Everything is in boxes now. Ma's stuff is in storage until Emily and I can go through it and figure out how to divide it up. I'm really only planning on taking the necessities with me, especially since I don't even know where I'm going. I decided California was off the table after my spat with Em. We both need this time apart to deal with things in our own ways.

I should be checking out places online. Applying for jobs, looking up facts and figures on Google about the best places for lonely ex-strippers to live. But I highly suspect that Google isn't going to have the answers to those questions. And something is still holding me back.

I grew up in this city. It's all I've ever known. Even with all of its wrongs, the thought of leaving it just doesn't feel right. When I've spent so many years having all of my decisions made for me through circumstance, trying to make them myself is overwhelming and even a little terrifying. This is my one chance to get out. Not to screw up my life anymore. And I've only got one shot to get it right. It's a lot of pressure to put on yourself.

I walk down the hall to finish packing my bedroom when I notice Ronan's old suit jacket still hanging on the door. Haunting me, the way he always does. And I can't look at it anymore. I can't have any of these things in my life, causing me confusion. From now on, I'm only going to move in one direction, and it's not backwards.

With that thought in mind, I grab the jacket from the door and stomp all the way down the hall and out the front of my apartment building. The first homeless guy I find when I round the corner is the lucky recipient of the jacket and everything it represents.

***

"You can't tell anyone yet," Mack whispers. "But I'm totally knocked up."

"No way." I glance down at her stomach, but there's no evidence there yet. She's glowing in her wedding dress though. I'm emotional again, and I don't know what to say. So I hug her.

"And married too." I tell Mack with tears in my eyes. "I can't believe you really did it."

"I know," she agrees. "I'm in it for life now."

I glance down at her hand, which still has a tiny amount of blood on it from the ceremony. Something I would have once considered strange and barbaric is now oddly sweet to me. Watching them pledge their love and devotion to each other in front of all of their friends like that. The words weren't enough. It had to be said in blood too. Not only is that the way of the syndicate, but that's how strongly they feel about each other.

Her devotion shines in her eyes every time she looks at Lachlan across the room. I'm happy for her, but a part of me is sad too. The last thing I should want or need is a relationship. Or the kind of wild, stupid love that makes people go temporarily insane. I never thought someone as jaded as me could be touched by a love like that. For the few brief times I was in Ronan's arms, I felt the way Mack looks right now. Dreamy and completely untouchable to all of the bad around me. The only thing she can see is him now.

At first, I wanted to warn her away from him. But now I know that I was wrong. Lachlan loves her too. Fiercely. And I feel truly sorry for anyone who ever tries to come between the two of them. I doubt there are any lengths they won't go to for each other.

"You better go to him," I tell Mack. "He'll just come to you if you don't."

"That's the way it should be," she tells me with a grin. "Make them work for it every once in a while."

I laugh, and then my eyes move on autopilot across the room towards Ronan. The smile on my face dissolves, and the only thing that remains is the act.

"You should go dance with Ronan," Mack suggests.

It's all I can do to shake my head because I doubt Mack has any idea of the events that have transpired recently. "Nah. He's not the dancing type."

"Yeah, you're probably right," she agrees. "He's more of the sit in the corner and brood type. Maybe you could go brood with him then?"

Lachlan sneaks up behind her as we're talking and it isn't long before he's dragging her away. I'm grateful for the reprieve from that conversation. I have no intentions of speaking to Ronan tonight.

When I turn around again, I'm surprised to find one of the Russians has descended on me though. He's a member of the alliance with the Irish, and a frequent client in the VIP area. I've seen him in the pit when I danced before and even delivered him drinks a few times.

His name is Niko, and although he's handsome in a rough way, he doesn't hold a candle to Ronan. Then again, nobody does.

"One must never drink alone." He greets me by wiggling a vodka bottle in my direction.

"Wasn't one glass enough?" I tease.

He shrugs and winks. "When the drinks are on the Irish, you take your fill before the bar goes dry."

I laugh and Niko pulls two shot glasses out of his pocket. Before I have another chance to decline, he fills them both up to the rim.

I take my glass and hold it up to his while he utters a Russian toast. Then we both toss back our shots and the burn feels good in my stomach.

"What does it mean?" I ask. "The toast?"

Niko flashes me a boyish grin. "May you get drunk enough this evening to think me handsome."

I'm smiling at him and shaking my head when a firm grip wraps around my arm. I look up to see Ronan, his eyes smoldering with barely contained fury.

His gaze flicks from me to Niko and back, filled with accusation. He yanks me into his side and leans down to whisper in my ear, never taking his eyes off Niko.

"Would ye like the lad to watch me give you a going over?" he asks.

"What the hell is your problem?" I fire back at him.

His response is to forcefully drag me away from Niko and pull me into an empty corner of the club, away from everyone else.

"Party's over," he says. "You'll be going home now."

"Like hell I will," I argue. "You don't get to decide that. Or who I talk to either."

"You were smiling at him," he accuses.

"So frigging what?" I retort. "We were just talking. At least someone around here knows how to use his vocabulary."

We stare at each other in silence, both of us fuming now. He's acting like a toddler. And after what he told Lachlan, he has no right.

I try to brush past him, but he just follows me. Niko has disappeared into the crowd which is probably for the best. So I take a seat at an empty table and Ronan pulls up a chair beside me.

We both stew in our own silences for a long time. I'm staring at the crowd, and he's looking at me. I can feel it, but I won't meet his eyes. Because my anger won't hold up under that gaze. And I need my anger right now.

But then he does something that I can't ignore.

His leg brushes mine, and it isn't an accident. It might seem like such an innocent gesture, but with Ronan, it definitely isn't. He doesn't flirt. Or do anything in half-measures. He comes to me for one reason and one reason alone. To take what he wants.

I can't recall a time he's ever touched me unless it was for a purpose. But right now, the heat of his leg is pressed against mine, and it can't be overlooked. I glance over at him, and he's still watching me.

There's a guilt and frustration in his eyes, but he doesn't apologize. Instead, he leans a little closer, and his breath fans my face. For a second, I think he's going to kiss me. My heart does a weird little flip, and I stare at him in confusion. I don't know what he's doing.

Apparently, neither does he. Because he looks as confused as I am. But his gaze isn't on me now. It's over my shoulder. Taking mental notes.

When I turn around, I catch sight of Scarlett and Rory across the bar. Sitting in the exact same position as we are. Rory is putting the moves on her, waiting for her to bite. And it occurs to me Ronan is trying to do the same.

"Are you mimicking him?" I ask.

A flush creeps up over his neck and he leans back in his chair. No answer. But what do I expect?

I could try to dissect his motives for following Rory's lead, but that was the old me.

The new me isn't supposed to care anymore.

"I'm going to have Conor take me home," I tell him.

I don't wait for his reply, and I don't look at him again.

Childish? Perhaps. But a girl has to be able to protect herself by any means possible. Even if it means using a silent wall of armor.

And until I'm burning rubber out of this city, I have no intentions on speaking to Ronan Fitzpatrick again.

Chapter Twenty-Two

Ronan

*"**Y**our strength has progressed considerably," Farrell observes.*

I remain silent as I was taught to do. Head bowed, knees resting on a bed of broken glass. The same ritual the trainees perform every day.

The pain does not bother me anymore. After a while, it became second nature, just as Farrell said it would. My training is going well, according to him. He believes I'm stronger than the other lads, but it isn't true.

I feel too much rage. That's where my strength comes from. The rage. It builds up inside of me until there's nowhere for it to go. I release it in small amounts when they let me. When they have me kill the men they send into the pit. It usually works. But I can always feel it building inside of me, and I'm afraid that one day the small amount isn't going to be enough.

They've stopped giving us the pills. A test of our loyalty. They question us. Beat us. Try everything to get us to break. They tell us we can have a pill if we just give them what they want. I can't stop shaking. Or puking. My skin is covered with sweat, and I'm burning up from the inside.

I want the pill.

But I refuse to break. Farrell moves to the lad beside me. Alex. He's smaller than me. Thinner. His body is slumped forward and his face is ashen. He wants the pill too. But Alex is smart. Smarter than me. He knows more about the outside world. He makes me question what they are teaching us here. He speaks of things that I try to block out.

It confuses and angers me. Sometimes, I just want him to stop. I tell him not to speak to me. But he does. And now I understand why we aren't supposed to talk. Because I worry what they will do to him today. How much more he can take. He's not my mate, but I don't want him to die. Sometimes, that happens in training. Sometimes, the other lads die.

But it isn't me. And that's why bonds are forbidden. They aren't supposed to matter. We should not be bothered if another lad dies because that means they were too weak to be a soldier. When I look at Alex, I do not see a soldier. I do not see him ever completing training. But I don't want him to die.

He's the only person who's spoken to me other than Farrell and Coyne. Sometimes, I think I'm going mad with nothing but the sound of my own thoughts. Down here in the dark, hungry and thirsty and tired all the time.

Alex makes me think that maybe I'm not going mad. But he says that's what they want. If I'm mad, then nobody will ever fuck with me. That's what he says. That's how they keep the compound safe.

He tells me stories. Stories from books that he remembers. And they take me away from this place. I like his stories. But he couldn't tell them to me for the last week because he's not well. He's been two days without water already.

But they just keep interrogating us. Trying to break us.

Asking us the same questions over and over. They say that if we are ever captured, they need to know we won't break. So they keep at it. The only time it stops is when they turn out the lights and put those screams on the speakers again. And then the rats. So many rats. They crawl over our skin. They crawl on me everywhere.

Today Coyne choked us until we passed out. And then woke up. And then passed out. I haven't a clue how long it went on for.

They just keep asking the same questions. Trying to test our loyalty. No pills. And the same questions. Over and over. I won't give them what they want. I won't break.

I want to smash my head into the concrete. But if I do, they will chain me up again. So I stare at the wall instead. But I can feel Farrell. He's looking down at me. And then Alex. He knows I won't break, but Alex is close. I think he will break. Because he wants the pills too much. He's shivering too. Sweating. And he's covered in vomit.

Farrell looks down upon him with obvious disgust. Before I can worry over the consequences of my actions, I blurt out something to distract him.

"I am only loyal to the cause."

His eyes dart to me, and they are filled with suspicion. He's onto me, and now he's going to make it worse. He reaches for his bamboo cane and walks behind me. I close my eyes as the cane cracks across the soles of my feet, and I don't move for the duration.

"Would ye care to take the lashings for your friend as well?" Farrell challenges.

"He's not well," I reply. "So I will take them."

Alex looks at me in horror, and I tear my eyes away. Farrell cracks the cane over my back and legs until I collapse into the shattered glass beneath me. But it isn't over. It's already too late when it occurs to me that I've only made it worse.

He drags Alex from the glass and forces him over the bench. Alex sobs, and I hate him for it. I hate those loud noises. Those cries. I want to cover my ears. I want to tell him to shut up. I don't want to see or hear any of this. Farrell pulls up his shirt and starts to beat him. He watches me while he does it, challenging me to speak out of turn.

When I don't, he hits him harder. And harder. The cane cracks across his head and face, and Alex collapses onto the bench completely. This is a test. Farrell wants to see if I will challenge him. But he's going too far this time. Alex has been without water. He is weak and malnourished. His body cannot withstand much more. I've watched the other lads hold up under torture. And I've watched the ones who didn't survive. But this time is different. Because Alex spoke to me. And I know him.

"Please," I say.

Farrell snarls at me and raises his arm again, striking out in rage across Alex's head. Alex stops moving. He stops making noise, and I'm holding my breath, silently pleading for Farrell to stop. He doesn't.

He continues to hit him. Again and again and again. Until blood sprays across his shirt and his arms.

Something about the sight of that blood makes all of that rage inside of me boil over just as I feared. I don't know where it comes from. I haven't any idea what I'm doing. But I'm moving

towards Farrell, and he tries to turn his cane on me. He's
unprepared for me to fight back, because I never have.

I take the cane easily from his grip, and I hit him with it.
Again and again and again until all I see is red. Beautiful, glorious,
red.

***

For as long as I can remember, women have always flocked to Crow.

Even as young lads in school, the girls were always coming up to speak with him. He told me how it worked and tried to get me to speak with them too. But I knew they didn't like me.

Nobody liked me. Except for Crow and his mammy.

I wasn't very good at school. By the time I finally went, I was already fourteen. I knew how to read and write, but I didn't know any of the other stuff. The other kids were always whispering that I was a freak. So I kept to myself. It didn't bother me.

When we came to the states, Crow offered to help me get a woman. Told me it was an important rite of passage for a man. He was always with a different woman. Said he didn't want to get attached. So I told him I was the same. I didn't need him to find me a woman, and I didn't want to get attached.

I'd followed Crow all my life. Did the things he did and tried to blend in. I thought it was all going okay, and I could have kept on with it for my whole life. But then I saw Sasha. It was her voice that caught my attention before I ever saw her face. I didn't usually look at a woman's face, unless I needed to. But Sasha had a gentle voice. I liked the way she spoke. She wasn't loud like the other women at Slainte, but always soft.

That night though, she was waiting tables in the diner where we ate breakfast. Her arm brushed mine as she filled up my coffee cup, and she looked right at me and smiled. Most women were afraid of me, I think, and they never looked right at me like that. But she did. And she wasn't laughing. She didn't treat me like I was different or make me feel uncomfortable. My arms were shaking, and my heart was beating fast. It reminded me of the pills they used to give us at the compound. And I hated that feeling. Hated her for making me feel that way again. But for the rest of the night I couldn't stop staring at her.

I wanted her.

I'd never wanted anything as much as I wanted her. She was the most beautiful thing I'd ever seen, and I wanted to touch her. For weeks, I couldn't stop jerking myself off thinking about the way she smiled at me. Wondering what it would feel like to have her beneath me. To be inside of her.

These sort of thoughts were doing me no good. I knew I couldn't have her. I was a murderer. Even though it was the only thing I'd ever known, I'd learned after I left the compound that it wasn't normal. And Crow explained that most women, they didn't like it. We had to keep that part of our lives separate, for obvious reasons. But I didn't know how to separate myself. I only knew how to paint the floor with blood and I could do that exceptionally well.

But I didn't know how to speak with her. What to say. When I imagined letting her touch me, and the things I was supposed to do to her, I didn't know what they were. There were some women at the compound. I remember Farrell told me they were whores and they were only there to bed the soldiers when they needed it. He said when I was sixteen, I'd bed one too. After I graduated training. But I never did. And I never wanted to.

But I couldn't get the notion out of my head when I saw Sasha. Only before I could sort any of that out, Blaine started grabbing her like he had a right to. Touching her and asking her out. She brushed him off, but I knew he kept going back. Because I followed him. And I followed her too.

I couldn't stop. At first, I just wanted to see where she lived. But then it wasn't enough. I broke into her apartment. Went through her things. Watched her whenever she came to the club with Blaine.

I wanted her. And I hated that I couldn't have her. Even when I saw Blaine hurting her, and I killed him, I knew I still couldn't have her. I was too fucked up. She'd never want me. A murderer. A freak. A mobster. The only thing I knew how to do was kill.

But I took her anyway. And I've never stopped thinking about it since. The first time I sank inside of her, I embarrassed myself. I was out of control with how badly I needed her.

I didn't like those feelings. So I kept away after that. But now, everything is changing. Sasha wants to leave. I don't want her to go, but I have nothing to offer that would make her stay. I'm well aware she hates this life. I see it on her face every day. She wants to escape.

I should let her.

But I don't want to.

When I walk into her apartment tonight and see the boxes packed up, it hits me hard. She really is going.

And now I know, I can't let her.

I walk down the hall to her bedroom and find it empty. She isn't here. My heart beats funny like the first time I saw her. Only it isn't good this time. There's nothing good about this feeling.

She's leaving. And I can't let her.

With that thought in mind, I do the one thing I despise more than anything. I sit down on her bed and try to work out the perfect lie. And when I spot the drawer across the room that has her knickers in it, I know exactly what it is.

I know how I'll get her to stay.

Chapter Twenty-Three

Sasha

When I arrive at the club the next night, I'm surprised to find the VIP room only has a few patrons. When Lachlan said they had an event, I was expecting a full house.

I don't give it too much more thought because I'm sure the place will be filling up before too long. At Slainte, the meetings can happen at all hours of the night. It hasn't been unusual for some of the dancers to be booked at times like four am on special occasions.

When I get to the dressing room, Jasmine is already wrinkling her nose in my direction. None of the other dancers have really liked me since Lachlan said I'm not to do lap dances anymore. I only ever did them for about a week before he put the kibosh on that without telling me why. Whatever his reasons, I was grateful. The other dancers however, didn't take too kindly to my special treatment.

It's not that the patrons in here are disgusting. They aren't just your run of the mill average Joes with a beer belly and a wife and four kids waiting at home. No, these guys are either mafia or mafia associates. And for the most part, a lot of them are pretty decent to look at. And besides Donovan, I've never really had any of the clients step too far out of line with me.

Lachlan told me when I started that I could always come to him if I had a problem with a guy, and he'd take care of it. But I guess after Donny started harassing me, I took that option off the table completely. I had trouble discerning where the boundaries actually lay. And I just kept telling myself that I hated this place so much I would be glad to be gone.

Looking at the familiar surroundings now though, I get a little emotional. This place is like some sort of big fucked up family. You have your competitive sisters and the guys that you go to when you need help, and then of course the creepy uncles. What family would be complete without the creepy uncles, anyhow?

I don't know.

I don't even know what I'm thinking. But when I rummage through my outfits, I decide I want to go out with a bang. I may not be the most popular dancer, or the prettiest, or even the one with the best moves. But I've worked the stage long enough to know what I do have, and how to work with it.

I change into a black jewel studded wrap around bikini set with thigh high black leather boots. It's more daring than my usual outfits. I tend to go with simpler themes. Items that are easy to maneuver in and easy to take off. But tonight deserves something special.

So on that note, I spend extra time on my hair and makeup. I do a smoky eye and a red lip and curl my long hair until it's smooth and sleek and falls softly down my back. All the while, I'm thinking about my song selection. I don't know if Ronan's going to be here tonight. But the songs I choose are a reflection of him. The only way I know how to say goodbye.

Flyleaf's *Set Me on Fire* and *All Around Me* followed by Starset's *My Demons*.

I hand them off to the emcee before my set. And then I have a 7UP to settle my nerves while I watch Jasmine perform. The room doesn't look any fuller, even after another hour has passed, and I have to wonder what's going on. Of course I can't actually ask Lachlan, because even though him and Mack couldn't take a honeymoon yet, I highly doubt he's here the night after his wedding.

Jasmine comes backstage, and the emcee makes my introduction with an entire spiel about this being my last performance. The music comes on, and I lose myself in the motions. My body and mind are tired, but right now, I've never felt stronger. I pull off all of my best moves and focus on the lyrics as each song flows into the next.

The men are cheering me on, and I feel good. I feel light. Like a huge weight has been lifted off my shoulders. Tonight, in this moment, there is no shame or filthy thoughts running through my mind. I just feel… free.

And then everything changes in the blink of an eye.

I barely have time to grasp what the commotion is about before someone tackles me and hoists me over their shoulder. When I open my eyes and my head stops spinning, my face is dangling down towards a pair of strong, muscular legs wrapped in nice trousers. A pair of legs I know well.

It isn't until the music cuts off that I realize he's yelling at one of the guys in the audience, all the while I'm tossed over his shoulder like a sack of potatoes.

"Ronan?" I squeak. "Put me down!"

His grip only grows stronger. "I'll fucking kill ye if you ever look at her like that again," he snarls.

His muscles are rippling with rage, pulling at the seams of his suit. He's itching with the urge to kill.

"What the bleeding hell is going on in here?" Lachlan's voice filters through the low din.

I try to crane my neck to see him, but I can't. Ronan's grip on me is so tight, I can't even wiggle an inch.

"He's having a wank right there in the bloody pit," Ronan shouts. "He was looking at her…"

His words are coming out broken and in between bursts of harsh breaths.

"My woman," he says. "He tried to touch her… and…"

"Alright, caveman," Lachlan says. "We get it, she's yours. Now fuck off out of here. I'll sort out the lad."

Ronan hesitates for a moment longer, and even though I can't see his face, I know his eyes are burning into whoever was staring at me. I worry that he's taking mental notes on who he's going to kill later. But then he turns around and carries me towards the back. And before we slip through the curtain and my humiliation is complete, I catch sight of Lachlan grinning. And then the bastard winks at me. He fucking winks.

Because he set this up. Set me up.

He knew Ronan would come in tonight, and he wanted him to see me. But I honestly could never have predicted the reaction I'm getting right now.

He takes me down the hall and finds the door to the basement. My head jerks with every step, and I try unsuccessfully to wiggle free one more time. When he finally stops at the bottom of the stairs, he doesn't even let me go. He just slides me down the front of his body and grips my ass with his palms before dropping me into a kneeling position before him.

I should be yelling at him, probably. Or something. But he's so angry. I've never seen him this way. He's fumbling with his belt, yanking down his briefs so that his cock springs free. It bobs once in front of my face before he shoves it in the direction of my mouth, bumping it against my lips.

Ronan and I have always had a fucked up way of going about things. The first time he fucked me, it was next to my dead boyfriend's body. The first blowjob, in a basement he uses to kill people. He isn't at all sweet. But if I wanted sugar, I'd eat a fucking cupcake.

I reach up and grab his thighs to anchor me as I drag him into my mouth. There isn't any uncertainty on his face tonight. There's nothing but ownership and wrath fueling this episode. But every time I draw him into my mouth, he groans.

His hands are in my hair, rough. He twists my head to suit his needs and uses me like a toy. If it were anyone else, I'd be pissed. But instead, I'm so fucking wet for him right now. I want him to use me. To take me. To be so out of control he can't help himself. I love it when he's like this. Harsh and dirty. I want him to use me up. I want him to toss me around and take me however he wants. The sex is so much hotter with Ronan because there are feelings involved. Emotions. I care about this man. And I want to serve him, right here in this dirty hallway.

I moan around him, and it only serves to rile him further.

"Is that good for ye?" he asks.

I mumble an affirmative around him, and he shoves my face deeper, making me choke on his cock.

"Is that the way ye like it?" His nostrils flare, and his fingers dig into my face. "Filthy like Donny used to do?"

I blink up at him in horror and confusion and jerk away, wiping my mouth. "What did you just say?"

"You heard me," he snarls. "Is that what ye like? Ye want me to treat you like a filthy whore?"

I shove him backwards as I stand up and he stumbles back a step. I don't make it two feet before he's yanking me back to him, trapping me between him and the wall. Ronan's never been gentle with me, but right now he's being downright caustic.

"Don't you ever fucking talk to me like that again!" I scream at him. "You fucking asshole…"

"I can do whatever I like with ye, Sasha," he announces. "Ye're mine."

And with that declaration, he tries to kiss me. I bite him, and it makes him bleed, but he doesn't stop. He grunts and devours me like he has every right to. And then he's pulling away, glowering at me. Like I'm the one who needs a frigging lobotomy.

"What the fuck is your problem?" I ask him. "You're acting like a lunatic."

He crouches lower and moves in on me, so that his gaze is directly across from mine.

"You let him touch you," he growls. "Ye fucking let him touch you."

And that's what all of this comes down to. Fucking Donovan. He put his slimy hands on me, and Ronan has the nerve to blame me for it. Pressure builds behind my eyes, and leaks out in the form of big, salty tears before I can get a grip.

"I didn't have a choice!" I yell in his face. "I've never had a fucking choice! You're all a bunch of fucking assholes. You just take what you want, and you don't even care…"

He kisses me again.

This time, it's gentle. His hands are on my face, holding me like I'm the most precious thing in the world to him. Like I wasn't just on my knees a moment ago blowing him in a dirty hallway while he called me a whore. And I know it's because I'm crying now. He made me cry. I said I wouldn't cry over a man again, but this one made me cry. And yet, when he soothes me from the hurt that he caused, I cling to him.

When he pulls away, his brown eyes move over my face, sad and torn and so beautiful it hurts to look at them. All of my anger melts away when he looks at me like this. It's foolish, but true.

"How do you do that?" I ask.

"Do what?"

"How do you look at me like that and just make me forget everything, Ronan? You betrayed me. You're mad because of what I did to protect you, but you didn't protect me at all. You told Lachlan our secret. And I want to be angry at you. I'm so fucking angry at you."

His face softens and his hands pull me closer, like I might try to flee at any moment. Even though he's the one that's usually doing the running. But he sees my frustration. My pain. He threw me to the wolves, and he has to know I'm fed up. This constant back and forth with him is making me fucking insane. And yet he disarms me with a single touch. Talks me off the ledge with the faintest of whispers. This man is pure agony. My descent to hell. In fact, I'm certain he must be Lucifer himself, because the poison he feeds me is too sweet to resist.

"I haven't a clue what Crow told ye," he says. "But it wasn't like that, Sasha."

"Then how was it like?" I demand.

"I don't want ye to worry about these things," he says softly. "It's all in hand."

This.

This is why I'm so deranged. This evasiveness. It took him two years after what happened to even talk to me, and now I'm lucky to drag one sentence out of him. He's so guarded, even from me. And it makes me question everything about him, but when I look at him, I do believe him. He believes he's protecting me by withholding information. By handling it. That's how things work in the mob. The men deal with business, and the women look the other way.

On some level, it's nice to be able to disconnect like that. To trust and have faith that the syndicate will protect you. That's how it works with the other girlfriends and wives. Unfortunately, it never worked that way for me. So it's hard for me to look at Ronan right now and just tell him that none of it matters. Because it does. It involves me. And I know there had to be a reason for him to tell Lachlan after all this time. A damn good reason because it was a very risky move.

"Just tell me one thing," I croak. "Tell me that you're safe and they aren't going to punish you for it."

"Ye're safe, Sasha," he replies. "I've made sure of that."

"I wasn't asking about myself," I answer. "And it's funny how you can say that, because I didn't exactly feel so safe when Lachlan was questioning me about it. Testing me when he knew the answer the whole time. What would have happened if I'd told him the truth?"

Dark clouds roll through his eyes, and something shifts in his expression. It looks like betrayal. And I feel a little guilty for even mentioning it though I shouldn't.

"He did that?" Ronan asks.

"It doesn't matter," I sigh. "I don't want to cause problems between you two. That wasn't my intention. I just needed to know that you were safe."

He's quiet for a long pause, and it's obvious he's still thinking about it. But whatever's actually going on in that head of his is still a complete mystery to me.

"Ye're done dancing," he says finally, in a tone like I have no say in the matter.

"I'm fully aware of that," I snap. "Tonight was my last night."

He grips my hair into a makeshift pony tail and tugs on it. His mouth hovers over mine, the heat of his every exhale skating over my lips.

"Nobody else gets to see you like that," he declares. "Ye're claimed."

His words douse me in gasoline. His eyes light the match. And when he grinds himself against me, all that's left to do is burn for him.

He crushes his lips against mine and kisses me so hard it borders on painful. His hands are tearing at the strings of my bikini, yanking them apart until I'm completely naked in his arms. His raging hard cock is still sandwiched between our bodies, at least until it isn't. He picks me up and the next thing I know, I've got ten inches of Ronan shoved inside of me. I cry out against him, and he feeds off of it, sucking his own choice of poison from the hollow in my throat. The taste of my skin is what gets him off. Being inside of me. Owning me. He drinks from me and gives me another lethal injection of his brand of narcotic.

"Why are you always doing this?" I pant against him. "Why do you always do this?"

His only answer is to fuck me into the wall. Being the psychopath that I clearly am, I come so hard I nearly black out. I want him. But he's so bad for me. The worst. And still, I clamp down around him, pulling him deeper inside.

He's putting me on display right now. Anyone could come down here and see us. I can only imagine what we look like. Him fully dressed, me naked and pressed against the wall. Lipstick smeared, mascara running down my face. Good and thoroughly used by him.

I wonder if Ronan's thinking about that too, when he groans and finishes inside of me.

Without a condom. Again.

Jesus. This fucking man.

His forehead falls against mine, and we both just hold on to each other until our breathing calms. And then he releases me and I slide down his body until my toes touch the floor.

His come is still leaking out of me when I bend over to pick up the scraps of my clothing. I attempt in vain to make myself decent while Ronan watches. He's already zipped and apart from his bloody lip, there's not a bit of evidence he just fucked me into next week.

"I hope you enjoyed that," I tell him. "Being that it was the last time."

He looks at me. And we both know it's a lie. This thing between us isn't over. I'll always be enslaved to this man. I'd serve him any day of the week and twice on Sundays. Because, fuck me, that's why.

He could just come out and say it if he really wanted to. Rub it in my face and tell me the ugly truth. Instead, he simply says, "Come on. I'm taking ye home."

Chapter Twenty-Four

Sasha

When Ronan said he was taking me home, the most logical conclusion would be that he meant to my place. So when we pull up to an unfamiliar house in Beacon Hill I stare over at his shadowed profile and wait for an explanation.

But Ronan being Ronan, he doesn't bother giving me one. Instead, he steps out of the car and comes around to open my side and then escorts me up the stairs. He's looking around the street, his eyes darting at every shadowed car and bush in the vicinity. And I'm used to him being uptight, but not like this. He's on high alert, and it's making me nervous.

"Is something wrong?" I ask him.

He glares at me. "Aye, something's wrong. You were flashing your tits and ass for all the lads tonight. After I'd taken you. Made you my woman."

I'm still staring at him in disbelief when he drags me through the door. And then I'm being attacked by the last thing I ever expected to see in his house.

A frigging Corgi.

I bend down to greet her, and she licks my hand before wiggling her butt back and forth and whining at Ronan. He calls her into the kitchen and gives her some food, but it's obvious she only wants his attention. Ronan doesn't seem to understand this… the most basic of emotions, and it's just so Ronan that I can't help but smile.

"She wants you to pet her," I tell him. "Hold her."

"How can ye tell?" he asks.

I want to tell him it's obvious, but the more I'm around Ronan the more I learn he actually does need things like this explained.

"That's why she gets so excited," I say. "When you come in the door. She does it every time, right?"

"Aye," he says. "I thought it meant she was hungry. That's what Crow said."

I roll my eyes and set down my bag. "No, Ronan. It means that she missed you. While you are out and about in the world and doing your thing every day, a dog only has interactions with you to look forward to."

"But why would she look forward to that?" he asks.

"Because she loves you."

He glances down at the little Corgi who is staring up at him with an expression I know far too well. It's the same damned expression I get when I look at him, too. Ronan moves to the fridge, and the dog comes running to me. I pick her up in my arms and smile.

"You and me, sister," I murmur. "We're just a couple of suckers, huh?"

"Would you care for a drink?" Ronan asks very formally.

"No," I answer. "What's her name?"

He comes back into view. "Her name is dog. And how did ye know it was a girl?"

I frown at him and shake my head. "You have to give her a real name. And it's pretty easy, Ronan. She doesn't have any balls."

He looks away uncomfortably and then sits down on the sofa. He's back to being stiff and unnatural and I have no idea what I'm even doing here.

I sit down in a spare seat and continue to play with the dog. "What about Daisy?" I ask him. "I think it suits her."

He watches the dog for a few moments and then shrugs. "That sounds... grand."

"You hear that, Daisy?" I coo. "You've been upgraded from dog. You have a real name now."

She whines and then gets overexcited, bounding off to go see her beloved master.

"Why am I here, Ronan?" I ask finally.

He won't look at me. And the tension in his body is only growing with every passing minute. He stands up and makes a gesture with his hand.

"Will ye come with me?" he asks. "I'd like to show ye something."

"Okay," I agree cautiously. He's acting really strange. Even more so than usual.

He walks down the hall, and for the first time I notice that the layout of his house is very similar to Lachlan's. But the furniture is much less prevalent, and I highly suspect that he pretty much never has company. This is a house designed for function only. Eat, sleep, and read from the looks of it. Everything is clean and tidy, but not overly so. There isn't much in the house at all for personal belongings. No photos, no knitted blankets or other personal effects that one usually collects over a lifetime.

When I stare at his back as he leads me down the dark and empty hall, it makes my heart ache for him. The only things this man has in his life are literally his brothers in the syndicate. And a dog that he didn't even know should have a name. I want to ask him more about his background, and there's a question on the tip of my tongue, but then he pauses in front of a room.

His room.

It's obvious from the scent alone that lingers there. It's Ronan's personal space. Where he sleeps at night. There's a bed with stark gray blankets and a closet full of suits and shoes and little else. A couple of books on the nightstand and a lamp to read by. That's it.

I look up at him and wonder if this is some misguided attempt at flirting with me. Or getting me into his bed, which doesn't seem likely. He's very fond of taking me up against walls and then making a quick getaway. He doesn't even like to remove his clothes.

"What did you want to show me?" I step inside the room and take a look around.

But Ronan doesn't follow. Instead, he shuts the door behind me, and a lock clicks into place from the other side.

"What the hell, Ronan?" I walk to the door and slap my hand against the wood. "What are you doing?"

"Conor is bringing over the rest of your belongings from your apartment," he says from the other side. As though this statement is totally reasonable and should explain everything.

"Excuse me?"

"And if ye need anything, you can call out for me."

"Ronan." I rub my temples in frustration. "You aren't making any sense. Tell me what's going on."

There's a long pause of silence, and I wait, hoping he hasn't disappeared. But then his voice is soft and slightly nervous as he explains.

"Someone broke into your apartment," he says.

"What? How... I mean how do you even know this?"

"Because they sent me a photo, to my phone," he replies quietly. "With a picture of your bed and your... um... your knickers and such."

A tremor moves through me, and suddenly I'm glad for the sanctuary of Ronan's house.

"Why would they do that?" I ask.

I don't understand. But the longer he remains silent, the more I start to piece it together.

"They know you," I speak into the wooden door. "Are they threatening me?"

Another pause, and I can almost imagine him taking off his glasses and rubbing his tired eyes the way he does when he's stressed.

"I fucked up," he says. "They've been watching me, and I came to your apartment. They must have had someone following me. I got the text tonight, and I went looking for you. And then I saw you at the club..."

His words die off, and I understand now why his reaction was so crazy. He probably thought I was dead. And then he saw me up on stage and snapped.

"Oh," I reply. "Well it doesn't matter. Because I'm leaving tomorrow, so they won't know where I'm going."

"Sasha," Ronan cuts me off, his voice agonized. "I can't allow ye to leave. They know your name. Your face. This isn't just someone I've pissed off. It's one of the blokes who worked for the Russians. Andrei, his name is. But he's better known as the butcher. I botched up the job I was meant to do, and now he's going to come after you to get back at me."

"I don't understand," I clip out, even though I do. I understand perfectly well.

"Ye're not leaving." He says through the door. "Ye're going to stay right here with me."

His footsteps move down the hall, away from me, and I slam my hand against the wood.

"This is called kidnapping, you know!"

Chapter Twenty-Five

Sasha

Accepting my fate, I slip out of my jeans and sweatshirt and raid Ronan's drawers for a tee shirt to sleep in. He does have them, which surprises me for some reason. Track pants too. I open up his other drawers out of curiosity and find several stacks of the same pairs of black briefs.

Even though he just locked me in his room and I'm annoyed at his fucked up methods of trying to protect me, I can't help imagining what he would look like in the briefs. I've never seen him naked. I've only ever been graced with a small glimpse of his powerful body. His chest and his arms, which were littered in scars and battle wounds that seemed worse than I expected.

I know what Ronan's job in the mafia is. I know that they call him the Reaper. And the day that I snuck down in the basement, I knew he was down there with Donny. But I needed confirmation. I needed to know for certain that he was going to be the one to kill Donny. Because a sick and twisted part of me wanted that. Wanted Ronan to be the one to exact vengeance on the piece of shit who treated me like a dog. Like a worthless whore who was only good for opening her mouth and getting him off whenever it suited him.

I knew Ronan would make him suffer for what he did. And I got off on the idea of it. Of the man who threatened both of us being wiped from existence. But what about the other men Ronan kills? I think about them often. Who they are, and if they're just as bad too.

I want to believe that they are. To justify what he does. I know Ronan has rage inside. I've seen it first hand when he killed Blaine. But even then, it was justified. And when I look at him, all I see is the calm. He's my anchor in the stormy sea. The one that keeps me from being pulled away into the chaos.

But Ronan needs an anchor too. Whatever caused those scars on his body, whatever caused him to be the way he is… so guarded, so untrusting, so quiet… it makes me question my own humanity. Because if I was faced with the men who did that to him, I would want to kill them too.

With a sigh I shut his dresser drawers and crawl into his bed. The sheets are stiff and not very comfortable. Shocker, I know. But they smell like him, and that makes me feel safe. I wonder what he's doing. Where he's sleeping. But these are dangerous thoughts to have. Because I can't get pulled back in.

This situation is only temporary.

That's what I keep telling myself as I curl up and bury my face into his pillow. I can't be angry at him though. My kidnapper and my protector are one in the same. He's trying to take care of me in the only way he knows how. And it's oddly fucked up.

Come morning, I will try to have a rational conversation with him. But until then, I allow myself to fall asleep in the sanctuary of his bedroom.

***

I stretch out on Ronan's bed and yawn.

The bed itself isn't very comfortable, but I slept better than I have in a long time. I can smell coffee brewing from somewhere inside the house, and I suspect he'll be in soon.

I pad across the room and decide to raid his drawers again since I don't see any of my stuff in the room yet. I pull open the drawer that had his track pants and grab a pair off the top. But then I feel something beneath them that catches my attention.

I flip through the rest of the cloth until I find a cardboard box hidden beneath. Pulling it out, my curiosity is riled. I bring it back to the bed with me and open it up. And my breath completely flees with what I find there.

The first thing I recognize is an earring I thought I'd lost forever. It's old and just a plain jane sterling silver braided hoop, but it's one of my favorites. I used to wear them all the time.

I slide my finger over the grooves and set it aside, digging through the rest of the contents. There are handwritten notes in there. Notes I left for the other dancers. Even a few I'd left in Lachlan's office regarding the schedule. They are nothing of significance, but Ronan kept them for some reason.

As I dig deeper, I find a napkin with my lipstick print on it. Another thing he must have retrieved from the club. One of my tank tops. Photographs of me from my apartment. Even a couple pairs of my lace panties. One pair in particular, I remember well. They are the same panties I was wearing when he killed Blaine and took me for the first time.

I'm still staring at all of it in shock when the door cracks open, followed by a sharp intake of breath. There's a pause, and then Ronan stalks over and starts shoving everything back into the box with his cheeks flushing a furious shade of pink.

He reaches for the earring, and I snatch it away.

"That's mine," I tell him.

He isn't looking at me. I've never seen him so embarrassed. So stiff.

"Ronan," I call out to him, and finally his eyes snap down to mine. "Why do you have all this stuff?"

He doesn't answer me. I want to hear him say it. He reaches for the earring again and I close my fingers around it.

"I like this earring," I protest. "I thought I lost it."

He stares at me like I just took away his favorite toy. And then with a huff, he takes the box to his closet and shoves it up onto the highest shelf where I can't reach and into the dark shadows. I'm staring at his back while I choose my next words carefully.

"I'm right here," I tell him. "Why do you need the earring when you have me?"

He turns around slowly and glances at me from across the room. And then his eyes move to the door. He's probably thinking about bolting and locking me in again. But I'm not about to let that happen. So I go to him.

One terrifying step at a time. Logic be damned.

When I reach him, I grab the lapels of his suit and smooth my hands over his chest. I wrap my arms around him, and he tenses.

"What are you doing?" he asks suspiciously.

"Hugging you."

He just stands there, arms hanging awkwardly at his sides. His hair is disheveled for the first time since I've known him. He's flustered. His breathing accelerated. And his eyes are darting over me, trying to anticipate my next move.

"Is this okay?"

He clears his throat. "It feels... okay?"

I drag my hands up and over his broad shoulders to the warm skin of his neck.

"Do you like me touching you, Ronan?" I ask. "Because sometimes I can't tell."

"Aye," he answers, his voice husky. "I like it very much."

He's quiet for a moment, thoughtful.

"When you touch me, it feels different," he adds. "Nice."

The gravity of that simple statement knocks me off balance.

"Hasn't anyone ever touched you in a nice way before?"

There are no words in response. But his body and his eyes tell me everything I need to know. Ronan Fitzpatrick is an iceberg. He only shows the world the smallest and safest parts of himself. But inside, underneath, is a wealth of hidden discoveries. I want to know them all.

I cling to him and lay my head against his chest. After a while, he seems to get the simple concept of a hug. His hands wrap around my waist and rest on my back. And even though it's the most awkward hug I've ever had, it's also the best.

"You don't have to keep me locked in the room," I tell him. "I won't leave until you say it's okay, Ronan. Because I trust you. I trust that you'll protect me."

He makes a small grunt of approval. But I'm honestly not sure he even heard me. Because he's staring at the place where my breasts are pressed against his chest. He likes that. Judging by the bulge digging into my stomach, he likes it a lot.

Knowing the way that Ronan is, I anticipate it's only a matter of time before he's throwing me down and fucking me again. But before things can even get that far, I reach for his hand and pull him back to the bed.

I tell him to sit down. After a moment's hesitation, he does. And when I drop down on my knees before him, I have his undivided attention. My palms rest on his thighs, massaging the solid muscle beneath before I go any further. His pulse drums against my fingertips, betraying how much he likes this too.

"We don't have a condom," I remind him.

My palms are slowly creeping up his legs while I speak, keeping his attention focused on how he feels instead of the words. When I reach the bulge straining against the zipper of his trousers, I palm him through the material and then tug. He makes another sound in his throat, and his eyes flutter shut.

I pull his cock free from his briefs, toying with it while I work up the nerve for my next question. He looks huge in my hands. Pure male perfection. And the thing is, he doesn't even know it. He just wants me. My touch. My hands on his body.

I let that go to my head a little. Because goddamn this man. He's hot as fucking hell. That's a fact. But if he tells me he's only ever been with me, I might go off the deep end completely. I need to know. I need to know just how much his dark obsession burns for me. Because I don't think I could ever let anyone else have him. He's mine, already. But the words… the words make it real. Make it true.

I swirl my thumb over the head of his cock and squeeze, milking the moisture that's already leaking out of him. His eyes are open now. Heavy and dark as they watch me taste him.

"Has anyone ever touched you like this before?" I ask.

His answer is a rough murmur.

"No."

I wrap my hand around his thick base and give it a couple more pulls, making his balls draw up against his body.

"Has anyone else got to have you, Ronan?" I ask. "Have you ever fucked anyone the way you fuck me?"

The resulting jerk of his hips makes me think he secretly likes my filthy mouth.

"No," he grunts. "Only you, Sasha."

A torrid fever builds inside of me, charging my blood with manic possession. Jesus. I nearly come just thinking about it.

This man is the walking definition of masculinity. Virility. If his crew were a wolf pack, he'd be the strong and silent Alpha. And yet I'm the only one who's ever touched this God among mortals. *Me.* A girl from the Dot with nothing to offer but my broken self.

"Good." My voice is hoarse, drunk on the knowledge of my claim. "Because if you ever touch anyone else, I'll murder them."

His eyes snap to mine, dark and hot like melted chocolate. They reflect my own right now. The way that I feel. Only, Ronan takes it a step further when a small boyish grin cracks across his face. I'm pretty sure I hear angel's singing, because holy shit that's a beautiful sight. It doesn't last long though, because as soon as I drag him back into my mouth, his head tips back and his eyes fall shut.

"Do you know what, Ronan?" I ask.

He's having trouble concentrating with his cock in my hand. But I tell him anyway.

"You deserve to feel good. And the fact that you never have is a fucking tragedy. I'm going to rectify that. Here and now."

His cock pulses in my palm, branding my skin with his heat as I suck him hard and deep, then soft and teasing.

"Tell me which way you like," I urge.

He hesitates. So I keep talking.

"Do you like me on my knees for you?"

"Aye," he answers in a husky voice. "Very much."

"Show me what else you like, Ronan."

He grabs the back of my head and surprises me when he thrusts up into my mouth roughly, the same way he did last night. Not only do I let him, but I get off on it. I reach down and cup his balls, and he makes another sound in his throat. God, I love the sound of Ronan coming undone for me.

He face fucks me with erratic thrusts, the head of his cock gnashing against my teeth and the back of my throat. This brand of roughness suits his personality. The way he dominates me. He takes me when he wants, without asking. Because Ronan can't help himself. He's starving for this. Has been starving for it for years. I see that now.

He pushes me all the way down on his cock and then explodes into my mouth. He isn't polite and doesn't ask if I want to swallow. He's an animal. So unpolished and not at all suave. But he's mine. My caveman.

When he pulls away though, uncertainty creeps across his face. The wheels are turning in his head again. Wondering. Thinking. Worrying. I won't let him get locked inside those thoughts. Those thoughts keep him away from me.

So I smile up at him and tuck him into his pants before zipping him back up. And then I move up and sit beside him on the bed, brushing my leg against his.

"So," I say lightly. "What are we going to do today, kidnapper?"

Chapter Twenty-Six

Ronan

*W*hen I spot the church on the hillside in the distance, a weak sound tears from my chest. It must be a sign. A sign that I am to stop running and bear punishment for what I have done. Alex spoke of this place. He told me how much he liked coming to the church. How they would help people. He told me it didn't matter what you had done, they would help you.

I hope they will help me too.

I've been running for days around this countryside. Weak with hunger and sick from drinking out of dirty puddles. I thought I could find someone to help me. That there was a life that still existed beyond the compound, like Alex talked about.

But the only thing I've managed to find is this church.

I stare up at the brick building and compare it to the church that Alex described. It does not look the same, but I can read the words and they clearly say it's a church. Something inside of me tells me to keep going.

But I've no choice.

My body is too weak to fight anymore. I'm filled with feelings I don't understand. I crawl up the steps and collapse near the door. I try to raise my fist to knock, or call out, but I cannot even manage that.

My head lolls back against the cold stone beneath me, and blackness takes over.

***

The priest is quiet as he sits across from me, examining me. He does not dress like the men at the compound. He does not look like a soldier. I've been here for weeks now. He's given me a bed, and warm meals, and has not pushed me to talk. He's been kind to me.

When he first asked me questions, I couldn't bring myself to answer him. My shame was too great. But I feel like I'm ready to speak now. And I think that maybe he can help me after all. I scratch at a worn line in the wooden table and open my lips for the first time since I left the compound. My voice sounds strange to my own ears when it leaves my throat.

"I've done something bad," I tell the priest. "And I know I must pay for it."

He is quiet for a long pause, and when I look up at him, he does not seem surprised by my confession. He's watching me closely, the same way Farrell used to do sometimes. It makes me uncomfortable again, but I don't let onto it.

"Tell me what you have done," he says.

I tell him. I tell him everything. Every awful thought I've ever had. I speak of the compound and the soldiers and my training. How I've come to enjoy the pain that was meant to provide punishment. How I don't understand my own thoughts at times, and my mind so often betrays me.

I admit that I took Farrell's life, even though he was my superior. We aren't supposed to kill our superiors. But I enjoyed it. I liked the way his blood painted the floor when I was finished. I speak of my confusion. Because I am a killer, and that was all I was ever meant to be. So maybe I'm not wrong. But I feel I should be punished for what I did to Farrell, and the priest agrees.

"Aye, lad. There is punishment for sins such as these. Severe punishment. There is only one way that you can save your soul now."

I blink up at him and listen carefully. I don't know what a soul is, but it sounds serious. I want him to help me, and I believe he can. That's what Alex told me. These places help people.

"Anything," I tell him. "Tell me what I must do. I am ready."

"It will be uncomfortable," he says. "You will not like it. I will not enjoy doing it either. But I must. In order to save your soul."

"I am ready," I tell him again. "I am ready for you to show me."

The priest has a grim expression on his face when he leads me to the back. It reminds me of the compound. Of Farrell. He was *always looking at me. Watching me. It made me uneasy, the same way the priest is looking at me now.*

"Pull down your trousers, lad," he says.

I recall my punishments at the compound. How Coyne and Farrell would take my clothes and use the cattle prod before they sprayed me with cold water. I didn't like being naked, but I got used to it. I think that maybe the priest is going to do the same.

I remove my trousers and cup my groin.

The priest frowns and then points at the bed. I sit down and look around the room. I don't see what he's going to hurt me with, and when he sits down beside me too, I'm even more confused. He pulls up his robes and then undoes his trousers too.

I swallow and try to look away.

"I told ye you might not enjoy it," he says. "But that is how punishment works, aye?"

That is how punishment works, but when he reaches for my arm, my stomach churns. He grabs my hand and pulls it away from my groin. And then he's touching me. I curl into myself and scramble back against the wall.

"I don't like that."

He grabs my leg and tries to pull me back, and when he stands up he has an erection. Vomit rises up my throat and then rage. His hand rubs between my legs, and I can't control the rage. I buck against him and throw my head into his.

He cries out in pain, but I do not care. I reach for the lamp from the bedside and crash it over his head. He backs away from me, his head bleeding and his eyes wide. He sees now. He sees the monster I am.

He flees towards the front of the church, but my training won't let him go. Neither will my rage. Alex said this place would help me. I don't understand. He was supposed to help me.

I chase after him, down the aisles while I shout out the same words.

"You were supposed to help me!"

He tries to leave. But I cannot let him. We are never to let an enemy escape with his life. I throw the lamp at the back of his head. He falls to the ground, and the rage finally consumes me. I cannot control myself any longer. I grasp the lamp in my hands and bring it down over his head.

And I hit him again. And again. And again. Until there is nothing but red.

It feels good.

"You were supposed to help me."

I repeat those words, until there is nothing left of his face, and my voice is nothing more than a whisper. And then I curl into myself and wish more than anything that I knew what to do.

I don't know how long I sit there for.

I only know that when I look up again, there is a woman standing over me with a trembling hand clutched over her mouth. Beside her, a boy my age is looking down at the blood around me. His eyes are wide, and his cheeks heated with embarrassment when they land on me.

I glance down at myself and work out that I'm still half naked, covered in blood. I have no explanation to give them. So I say the only thing I can.

"He was supposed to help me."

***

Sasha is in the kitchen and I'm at the table.

I have a newspaper in my hands, but my eyes are on her. Watching her move around as she cooks. I don't know what it is, but it smells good. And she keeps feeding the dog -Daisy- little scraps.

I haven't worked out what to do with her. I can't stay at the house all the time. But I can't let her leave. She believed me. She believed my lie so easily that it feels wrong. But when I watch her moving around my home, and smell her scent around me, I cannot be sorry.

She is so beautiful.

She looks over her shoulder and catches me staring. I look away, but before I do, she smiles.

"It's ready," she says.

A moment later, she's pushing a plate in front of me. I stare at it too long, and Sasha looks worried.

"It's an omelet," she says. "You like eggs, don't you?"

"I've never had them this way," I admit.

"Really?" she smiles again. "Well then you won't be disappointed that it's only cheese and veggies. You don't have much in your fridge."

She sits down and starts to eat, and I bring the plate to my nose and sniff. Her fork clatters onto her plate, and when I glance up, she's watching me with a strange expression. I tear my eyes away and take a tentative bite.

"I haven't poisoned you, Ronan," she laughs. "If that's what you're thinking."

I frown, and her face grows serious. "Did you really think I might have poisoned you?"

I don't like seeing her upset. And I made her that way. So I take a bite. And it's good. I tell her so, and she relaxes again. I make a note to tell her the food is grand any time she cooks for me.

"I'll have Conor do some food shopping today," I tell her. "You can make a list if you'd like."

"Okay," she agrees.

We eat in silence, and I finish before her. When I look up at her she seems happy. And I think maybe having her here with me will be okay. But that changes when she asks her next question and reminds me of the things I can never have.

"Tell me about your childhood," she says softly.

"I lived with Crow," I answer.

She waits for more, but I don't know what else to say.

"No, before that."

I shift in my seat and focus my attention on Daisy, who's sitting on my foot again. "Why?"

"Because I want to know you, Ronan. Is that okay?"

I don't answer her. A flood of images come back to me, but I don't know how to sort them into words. I don't think I could even if I tried. I've tried with Crow. Sometimes I've been able to explain things. But even he doesn't know everything.

Sasha reaches across the table and grabs my hand. I stare at her fingers, observing how small they are against my own. How soft she is compared to my skin. Like silk.

"It's okay, Ronan," she says. "You don't need to tell me right now."

She takes our plates to the sink and then comes back a moment later.

"Hey, you can get prescriptions, right?"

"Aye," I answer, relieved that I can actually do something she asks.

She pulls out a piece of paper from her pocket and hands it to me. I don't recognize the name of what she's scribbled down, and I worry that something might be wrong with her.

"Can you get me that?" she asks.

I nod, but already I'm making other plans. I don't want anything happening to Sasha. So I'll get her a prescription, but I'll bring her a doctor too.

Chapter Twenty-Seven

Sasha

When I finish with my shower, Ronan shows me to the room where Conor stored all of my belongings. It's strange, having them in his house. I didn't even get to say goodbye to my apartment.

It's a silly thought, but that dingy little box was the place where I grew up. The place where I had some of my best memories. I wonder if Ronan would take me back there one last time. Probably not. He says it isn't safe, and I doubt he would understand the emotional connection I had to it.

As I knot my towel around my chest, I bend over to take a peek in one of the boxes that holds my clothes. But when I do, I notice Ronan's dress shoes behind me in the doorway. I crane my neck to look at him and catch him staring at my ass.

I smile.

Sometimes he seems so unsure of himself, but right now he's as close to a man as any other. He catches me staring and his eyes move to the blue thong dangling between my fingers.

"You should wear the black ones," he says. "With the red bows."

I'm pretty sure my mouth is open, but there's nothing coming out of it. I don't know whether to be flattered or think he's totally nuts for knowing what all of my underthings look like.

"I'll do that," is the only thing I can think to say.

"The doctor will be here in ten minutes," he adds.

His voice is back to being formal, and it makes me want to ask if he will ever feel comfortable around me. But before I get a chance, he disappears down the hallway.

I dress in a pair of yoga pants and an off the shoulder sweatshirt and braid my hair. It isn't until I look in the mirror that I realize that though Ronan may not be comfortable with me, I am with him. He's seen me in pretty sorry shape a few times now. I don't feel the need to dress up to impress him. But a part of me does wonder how his hands would feel roaming over the tight material of my leggings and up beneath the loose material of the sweatshirt.

When I hear the front door shut, I walk down the hall and wonder if the doctor can prescribe me something for my obvious insanity. Because I seem to be forgetting that this situation is only temporary, and I don't have the luxury of fantasizing about Ronan like that.

In the parlor, I stop and cover my mouth to stifle a laugh when I catch Ronan carting the Corgi up the stairs beneath his arm while she tries to lick at his face.

"What are you doing?" I ask.

He sets her down at the top landing and smooths out his suit.

"Her legs are too wee for the stairs," he explains as he points at the offending limbs. "She can't get down them to go outside."

I laugh and he stares at me in confusion.

"She's got you wrapped around her little paws," I tell him.

A knock sounds at the door, and Ronan is grateful for the interruption. On the other side is a female doctor which surprises and relieves me. I half expected the same guy that tended to Ronan after the fights to show up here.

"Sasha, I presume?" the doctor walks up the steps and holds out her hand.

"Yes, that's me."

"Is there somewhere we can speak in private?" she asks.

I look at Ronan, and he's already edging towards the door. "Conor's just outside," he says. "I'll be back after."

After what, he doesn't say, but I presume it's probably mafia business.

The doctor takes a seat on the sofa and pulls out a notepad with the name of birth control I requested scribbled on it. She goes through a whole host of routine questions about my health and dates of last exams and I'm suddenly grateful Ronan did leave. I don't think he could have handled this part.

"Have you taken this medication before?" she asks.

"Yes," I tell her.

"Okay and did you have any issues with it?"

"Not that I can remember."

"Great, well unless you have any other questions for me, I'd be happy to write you a prescription."

"Perfect." I smile and wait for her to write the prescription. But instead, she reaches inside of her bag and pulls out a cup.

"We just need to do a routine pregnancy test first," she says.

"Oh." I swallow down my nerves and take the cup with trembling fingers. "Right."

I'd forgotten about this part. The last time I was on birth control was when I was with Blaine. I don't know how many times Ronan has finished inside of me now, completely unprotected. But I won't soon forget the panic on his face when I mentioned the possibility of getting pregnant.

As I walk down the hall to the bathroom and go through the process, I tell myself it's not even possible. I mean, it was only a few times. And he did use a condom once. But then I try to count the dates in my head, and I start having a mini panic attack.

I haven't been eating properly, and I've been a jittery stress head. I think I did miss my period last month, but now I'm not really sure. By the time I get back to the doctor, I'm a nervous wreck and she reads it on my face.

"I'll do it right here," she says, going about the process.

I don't watch. I sit down on the couch and stare up at the ceiling. I was supposed to be leaving. If things had gone to plan, I'd already have been gone. This wasn't supposed to happen. Because I had a plan. A light at the end of the tunnel. But before the doctor even says the words, I know it's coming. And then she confirms it with her words, and everything swirls around me.

I'm pregnant.

With Ronan's child. And if he finds out there's a good chance he'll either freak the fuck out or imprison me in this life forever. I don't like either side of that coin toss.

The doctor reaches out and gently squeezes my shoulder.

"Are you alright?"

"I'm fine," I reply with a jerky nod. "But this stays between us, right?"

"Of course," she says. "I'd be happy to schedule you an appointment in my office if…"

"That's okay." I rush to stand up and almost fall over in the process. "I'll make one later. I can do that, right?"

"Of course," she says. "But I wouldn't put it off too long. You'll need a blood test and…"

"Okay," I cut her off.

I know I'm being rude, but I just want that pregnancy test gone. She walks to the kitchen and cleans up and I pace the length of the dining room, staring out the window. I don't know what I'm going to do.

Oh God, what the hell am I going to do?

I don't even wait for the doctor to leave before I shuffle down the hall to my room and scramble through my purse for my cell phone. But it isn't there. And after digging through the rest of the boxes, I can't find it anywhere.

A throat clears behind me, and I spin around to find Ronan in the door frame.

"All good?" he asks.

His gaze is probing, his voice tense. And it almost makes me want to tell him. Almost. But then there's that boyish innocence in his eyes. God, how can one man be so contradictory? He's a killer, a cold-blooded murderer for the mafia, and yet he can be so innocent sometimes.

"Where's my phone?" I ask.

My question makes his eyes turn down, which puts me on guard.

"I had to get rid of it," he answers. "It wasn't safe."

I don't even have the energy for that argument, so instead I ask for his. When he hesitates again, I get irritated.

"I need to call Mack," I snap. "Is that alright? Or can you have her come over? I want to see her."

He still isn't moving, or responding, and I feel as though I need to explain further for some reason. Like he can see right through me.

"I didn't get to see her after the wedding," I tell him. "She'll think I just left town without saying goodbye."

Finally, my words seem to find a crack in his armor. "I'll sort something out," he says.

Chapter Twenty-Eight

Ronan

"Are you going to kidnap and kill me?" Mack asks from the passenger seat.

My grip squeezes the wheel as I keep my eyes fixed on the road.

"If that were the case, do ye think I'd answer that question honestly?"

"Well, Ronan," she says. "Yes, I actually think you would. You're weird like that. I don't think you really have it in you to tell a lie."

Her words feel like an accusation though I know it's just Mack's personality. She doesn't know how wrong she is in this case though.

"So what's with all of the secrecy?" she asks. "I don't like hiding things from Lach. We're not doing that stuff anymore. So unless you give me a good reason…"

I glance at her across the car and I know she's right. She'll tell Crow, and he'll rip me a new one even though he was in the same situation not too long ago.

"I needed Sasha to stay a little longer," I tell her.

Mack stares at me and the car is silent for a long pause before she bursts into laughter. "Oh God, Ronan. What did you do?"

"Why does it matter?" I reply. "You wanted her to stay."

"Of course I did," Mack answers. "But not through coercion, or kidnapping, or whatever it is you've drummed up."

"There are people that might have seen her with me," I tell her. That part isn't really a lie. Even though I would have noticed. And I would have taken them out the first chance I got. "I just need her to stay a little longer."

"Right," Mack says. "And she thinks she's in danger, meanwhile. That's a great plan you've got there, Ronan."

I slam my lips shut and regret my decision to go get Mack.

"You know she's my friend too," she says.

"Aye. So you should want what's best for her."

"Oh please," she laughs. "Ronan, I'll give you a week to come clean. That's all you're getting."

"Two," I bargain.

Mack is quiet again for a moment and then sighs. "You need to tell her how you feel. If you care about her, then she needs to know that. She's not a mind reader. And the only way she'll ever decide to stay on her own is if you give her a damn good reason to."

I mull over her words as I park the car on the street and leave it idling. Conor is standing at the front door, watching over the house.

Before Mack gets out, she twists in her seat to look at me. "Two weeks Ronan. And I want Dunkies delivered every morning."

"Fine," I grumble.

"But it has to be decaf," she adds. "Or else Lach will go nuts. He doesn't want me drinking so much caffeine these days."

I nod in concession, but Mack just continues.

"And I want choices. I'm talking lots of donuts, capiche? I don't want to get bored with the selection."

I scowl at her and she smiles. And then she pokes me in the chest and skips up the front stairs to the house.

I'm still thinking about her words when Crow texts me and asks me where the hell I am. He's got a lead on Andrei, and we're going to follow it up together.

Chapter Twenty-Nine

Sasha

When Mack comes trotting into the parlor with a happy expression on her face, it dies off quickly when she sees the expression on mine.

"What's wrong?" she asks.

I grab her by the arm and yank her down the hall to Ronan's room.

"Where is he?"

"He had to go to Slainte," she answers, then pokes around the room in curiosity. "So this is where the Reaper lays his head at night, huh? Go figure. This place has absolutely zero personality."

"Ronan has plenty of personality," I snap.

Mack frowns at me and I scrub my hands over my face in frustration. "I'm sorry," I tell her. "I know it was a joke. I'm just freaking out right now."

Mack sits down on the bed, her voice calm and her words careful. "And why is that?"

"Because," I whisper hiss as I point to my stomach. "He put a bun in my oven."

Mack blinks. And then blinks again. I think she's in more shock than I am.

"Mack?"

"Right." She jumps up on her feet and tries to comfort me with an awkward hand pat on the shoulder. "I honestly have no frigging clue what to say, Sash. I had no idea Ronan actually banged you. Damn. That's so weird. I can't even imagine…"

"Okay, well please don't try," I cut her off. "I don't know what I'm going to do. He's going to freak if he finds out. But he deserves to know. But then if I tell him he's going to keep me trapped here in this life forever."

Mack sighs and collapses back onto the bed. "And let me guess, you want me to keep my mouth shut too?"

"Obviously."

"This double agent thing is not all it's cracked up to be," she mutters.

"What?"

"Nothing," she says quickly. "Listen, Sash. I don't really know what the deal is with you and Ronan. I think I'm still in shock that he actually had sex. I mean the man is like a fucking ice cube. Does he ever warm up?"

"He's very… intense," I tell her.

Mack holds up her hands and shakes her head. "Okay never mind, that's too weird. He's like a brother to me or something. I can't think of him that way. So let's focus on the important thing which is the tiny human growing inside of you and the fact that I have no fucking clue on how to advise you in this situation."

"That isn't helpful," I groan.

"I know," she says. "I suck at this stuff. Is it wrong that I feel happy? Like giddy. We're both preggers at the same time. And we're both with guys that we probably never in a million years thought we'd end up with, but at least we'll be going through it together."

I smile at her and shake my head.

"Ronan and I aren't really together, together."

"Well, regardless," she beams. "You're having his baby."

Her happiness is contagious. I've been so busy freaking out over it that I never really stopped to think about that simple point. My hand moves over my belly and I blink back the tears knowing that Ronan and I created this.

It isn't wrong. No matter how fucked up this situation is, or how badly I wanted out of this life, this baby could never be wrong. I love it already. In fact, the enormity of my sudden love for something I only just found out existed hits me hard and fast.

"God, Mack, I'm having his baby."

"You are," she agrees.

"I love him," I blurt. "I know it sounds crazy. But I really do. I've been in love with him for so long. We are so fucked up together, but I love him."

"Welcome to the loony bin." Mack smiles. "Come in, sit down. Stay for a spell."

I half-laugh, half-cry. Mack always has a way of making me feel a little better.

"But seriously though," she says, "you should tell him."

"I can't," I croak. "I don't think… I mean I don't know if he feels the same. He barely speaks. I have to drag every little word out of him."

"Sash, let me tell you something. I went into Slainte thinking every single person there was sheisty as fuck. And I watched them all, Ronan included. But do you know what?"

"What?"

"He was so busy watching you that he never noticed anything else in that club. When you were there that was the only thing that existed to him. I know you said you wanted out of this life, and I get it, I really do. But are you running away from the life, or from him? Because you sort of seem to lump him in with all the other mob guys when we both know that's not really the case."

I blink up at her and feel pressure behind my eyes. Even though Mack is sarcastic and deflective most of the time, she really is very perceptive.

"I think he would take good care of you, Sash," she says softly. "I think no man would ever dare look your way again if you were his. And he would never, ever hurt you. Because if he did, I would frigging murder him."

"I don't know." My thoughts are too jumbled up right now to make sense of.

"You're both avoiding each other, Sash. Avoiding the elephant in the room. How long has this been going on for?"

"Years," I answer honestly.

"Right," she says. "And it's kind of ridiculous, huh?"

"Well, when you put it like that."

Mack smiles and reaches over to hug me. She's getting better at the hugging thing. "Talk to him, Sash," she whispers. "That's all you can do."

Chapter Thirty

Sasha

When Ronan gets back, I've got a whole feast prepared for dinner. Conor delivered the groceries I asked for, and I didn't have much else to do besides wash and play with Daisy.

It turns out, Ronan doesn't even have television or internet in his house. Just books. And after being here only one day, I can't imagine how he handles the silence all the time. It has to get lonely. I wonder if that's why he got Daisy. It doesn't really make sense, him having a Corgi. So when we sit down to dinner, I decide to ask him about it.

She's pawing at his leg, and he's petting her head awkwardly. Most people probably wouldn't notice it, how unsure he is with such simple things like that. Ronan always comes off cold and well put together, but if you look closely, you can see it in the little things he does.

"I take it you never had a dog before?" I ask him.

He looks up at me and shakes his head. "No."

"So how did you end up with Daisy?"

"She was at Donovan's house."

And with that simple statement, the subject is dead in the water. I'm not new to this life. These guys aren't in the habit of talking about men they killed. Once they're dead and buried, that's it. It's like they never existed before. And judging by the way Ronan's looking at me he prefers it that way too. But I do wonder if it's because he killed him or because of what Donny did to me.

The room is quiet, and I'm trying to think of something else to talk about. Ronan's staring at the pot roast and does that thing where he sniffs it before he eats it.

"Why do you do that?" I ask.

He blinks up at me and his cheeks flush under my scrutiny. "I don't like a certain sort of foods," he says.

"Okay…" I draw out the word, choosing my next ones carefully. "Like which sort?"

"I don't know."

If it were anybody else, I might think they were being intentionally vague. But Ronan's answer is an honest one, and I have a feeling that most of the time his answers only make sense to him. He doesn't understand the need to elaborate. I always took it as a sign he didn't want people to talk to him, his being so short and blunt. But then I think about him and Crow, and how close they are. Crow always pushes him for more answers, and I've never seen Ronan get angry with him for it.

So I decide to test it out myself.

"Why don't you know, Ronan?"

He eats a potato and thinks about his answer before he replies.

"Where I was reared, there was sometimes a sort of strange smell in the food. I don't know exactly what it was. But it made us sick. So I always check, just in case."

"Oh."

The room is silent again while I gather the courage for my next question. "That was at the compound, right?"

He sets his fork down. And I can't read his expression. I never know what he's thinking. But I know that I never will if I don't work at it.

"Lachlan said you were raised in a sort of training camp," I add, hoping he will explain further.

"Aye," he answers. "I was."

"Would you tell me about it?" I ask softly.

He frowns, and then, "what would ye care to know?"

"Did your parents live there with you?"

"Maybe," he says. "I only met my father once. Never met my mammy."

There's no emotion in his voice. It's like he's telling me the weather outside is cold. Or it's Monday. It's just a fact to him. Nothing else. And that devastates me.

"So who raised you?"

"A lady," he says. "I didn't know her name. She reared us until we were eight, and then our training began."

"Training for… killing, right?"

"Aye." He nods. "But mostly just war. They believed a war was coming. And they were making us into soldiers."

"So how did you meet Lachlan?"

"I met him in a church," he explains. "After I left the compound. His mammy took me home and looked after me until she died."

This time, there is warmth reflected in his voice. Even though he doesn't say it, it's obvious he cared for her very much. His relationship with Lachlan becomes so much clearer with those simple words. And I find myself wishing that his mother were still alive so I could hug her and thank her for helping Ronan. For raising him to be the man that he is today.

"Will you tell me what kind of things they made you do at the compound?"

He's quiet, and his eyes are dark again, shutting me out. This is a question he doesn't want to answer. And I have to accept there are just some things I may not ever know. It's up to him to tell me if he wants to. But I will break down his barriers, one by one.

"You could show me," I offer instead.

"How do you mean?" he asks.

I leave the plates on the table and stand up, taking his hand in mine. Ronan stares at our linked fingers for a moment before he relaxes in my grip and follows me where I lead him. To the bedroom.

I release his hands and step in front of him, nervous.

"I want to feel you," I explain. "All of you, Ronan. I want to feel your skin against mine. To know you. Will you let me?"

He's frowning. His eyes are downcast, and I can't get a read on him. I'm afraid he's going to say no. So I reach up and touch his face, stirring the magic that lingers between us every time we come together. I want him to feel it too. To take comfort in the knowledge that he's safe with me. That I would never hurt him or judge him. Because at this point, I can no longer deny that we are connected on some strange level. And I know I can't be the only one who feels it.

"Tell me what you're worried about," I say.

"I don't know," he answers.

"But you like it when I touch you?"

"Aye," he says.

"Do you trust me?"

He nods without a moment's hesitation. I stand on my toes and brush my lips against his, giving him the softest of kisses. His body relaxes into me, and he tries to pull me closer, but I stop him.

"I want to feel you," I insist.

Our gazes lock, and then finally, he nods. That mournful look is back in his eyes again, and a part of me hates that I'm making him uncomfortable. But the other part of me, the one that wants to help him see there's nothing to worry about, wins out.

I unbutton his suit jacket and slide my hands inside, over his broad chest. I peel it back off his shoulders and then go to work on the buttons of his undershirt. Once I've got that off too, I grab his hands and guide him backwards to the bed. He follows and sits down, and I kneel before him to remove his shoes and socks.

My palms slide up his trouser clad legs, soaking in the full power of his strained muscles before I reach his belt. I unbuckle him and tug down his zipper. He's wearing black briefs beneath, swollen from the outline of his hardened cock. My instinctive urge is to touch him. To please him. But first, I want to explore everywhere he's never let me venture before.

He lifts his hips and helps me with the business of removing his pants. Then I stand before him and remove my own. I've done this hundreds of times at the club. For an audience of other men. It meant nothing then. But it means everything now.

Ronan watches closely as if he might miss something should he even blink. He's seen me naked plenty over the last two years, but he still looks at me like it's the first time. Like I'm not dirty or wrong or broken the way I often think I am.

His tendons are strained from how badly he wants me. How much he's struggling to maintain his self-control. So I don't make a long production of it. Tonight's not about putting on a show for him. Tonight's about learning the landscape of his body. Connecting with him in a way that's more intimate than any other. Knowing his skin. The story only his body can tell me.

My fingers burn with the need to have those things.

I crawl onto the bed and move around behind him. His back is rigid, and I have to withhold the sharp intake of breath when I understand why. Upon seeing the large tattoo carved into his flesh, my stomach churns with dread. For Ronan.

The words are distorted, but I can still make them out. The codes of his militant cult. They are engraved onto his skin as a permanent reminder of the horrors they never want him to forget. The stretched lines make it apparent they were done many, many years ago. When he was only a child, and not even close to done growing yet.

My eyes sting from unshed tears, but I don't let them fall, and I don't make a sound. I told Ronan he could trust me, and now I understand his fear. His fear that I couldn't handle seeing these things without losing my shit.

That thought alone propels me to touch his shoulders. They are warm and muscular beneath my palms, a testament to the many hours he spends boxing with Lachlan.

This man is a fortress in his own right.

Immovable. Unstoppable. Formidable.

He is the very thing they created him to be. A killer. A machine. But he's also a protector. A man who can be as human as any other. I've seen his true nature. And I've never felt safer than when I was in his arms. So these people- the ones who hurt him- they didn't win. Ronan might not know it, but I do.

"Is this okay?" My fingertips move over him in a gentle cadence, massaging him lightly. A full body shudder moves through him, and his voice is a rough whisper when he replies.

"Aye."

"Have you ever had a massage before?" I ask.

"No."

My eyes rove over the skin on his back, riddled with scars and a lifetime of more pain than any one person should ever have to bear. It looks like he was whipped, stabbed, burned, and shot at... among other terrors my mind probably couldn't even conjure. These wounds tell the story his lips can't. And even if I don't know all of the details, I'm glimpsing a piece of Ronan that I doubt very many ever have. It isn't something I take lightly.

My fingers crawl up the nape of his neck and dissolve the tension from his muscles there and into his hairline. Ronan's only response is a small grunt of approval, but it plays like the sweetest melody I've ever heard. I massage his scalp and press a gentle kiss to his shoulder.

"I'm messing up your perfect hair," I say.

"I don't care," is his reply.

When I move lower, I notice a deep scar on the side of his head. My stomach flips when I trace over the raised flesh behind his ear.

"What's this one from?" I whisper.

"Another lad tried to cut it off," he answers. "And then I killed him."

I nod even though he can't see me, because I'm afraid if I speak my voice will betray me.

So for a while, I just touch him. Coaxing the stress from his body and watching the magic of Ronan melting into me. He's enjoying this. He trusts me. And I know without a shadow of a doubt now that I'll never be able to let him go.

I direct him to lay down on the bed. He does, and this time, I kneel beside him and work on his feet. Like every other part of him, they are well cared for and clean. But on the bottom of his soles, I uncover another score of long healed scars. More burns and slices. Deep and unforgiving. The amount of pain he must have endured to conceive such mutilations is unfathomable.

"Do they still hurt?" I croak.

"Sometimes," is his murmured reply.

His voice is sleepy. Content. The shock of what I'm witnessing no longer fazes him. He's under the spell of my fingers, completely oblivious to anything else. I forge on, choking my emotion down as the horrors of Ronan's childhood are laid bare. Scars on his knees. His thighs. His stomach, chest and shoulders. There isn't a single part of him that's been untouched by the violence he has known.

I'm trying to hold it in. Tamp it down. Keep control of myself. But the more I see, the harder it becomes. So many times, I've questioned this man. Who he is and what reasons he had for his behavior. I couldn't have known. My mind would never have taken me to such a dark place. But I get it now.

I get it so much that silent tears of shame and anger bleed from my eyes, burning me like acid. A sob drags from my lungs before I can stop it, and Ronan blinks up at me in confusion. I swipe at the mess that is my face and shake my head.

"I'm sorry," I tell him. "I'm so sorry. I don't mean to cry. It's just, I hate them. I hate them for what they did to you. And I slapped you. I should never have slapped you…"

Ronan reaches for my hand and tangles our fingers together. He stares at that connection, and he likes it. Things that I've always taken for granted, the small kindness of a human touch, must be so foreign to him.

He's never had them. Any of them.

I'm going to make it up to him. I'm going to rock his world and make him feel everything. Everything good.

I straddle his hips and lay my body down across his much larger one, gazing up at him.

"Will you take off your glasses?"

He does. His eyes are soft and intense, soaking up every detail that comprises the woman on top of him. He knows me already, but it's time for me to learn him. So I touch his face, mapping out every arc and bow. The fire that forged him was monstrous and cruel, but I've never seen anything more beautiful in my life. When I tell him so, he frowns.

"I'm a man," is his reply.

I slide my hand down between us and grip his cock.

"I know."

I tug on his shaft twice to provoke him. My exploration is over, and the time for talking is done. Ronan is already a step ahead of me when he grabs me by the hips and flips me over. He settles between my legs so that he's in the dominant position, exactly where he belongs. He presses my stomach into the bed and arches my hips as he slides up into me.

I'm full, content, and greedy at the same time. Clinging to his arms and breathing him in. He connects with me in a way that nobody else ever has. My body was dormant, and he brought me to life again. We're a symphony of madness. Dark thirsts and wild obsession. My love for him burns hotter than the sun. It's sappy. It's fucked up. And more than anything, it's real.

I wrap my legs around him and tug his face down to mine. Ronan wrecks me with a kiss. And then his lips are on my throat, indulging in the taste of my skin. He couldn't know how close I am already when he reaches down between us and touches my clit.

It sets me off like a bottle rocket, and he's right behind me. He comes inside of me again. And in one aspect it's a relief that I don't have to worry about it anymore. Instead, I'm wondering what he's going to do when he collapses beside me. Because this is usually the scene where he bolts. Only now, I'm in his house. His bed.

He looks over at me with lazy eyes and pulls me against him, kissing me on the forehead. I relax into him and draw circles on his chest and my own eyes grow heavy too.

"Don't go anywhere," I murmur against him as I fall to sleep. "Just stay with me."

And he does.

Chapter Thirty-One

Sasha

When I wake up again, at first I think that Ronan is gone. But then I look up to find him propped against the headboard, reading.

At some point he must have gotten dressed, only he's wearing a tee shirt and a pair of sweat pants. His hair is still mussed from where I massaged him, and he's never looked sexier.

He feels me watching him, and his eyes move to mine. They are unguarded and at peace, and it makes me relax too. I worried that after what we shared tonight, he might try to shut me out again. But so far, he seems perfectly content to have me here with him.

Then he gives me one of those small smiles of his. And everything inside of me just melts. Ignoring the book in his hand, I crawl into his lap and kiss him like crazy.

But before we can get too carried away, I pull away and grin back at him like an idiot.

"I'll be right back," I tell him.

He watches me as I walk over to his dresser and raid his drawers for a tee shirt before trotting out the bedroom door. I go to the kitchen and grab the pint of Ben and Jerry's I made Conor buy along with two spoons and head back to the bedroom.

When I sit down on the bed next to Ronan again and he's looking at me like I'm crazy, so I feel the need to explain.

"I didn't get to finish my dinner." I wiggle the container in his direction. "Ever had it?"

He checks the label and shakes his head.

"Oh God, you've got to try it," I insist.

I grab a heaping spoonful for him and try to hand it to him, but he hesitates.

"Do you want to smell it first?" I ask. "I think you'll like it. Brownies and cookie dough. The best of both worlds."

"But there's sugar in it," he says.

"So?"

"So, sugar is…" his words drift off, and he frowns again.

I'm sensing another hang-up here that has something to do with his childhood.

"Will you try it for me?" I ask.

His eyes move from the ice cream to me, and then he nods. And I learn something new about Ronan. I think that if I phrase just about anything that way, he will probably say yes.

I move the spoon to his mouth and he takes a bite. After a moment, his features morph from curious to something else.

"Good?"

"Aye." He nods. "Very good."

He takes the spoon and dips it back into the container, gathering some more. And he looks very much like a child who's just had their first taste of ice cream.

I feel protective of him, in this moment. And I never want to let anything hurt him again. I know Ronan can handle himself. He can handle anything this life would ever throw at him because he's already been through hell and back. But watching him experience things for the first time, such simple things, at his age… makes me realize he also needs someone to experience them with.

And it occurs to me that I want that someone to be me. For now and for always.

When he looks up at me with chocolate on his lips, I smile at him. He offers me a smile back. And goddamn, it's a beautiful thing.

I am so incredibly fucked.

Chapter Thirty-Two

Sasha

Over the course of the next week, Ronan and I fall into a sort of pattern. He gets up every morning and goes to work just like any other man with a normal job would.

I don't know exactly what else his job in the mafia entails, only that he does whatever Crow needs him to. Lately though he's been taking on more responsibility. I've noticed a change in him, even just around Conor and Rory. He gives them instructions- mostly regarding watching over me- with an authority in his tone I've never heard before. Ronan's always been the kind of guy that you didn't fuck with, mostly because you could tell just by looking at him that you'd be wise not to. But now he's carrying himself differently. Speaking more. And when he comes home at night, he's exhausted.

He hasn't let me leave the house, and when I try to ask about Andrei he gets very tense. So I've let the subject stay dead for now. I've kept myself occupied by drawing and cooking a lot. Ronan seems to like what I make him, and he's even stopped sniffing everything before he eats it.

Those little signs of his trust in me mean so much more than he could ever know. It makes me think that maybe we could actually make this work between us. That he could be excited about this baby when I tell him.

But he's also still holding back a part of himself. I've noticed every night after I fall asleep he disappears, and when I wake in the morning, he's already dressed. It's happened every night this week, and I'm not really sure what he's doing.

So when we crawl into bed this evening, I have a plan. Ronan's handsome face is marred by the dark circles under his eyes, but it still doesn't stop him from mauling me. He's getting more comfortable with that too.

When we finish and he collapses on the bed beside me, I curl up in his arms and close my eyes. And then I wait. And wait some more. My breathing is steady and even when he finally slips out from beneath me and covers me over with the blankets.

He grabs some clothes from the dresser before his footsteps move down the hall. I give it a couple of minutes before I go to investigate. And when I find him lying on the couch, staring up at the ceiling, I frown.

"Do you not want me in your bed?" I ask.

My voice startles him, and he glances up at me in confusion. "I do," he answers. "I want ye in my bed, always."

"Why are you out here? Is this where you've been all week?"

He glances down and blows out a breath. "I'm sorry," he says. "I thought it was better this way."

My hands tremble as I wrap them around myself. I don't expect Ronan to know I'm upset, since he's not very good at understanding emotions. But he gets up and walks to me, pulling me into his arms and kissing me on the forehead. It's a gesture so sweet and unexpected, it dissolves the fear right out of my mind.

"I don't mean to upset you," he says. "I worry that I might hurt ye. Like last time. I could not live with myself if I did that to you again, Sasha."

I reach up and stroke the dark circles beneath his eyes with my fingers. "You should have told me, Ronan. You've been losing sleep. We could have talked about it."

"Why?" he asks.

"Because I know that you aren't going to hurt me. That night, you were on medication. And I shouldn't have been touching you when you were so out of it. It wasn't your fault."

"I hurt you," he repeats.

"It won't happen again," I assure him.

He shakes his head, and I can see this is going to be another battle with him. But it's one I'm willing to fight. I grab his hand and thread my fingers through his, leading him back down the hall to his bedroom.

"Lay down, please."

He hesitates, so I climb onto the inside of the bed and pat the space across from me. Eventually he gives in, but it's only to appease me. He plans to leave again once I fall asleep. Too bad for him, I've got plans of my own.

I reach out and run my fingers through his hair, and he closes his eyes. I gently massage his scalp and then work my way to his neck and shoulders. The tension drains from his muscles, and within minutes, he is asleep.

I nestle close enough to feel his warmth but am careful not to touch him anywhere else. And when I close my eyes, I feel safer just knowing he's there.

***

I wake up to the sound of heavy breathing.

Ronan's body is rigid against mine, a sure sign he's in the throes of another night terror. He's not making a sound, but by the way he's jerking against me, it's obvious he's reliving one of his horrors.

It's nearly dawn, so I can just make out his features in the early morning light. His face is contorted in pain. And I want it to stop. I don't want him to live through this agony anymore.

My mistake from last time is still fresh in my mind and makes me consider my next move carefully. I crawl from the bed and stand at the end of it, so there's enough distance between us if my waking him does trigger a reaction.

"Ronan," I call out.

He doesn't stir from his nightmare, so I call out to him again. And on the third time, his eyes snap open and he sits up in bed, drenched in sweat while his eyes dart around the room looking for threats. When they land on me, they fill with confusion and then disappointment.

"Hey." I walk over to his side and crawl onto his lap. "It's okay."

He won't look at me. His eyes are dark and closed off and far away. He's angry with himself. I place my palms on his jaw and tilt his face up so he has to meet my gaze.

"Come back to me," I tell him as I smooth my fingers over his skin in a soothing gesture. "Always come back to me. We can slay those demons together."

His arms wrap around my waist and he buries his face in my neck, breathing me in. When he speaks, his voice is filled with a conviction that doesn't leave any room to wonder.

"I'll always look after ye, Sasha," he says. "Protect you. You never have to worry about that. Nobody will ever hurt ye again."

"I know," I whisper.

And then I kiss him. Because I know he means it.

There isn't a thing on God's green earth that Ronan Fitzpatrick wouldn't do to protect me.

Chapter Thirty-Three

Ronan

I've just turned on the shower when there's a knock at the front door.

Before I can even get my briefs back on, Sasha calls out as she walks down the hallway.

"I've got it."

I call out to her and tell her not to answer, but I know it goes unheard through the wooden door. I'm right behind her and only half dressed when she opens the door to Crow. He blinks at her for a second, and relief washes over his face when he sees her standing there. Then his gaze moves to me, and immediately, I know this visit isn't bearing good news of any sort.

"Sasha." Crow dips his head at her. "I didn't realize you were here."

She doesn't catch the strain in his eyes or shoulders, and I'm glad for it. But there's still the potential for my lie coming unraveled, and I haven't any idea what I'm supposed to do.

"What do ye need?" I bark at Crow.

Both him and Sasha look at me in surprise.

"I need a word with ye in private," Crow answers, his gaze roving over my unkempt state.

He's smirking now.

"Looks like I caught you two playing house," he adds.

Sasha gives him a funny look and then glances in my direction.

"We can speak outside," I tell him. "Just give me a moment and I'll meet you out there."

"I can wait here," he says. "It's fecking freezing out there this morning."

"I'd rather you didn't," I argue.

"Ronan?" Sasha walks towards me and rubs her hand over my arm. "It's okay. I was going to hop in the shower anyway."

I'm relieved when I don't see any questions in her eyes. I'm not ready for her to leave. And I'm not sure now that I ever will be. She leans up on her toes and kisses me on the cheek, right in front of Crow. It's only after she's walking away that I've worked out it doesn't bother me. Crow clears his throat, tearing my attention back to him.

"What's she doing here, Fitz?"

"That's not your concern," I answer.

"What's got your knickers all in a knot?" he asks. "It was an honest question. She was supposed to be leaving, last I heard."

I glance down the hallway and gesture for him to sit down. He does. Daisy sniffs at him and he pats her on the head a couple of times before she jumps onto my lap.

"She's just staying with me for a bit," I tell him. "It's not a big issue."

"Ronan," Crow says in a solemn voice. "I came here to tell ye that Andrei knows about her."

"What?" My eyes snap up to his. "That's not possible."

"Anything's possible," he says. "And he does."

"How do ye know this?" I ask.

He glances at the floor, and his eyes glaze over. "Someone attacked Jasmine after she left the club last night," he explains. "And dumped her body in the alley for us to find this morning."

He hands over his cell phone, and I stare at the photograph of the mangled dancer. The butcher has left his calling card all over her body, and even to someone such as myself it's a shock of violence. I've no stomach for this sort of act being carried out on a woman. But the most disturbing thing about it, and the one I can't look away from, are the words carved into her chest.

Where's Sasha?

"She can't know about this." I shove the phone back towards Crow so I don't have to see it. But I'm still thinking about it, and that won't go away.

Crow tilts his head to the side and studies me for a moment. He reads the expression on my face clearly. This thing with Andrei has just taken on a whole new urgency that it never had before. And Crow thinks I'm going to do something stupid. He's probably right.

"I'm going to find him," I tell him.

"Ye're not going anywhere alone," Crow answers. "He'll be expecting ye."

"I always work alone."

"This is not up for debate, Fitz." He rises to his feet. "And if I were you, I'd reconsider telling Sasha."

I take off my glasses and rub my tired eyes. "She already sort of knows."

He looks down at me and nods. Crow knows me too well to have to ask why.

"See to it that Rory's here to watch over her," I tell him. "Conor can come with me."

"Conor's too green," Crow argues.

"Which is why he won't be staying here alone with Sasha."

Crow looks set to argue, and it riles me. "I recall a time not too long ago that ye didn't want to leave Mack's care in Conor's hands either."

He smirks and shrugs, and I know I've won. Rory and I have a mutual respect for each other. I trust him. And if I have to leave Sasha alone with anyone who isn't me or Crow, I'd rather it was him.

Crow's face clearly betrays how little he likes it, but he knows I'm right. We don't have enough men to watch over all the dancers, maintain normal operations, and chase after Andrei.

"I'll send him over then," Crow says as he reaches the door. "And Ronan?"

"Aye?"

"Quit sending my wife so many bloody donuts," he says. "It's not good for the baby."

***

After a quick shower, I head off before Sasha can even finish breakfast. I think she's worked out that something's not right, but she didn't ask.

That's what I like about her. She never pushes me. She lets me do what I have to, and then she waits until the right moment if she has a question. If she thought it was odd that Rory showed up to watch over her, she didn't say so.

Now Conor and I are in the car, driving to all of Andrei's usual haunts trying to chase up leads. By lunchtime, we've already been shot at twice and nearly stabbed as well. Conor handled himself pretty well, and I told him so. He's young, but he's learning fast.

"It seems kind of pointless to go to all the same places he usually hangs out," Conor notes. "If he's taunting you, how likely do you think it is that he's going to be somewhere he knows he can get caught?"

"Do you have a better suggestion?" I clip out.

Conor shrugs and then stares back out the window. "Well if he's looking for Sasha, I would assume that he's probably somewhere near her apartment and the club. Even if he isn't, some of his men would be. Do you know who any of them are?"

His words spark a memory. The familiar face that I couldn't kill the last time I saw him. The young lad who looked like Alex.

I hit the brakes and turn around, heading towards Sasha's old apartment. Conor glances at me, and he's got a stupid grin on his face.

"I said something helpful, didn't I?"

"Aye, lad," I tell him. "Ye're learning."

For the next three hours, we drive around Sasha's neighborhood and some of the places near Slainte where they might be hiding out. The problem is that the area has an abundance of seedy places to hide. I never liked that she lived in this neighborhood, but there was little I could do about it.

I don't think we're going to find Andrei today, and it grates on my nerves. But then I spot a lad on the corner of Sasha's apartment building from across the lot where we're parked. He's not the same lad who I saw that night, but he's about the same age. Young, dumb, and obvious as shite.

He keeps glancing over his shoulder as he walks. I count each occurrence, and by the time he reaches the main door, he's done it six times.

"Him," I tell Conor.

Conor scrunches up his brows and shakes his head, doubtful. "You think so? He just looks like some young punk to me."

"Sort of like you," I remark as I climb out of the car and shut the door behind me.

Conor follows me into the building and we keep a safe distance, stopping on every landing to listen to his footsteps above us. I'm not at all surprised when he stops on Sasha's floor and turns.

His footsteps grow distant as he walks towards her apartment, and that's when we rush him.

Just as he's opening up the door, I hit him from behind, holding him in front of me as a shield. But when the door swings open, the only other man inside is taken by surprise. He raises his gun, but my weapon has already discharged and lodged a bullet in his head before he even gets off a shot.

The lad in my arms is shaking now, pissing himself with fear. And I almost feel bad for what I'll have to do to the young one to get information out of him. Until my gaze swings to the far end of the room, where a girl who looks familiar is cuffed to the radiator.

She's beaten pretty badly and already has a few slashes over her body that no doubt came from Andrei. He likes to play with his toys before he finally kills them. It's a long process, and I have to wonder how long he's been toying with her for. Her face is so swollen I can't place where I've seen her before. But Conor knows. He rushes towards her and kneels down to help her.

"Scarlett?" he whispers. "Is that you?"

She makes a sound somewhere between a moan and agreement.

"She's handcuffed," he says, glancing back to me. "Can you pick the lock?"

"Aye," I tell him. "I could. Or ye could probably just grab the keys from the dead arsehole on the floor just there."

Conor blinks and then scurries over to the body as I check the hallway and then pull the young lad across the room. Once Conor's got the cuffs off Scarlett's hands, I gesture for them and lock them into place on their new prisoner. I can't torture him here, because I don't have any of my tools or the things I'd need to keep him quiet. Not to mention that if two of Andrei's men are here, there are bound to be more on the way. And since I can't be two places at once, I'll have to make do.

"Take her down to the car," I tell Conor, tossing him the keys. "And then meet me at the rear fire exit door."

"Okay." He nods and helps Scarlett to her feet.

She looks at me, and I feel a stab of something in my gut at the obvious trauma she's been through.

"Did this lad hurt ye?" I ask her before she goes.

Her eyes move over him, and there's no fear there. She just nods, like she's seen men such as him a thousand times over. She knows she's signing his death warrant, but doesn't care.

"Conor will take care of ye," I tell her. "Nobody else is going to hurt ye now."

"I know," she answers. And before she goes, she adds, "make him suffer."

***

When Conor showed up at Slainte with my prisoner in tow, I knew it'd only be a matter of time before Crow came round.

I don't even bother asking him how the hell he knew where I was watching the apartment from. He sits down beside me in the vacant building across the street and whips out a pair of binoculars.

"Any movement?" he asks.

"Not as of yet," is my reply. "But they'll come calling soon enough. Andrei won't let a good woman go to waste."

"Ye should have rang me," he says. "You don't fecking listen, Fitz."

I shrug and the room around us goes silent for a pause.

"How's the girl?"

Crow sighs. This whole situation is only adding to his headache, I'm sure. That girl was a mate of Macks, but she isn't under our employ. And she's also now a witness to a murder. It's a complication for him. Even if I were to tell him not to worry about her, that I trusted her to keep her mouth shut, that isn't the way it works.

"Rory's going to keep an eye on her for a bit," Crow answers. "But Mack doesn't know that."

"She won't hear it from me," I tell him.

He nods and sets down the binoculars after scanning the street, kicking back in his chair.

"Seems Rory fancies her anyway," Crow notes. "But she wouldn't give him the time of day. He was all over the babysitting gig when I mentioned it."

"Aye," I agree. "Glad I don't have to do it."

"You've got your own woman to worry about, Fitz," he says. "What's the craic with you and Sasha?"

I ignore him because it's none of his business. Crow is always suspicious of the dancers, but I think he's been even more so with Sasha because of what happened with Blaine. Regardless of what her reasons for lying were, Crow will still probably always be suspicious of her. But I know Sasha. I've been watching her for three long years. Wanting her. Learning about her. I know everything there is to know about her, from how well she sleeps to the type of food she likes to eat.

A man doesn't get to know these things about a person without coming to some conclusions of his own. Sasha is as loyal as they come. I always suspected that Blaine was threatening her somehow. Manipulating her. But without her coming clean about it, there wasn't anything I could do about that either. Until I did. Until I saw it firsthand.

I don't expect Crow to ever understand that. So he can keep his opinions to himself for all I care.

"Why don't ye make an honest woman out of her, Fitz?"

I glance over at him, expecting sarcasm on his face. But it isn't there. He's serious.

"I don't know if she'd have me," I answer him honestly.

"Well there's only one way to find out," he says. "Isn't there? Do ye honestly believe you can just let her walk away? Because I don't think ye can."

He's right, and we both know he's right. So I just nod.

And then I catch movement on the street. I use the scope of my rifle to have a look, and Crow follows suit with the binoculars.

"Looks like we've got a couple more bites," he says as we stand up. "Hope ye're wide awake, Fitzy. Going to be a long night for the infamous reaper."

Chapter Thirty-Four

Sasha

Rory's pacing back and forth through Ronan's house, on edge after the phone call he took earlier. He keeps glancing at the door, so I know he's expecting someone, but I don't ask him who it is.

Rory's always been respectful towards me, but being that he didn't hang out much in the VIP lounge at Slainte, I don't know him very well. It's strange to have him watching over me, but one look at the guy and it's clear why Ronan picked him.

He's ripped as all get out. A large, solid frame that I know frequently does some major damage at the underground fights. He's a boxer through and through. Rough around the edges but has a sense of humor too. He's always cracking jokes and messing around. So to see him serious makes me a little edgy.

"What's going on?" I finally cave in and ask.

Before he can answer, Conor opens the front door. He ushers in a girl who someone obviously used as a punching bag, and a nervous tremor runs up my spine when I get a good look at her. It takes me a minute, but I recognize her as Mack's friend. Scarlett.

Before I even get a chance to offer her some help and ask who the hell I've got to murder, Rory is at her side. His hands are twitching, and it's obvious he wants to touch her, but he keeps himself in check. Barely.

"The doc is on his way," he tells her. "Sasha can get you some clothes. Tell me what you need. A shower? Pain killers? Name it, sweetheart."

She waves her hand at him dismissively and tries to smirk, but it's obvious that it's painful for her to even attempt it.

"Jaysus," Rory mutters. "I'm going to torture the motherfuckers who did this to you."

Scarlett tilts her chin up and puts on a brave face. She might be fooling the guys, but I recognize the exhaustion in her eyes. It's the same expression I wore on my face every day that I had to deal with Blaine.

"Just go, Rory," she tells him. "I'll be fine. Or maybe not. I guess whatever you decide being that you took the choice from me."

"It's for your protection," he tells her in a soft voice.

His fingers brush over her arm and she shrugs him off, her eyes meeting mine.

"Would you mind giving me a hand?" she asks. "I need to get out of these clothes. And a shower does sound good."

"Of course."

I walk over and join her and Rory frowns when I lead her away from him. He's wearing a helpless expression on his face, but it doesn't last long. It's quickly replaced by determination. It doesn't surprise me in the least. These guys live by a code, and I don't feel the slightest bit sorry for whoever's about to befall their wrath tonight.

I help Scarlett into the bathroom and out of her mangled dress. Her entire body is covered in bruises, and there are some deep cuts across her arms and chest. I know it's a stupid question, but it's the first one out of my mouth anyway.

"Jesus, honey, are you okay?"

She tries to shrug, but winces again. "I've been through worse."

"God," I mutter as I walk to the shower and turn it on for her. "I'd kill them myself if I could."

"Looks like we've got a few Irishmen on the job already," Scarlett quips. "Although I suspect they have ulterior motives."

"What do you mean?"

She blinks at me, and doesn't even try to bullshit me, which is nice for a change. "It's you they're after, dollface."

"What?"

I reach for the counter to keep my balance. "How do you know that?"

"Because I was in your old apartment," she says. "And they were grilling me about you."

"Oh my god." I throw a hand over my mouth and barely make it to the toilet before I vomit.

Scarlett just watches like she sees this sort of thing every day. She's so blunt that I don't really know what to make of her.

"Sorry," I groan.

"Pregnant?" she asks.

My eyes widen, and she shakes her head. "Don't worry. I'm not going to tell anyone. Just like I wouldn't tell those dickheads anything about you. Not that I know anything, anyway."

"I didn't know how bad it was," I admit. "I just thought I had to stay off the streets and out of the club and I'd be okay. But now they're torturing people, because of me?"

"It's not because of you," she tells me. "But you already know that. Doll, the quicker you learn that women are nothing but pawns in this male dominated world, the better off you'll be."

"Trust me," I tell her as I wipe my face. "I'm already very much aware of that."

Chapter Thirty-Five

Sasha

By the time Ronan gets home, Scarlett is passed out on the sofa. I was admittedly drifting off too, unable to fight the exhaustion of the night any longer. But Rory was even more antsy than usual. Especially after he heard Scarlett tell the doc she needed a plan B pill.

Ronan walks right up to me and barely acknowledges Rory, except to say, "I saved one for you."

Rory is up and out of the door like his pants are on fire, and I tell myself I don't even want to know.

Ronan collapses beside me on the sofa and pulls me into his lap. He's got Jameson on his breath as he kisses my face and smooths his large palms over my hair. Pretty soon, he's made short work of my shorts and tee shirt, and he's carrying me down the hall to his bedroom.

He fucks me like crazy into the bed and then collapses beside me when we've both finished. My hair falls over his chest and he plays with it, his gaze quiet and thoughtful.

"Stay with me," he says quietly. "Be with me."

My pulse explodes, flooding my entire body with warmth. I can't stop touching him. Looking at him. I don't know whether to blurt how much I love him or that I want more than anything to be with him. What comes out instead is, "I'm pregnant."

And the moment is officially over.

Panic seeps into his features, washing away any progress we've made over the last few months. His eyes flick from my face to my stomach and back about ten times before his expression falls completely flat.

He doesn't say anything. Not a word. He just gets up and dresses himself.

"Ronan?"

My voice is weak, and I can't find the words to beg him to stay. So he walks right out the door.

Chapter Thirty-Six

Sasha

I glance up at the clock again for the hundredth time in the last ten minutes. I don't know what to do at this point. But I'm going frigging nuts sitting in this house, just waiting for him to come back.

Scarlett's still sleeping off her injuries on the sofa where she insisted she would stay. Rory tried to argue, and the end result was him hovering out the front of the house where he could keep his frustrations to himself.

I know he's only just outside, parked on the street in his car. I could walk out there and demand he take me to Ronan.

Or, I could just leave altogether.

That second option no longer appeals to me. The thought of leaving him now feels like its own sort of prison. I like being here, in Ronan's house. Sleeping next to him. Breathing him in when he holds me at night. I don't know how I could give that up. Give him up.

We've come so far together. I don't want to turn back now. But then I just keep thinking that he left me. Again. And maybe this time, he really doesn't want to come back. Maybe it's all been for nothing.

My new phone rings, startling me from my thoughts. When I see Mack's name, I pick up without hesitation.

"Sash," she yells through the phone. She sounds totally freaked. And Mack never sounds freaked. It puts me on edge too. "Something's going down."

"What do you mean?"

"Some feds just came and arrested Lachlan. I tried calling some of the other guys, but I can't get through to them. Is Rory still there?"

"I don't know." I walk towards the door. "I'm going to check now."

"Wait!" Mack says. "Grab your purse and some clothes. Tell Rory to bring you to the safe house. That's where I am."

"I can't," I argue. "I have to wait for Ronan to get back."

"Sasha, this is protocol," Mack insists. "He'll know exactly where you are, and he'll come to you when he can, okay? But for right now, we don't know how many of the guys are in custody, and it isn't safe to be in the house unprotected."

I think of my baby, and even though I want to wait for Ronan, I know she's right.

"Okay," I tell her. "I'll grab some clothes."

"Be quick," Mack urges. "I have a really weird feeling about all of this. I'll stay on the phone with you until you're in the car with Rory."

"Alright, but I've got to grab Scarlett too."

"Scarlett?" Mack echoes through the phone. "What's she doing there?"

I don't answer because I'm pretty sure if she doesn't know already then I wasn't supposed to say anything. But I really don't care.

"I'll let her tell you herself," I answer. "When we get there."

"Ugh," Mack groans. "Fine, whatever. I'm going out of my mind, Sash. Just hurry."

I pack quickly, and Mack repeats the evening's events to me while I do. She explains how Lachlan had just come home from the club when the feds started banging down the door. It was odd timing, like they intentionally wanted him to be away from the others so he couldn't warn them.

"You haven't heard anything from Ronan?" I ask again. "I've texted him and he won't respond."

"No, Sash," she answers. "I'm sorry. But if anyone knows how to evade these guys, it's Ronan. I don't think you have to worry about him. We'll figure out what's going on."

Her words do nothing to comfort me, so I focus on the task at hand. I rouse Scarlett from her sleep and explain that we have to leave. To my amazement, she jumps up without delay. And it occurs to me this girl's natural fight or flight instincts are kicking in, a sure sign this isn't the first time she's had to run for her life. We reach the front door and I scoop Daisy up, tucking her under my arm when something occurs to me. Her leash is still in the kitchen, and we're going to need it.

"Can you take her to the car?" I ask Scarlett. "I'll be right behind you."

She nods and Mack grumbles in my ear, obviously on edge.

"What's taking so long?"

"I've got to get Daisy's leash. Ronan doesn't let her outside without it."

"We can get a new leash," Mack protests. "Just get your ass in the car."

"Alright, I'm going, I'm going," I tell her. "Let me call you right back."

She's still protesting in my ear when I hang up and glance around frantically for the leash. I know how particular Ronan is about Daisy going outside with it because he doesn't want her to run off. But I can't find the stupid thing anywhere.

Just as I'm about to give up, I find it hanging over one of the chairs. I yank it off and race towards the front door and down the steps.

But I don't even make it ten feet before a car pulls up and a flurry of activity ensues. My phone falls onto the sidewalk in the chaos, and my gaze drifts to the car parked down the block. Where Rory and Scarlett are.

Their faces are panicked, and I know it's too late for me already when the uniformed agents converge on me. There's nothing they can do for me at this point without alerting the feds that they're here too. So I tear my eyes away and focus on what's in front of me.

A woman decked out in FBI field gear approaches me first, gripping me by the arm.

"Sasha Varela." She holds up a piece of paper. "We need you to come with us."

I don't even get to see what's on the paper before she yanks it away. I hesitate when she tries to usher me to the car, and the other agents move towards their guns.

"I don't want you to get hurt," she says. "But I will cuff you if you don't come willingly. Let's not go that route, Sasha."

I glare back at her and she shoves me into the back of a sedan. The female agent piles in beside me and we peel off down the street.

"Where are you taking me?" I demand. "What am I under arrest for? I need to know…"

"I'll explain everything very soon," she says. "But I can promise you, Sasha, this is probably the opportunity you've been waiting for."

***

The agents take me to a white house in the middle of suburbia. And the entire time, the guy that's driving keeps staring at me in the rearview mirror. He's giving me the creeps, and nothing about this situation feels right.

When we park the car, my rational thought process starts to come back to me. They can't just do this kind of stuff. I have rights, and I'm pretty sure they've already broken half of them.

"What are we doing here?" I rant. "You can't just arrest me without telling me what it's for. I want a lawyer. I have somewhere to be… I need to post bail, and I know my rights…"

"Sasha." The female agent grins smugly. "Just calm down. I'm going to explain everything right now."

They take me inside of the house and seat me at the kitchen table. The female sits across from me, looking way too self-important as she folds her hands across the glass.

"Sasha, my name is Agent Reed, and believe it or not, I'm here to help you."

"Help me how?" I demand. "By holding me hostage? Am I under arrest or what?"

"You're not under arrest," she says. "Yet. But that could change, depending on how the rest of this interview proceeds."

"What the hell does that mean?" I snap.

"We've had a good Samaritan tip us off on some criminal activity within the club you work for. Leads in some missing person cases as well as a written witness statement by one Donovan O'Connor."

"Oh you've got to be fucking kidding me." I shake my head and a maniacal laugh bubbles up my throat.

Am I never going to escape this frigging asshole? He's dead, and he's still fucking with my life.

Agent Reed purses her lips and acts genuinely surprised by my outburst. "I'm really not. Included in that witness statement are some very interesting things about you Sasha. It seems you are implicated as a potential accomplice yourself to some of these crimes."

I sit back and cross my arms while I stare at her. "First of all, Donny is frigging deluded. So if you buy anything he's trying to sell you, I feel sorry that he's wasting tax payer's dollars sending you on these types of goose chases. And second of all, I don't know anything about any crimes. I'm just a dancer. A freelance one at that. So technically, I'm not even employed by that club. And unless you're going to place me under arrest, you better take me back to my house."

The agent sighs and gestures for the other man who is still watching me closely. He's clearly an agent too, but something about him doesn't feel right. I don't like the way he keeps looking at me. Like he knows something I don't. Like all of this is just for show.

He opens up a drawer and hands agent Reed a file which she then tosses onto the table in front of me.

"Donovan O' Connor has been missing for some time now," she says. "And by his own account, he suspected this might happen. He was prepared for it."

She opens up the file and leaves me to have a look on my own. I swallow down my nerves as I slide it across the table and begin to flip through the pictures. Immediately, I know exactly who and what they are.

The photos themselves are grainy, and there's no clear shot of his face. But it's undoubtedly Ronan shoving a large roll of carpet into the trunk of a car behind Slainte. I take my time studying each photo. I'm trying to see if Donny actually captured anything of use.

The photos were obviously taken on a cell phone, and there are no lights in that part of the lot, so almost all of it is in shadows. There's nothing that can identify the car that I can see because Ronan is blocking the plate itself. The photos have obviously been altered as much as they can to try to identify the subject, but a fat lot of good it did.

If I didn't know it before, these photos only confirm what an idiot Donny was. He thought this would be his smoking gun. But it's obvious that if they have me here they need me to corroborate his story. And without him being here to talk, I have to doubt they have anything else to go on.

"Before you say anything," agent Reed interrupts my thoughts, "I think it's pertinent you know Sasha, that you can be brought up on charges as well if you don't cooperate. Alternatively, you can have the slate wiped clean. Move into our WITSEC program and begin anew. New name, new city. A chance to make a life of your own. I know that the last few years have been difficult for you. Supporting your mother during the final stages of her cancer could not have been easy. And then going to work at Slainte every night, knowing that you could never leave. You can't tell me you haven't thought about it. I'm giving you that opportunity now."

I take a slow, controlled breath and look up at her. For the last three years, I've managed to fool everyone who ever asked about Blaine. He's the fucking nightmare that just won't go away. And this agent thinks I'm just a dumb stripper who doesn't know what she's doing. She thinks she can fool me with her sweet talk. Her promises of a new life. I know better. I know her sugar coated lies are really laced with venom.

Even if I had nothing and nobody to lose, betraying the syndicate is the last thing I'd ever do. It's a death sentence, no matter which way you spin it. If it had been Blaine I was selling down the river, I might have felt enticed. But it isn't. It's Ronan and everyone else who has done right by me. And if I can stand up to Lachlan and his questioning, I can sure as hell handle this dumb broad.

"Look," I tell her. "It's obvious you think I know more than I do. But I don't know what you want me to say. I have no idea who's in those photos. Even if I did, it's kind of hard to tell what he's doing. I mean, it looks like he was doing renovations for all I know. So I'm sorry, but like I said before, I can't help you."

"That's a shame," she sighs. "We were really hoping that you'd be willing to cooperate with us on this."

She remains calm, opening the other file in front of her and sliding it across the table in my direction. I give it a cursory glance and feel my own resolve fracturing just a little.

"The way I see it," she says, "there's only one obvious choice. Either you take the deal I'm offering… or you'll be going down for multiple crimes that involve aiding and abetting a criminal organization."

She points at the second piece of paper in the file to prove her point and then arches a brow for emphasis. "Those are all felonies, by the way. Not that it matters. It makes no difference which prison you end up in. The Irish have reach in all of them, I'm told."

My eyes snap up to hers, and I seriously debate lunging across the table and choking her to death right here.

"This is making you feel really fucking important," I snarl. "Isn't it?"

She brushes off my comment with a wave of her hand. "So what's it going to be, Sasha? You better think quick. This is a limited time offer."

I sit back in my chair and contemplate my options. My airway is growing smaller by the second, and I know I need to ground myself. But I look around this room, and there's nothing familiar. It doesn't help the way it usually does. Panic is seeping into my every ounce of flesh, and I don't know how to stop it. I'm pregnant. I can't go to prison. But I can't sell Ronan out either.

Agent Reed and I stare at each other across the table, neither of us speaking a word in the stilted silence. But there's a smug smile on her face. Because she knows she's caught me in her web. Fucking bitch. Fucking traitor bitch. She doesn't give a fuck about anything but how good this will look on her record. This is all about her job accolades and what it will do for her.

I honestly have no idea what to do.

But as it turns out, it doesn't matter. Because a moment later, someone busts through the back door and gunfire erupts throughout the house. Agent Reed shoves me under the table and I grab a chair for cover and squeeze my eyes shut.

I take three deep breaths to calm myself before I peek out to see agent Reed hiding behind a partition as she fires off shots in the direction of the intruders. A pair of leather shoes walk up behind her, and all I can see are the man's legs.

A gunshot goes off, and she collapses to the ground. Dead.

And I'm officially in a full blown panic attack. There are some murmured words in Russian when more shoes converge in the kitchen. One of them crouches down a moment later and smiles at me. It's the same creepy agent who was driving the car.

A corrupt fed. Who just watched these guys murder one of his own and is probably going to kill me too.

He grabs me by the arm and yanks me out from under the table. Two other men join him, and I know just by looking at them they aren't who I want to be leaving here with.

"Where are you taking me?" I try to resist as they pull me out the door and shove me into another car, but it's futile. The fed says something in Russian to the other guys, and confusion washes over me.

The Irish have an alliance with the Russians. Maybe they are helping me. I cling to that hope for all it's worth. Until they put zip ties on my wrists and duct tape over my mouth.

Then I watch in horror as the two guys punch the fed in the face a couple of times until he's banged up pretty good. I'm no genius, but I don't need to be to see what's going on here. He wants to make this look good to his colleagues. Which means he doesn't plan on me being alive to contradict it.

The fed crouches down and winks at me.

"Have fun, kitten."

Chapter Thirty-Seven

Ronan

"That one there." Rory points ahead. "The black Denali."

My eyes scan the road and focus on the distance between us and them. By the time I was able to get to Rory, Andrei's crew already had her in their possession.

Part of me wants to lash out at Rory for not stepping in sooner. But the rational part of me knows I wouldn't have the first clue where she was if it wasn't for him.

I've failed her. Allowed my fears to overcome me and walked away at a time when she needed me the most. And now she's in a car with Andrei's men, who I have every intention of slaughtering like the pigs they are.

"I will protect her," I say aloud.

"I know, Fitz," Rory replies. "We're going to get her back, mate. Don't ye worry about that."

"You shouldn't have left her behind in the first place," Scarlett chimes in from the back seat.

"I was protecting you," Rory growls. "Which you seem to keep forgetting."

"I don't need your protection," she answers.

"She's having my baby," I tell no one in particular. I just need to hear it spoken aloud. So they understand the gravity of this situation.

"Congratulations, Fitz," Rory says. "I never pegged you for a fatherly type."

My hand twitches on the gear shift. "I'll protect her," I repeat. "I'll look after both of them."

"I know," he agrees. "I don't doubt you, Fitzy. You'll do a grand job of it."

The car ahead of us changes lanes, and I finally get a clear view of the Denali. The one that has Sasha in it. My Sasha. And my baby. Because I'm going to be a father.

I haven't had much in my life. Crow and his mammy and the syndicate. I made do with that before, but things are different now. My whole life is in that car up ahead. I'm going to slaughter the men who thought they could take that from me.

"Keep your distance," Rory warns. "We don't want them to work out they've got company just yet. Remember the bigger picture, Fitz."

"I need to get Sasha."

"You do," he agrees. "But you also need to get Andrei. Settle this once and for all. And having a showdown in the middle of the freeway won't do."

He's right, there's no argument about that. But I have an intense pressure inside of me which only breeds every moment she's trapped in that car. It's the same pressure I felt when I killed Blaine. When I saw him hurting her. I don't understand this emotion. I don't know how to sort it out or even what to call it. I only know that when it comes to anyone hurting Sasha, I will always feel this way. The only balm for the fire inside is to eliminate the threats against her. To destroy anyone who thinks they can touch Sasha.

It's the single thought keeping me from going mad right now. Planning Andrei's murder and bathing the floor with his blood. I will make him suffer. I will make his death a thousand times worse than any he's ever saw fit to dole out. The butcher will know real pain when I'm finished with him.

The car ahead exits off the freeway, and I follow. Daisy starts to whine in the backseat and Scarlett pulls her into her lap.

"This dog looks familiar," she says.

I ignore her because my attention is focused only on the Denali. They're driving into a rural area. A sure sign they're leading us directly to Andrei. When they turn off onto a dirt road, Rory taps the dashboard to get my attention.

"You need to slow down, lad. It's only going to put Sasha at risk if they catch onto us. We're not going to lose them."

I pull my foot from the accelerator and attempt to calm myself. The rage is coiling tighter inside. I'm losing control. And all I can think of is Sasha and my baby. These pigs might do something before I can get to her.

"No." I push my foot back down and focus my attention up ahead. "It has to be dealt with now."

"Fitz," Rory tries to argue, but I'm past the point of being rational.

Scarlett doesn't seem to have an opinion on the current events as she continues to talk about the dog. I'm not listening much, until some of her words capture my attention.

"Princess," she says. "That's what her name was."

"Her name is Daisy," I argue. "Sasha picked it."

"But where did you get her?" Scarlett asks.

Rory glances at me when I don't answer because he already knows. Conor's been giving me shite about it in front of the lads every time I go to the club.

"Being as ye're not going anywhere..." Rory meets Scarlett's eyes in the mirror. "I suppose it won't hurt to tell you this was Donny's dog."

Scarlett wrinkles her nose and glares back at him. "Keep trying to find reasons to make me stick around. I promise you'll get sick of me soon enough."

"I doubt that very much," is Rory's only reply.

The car falls silent, and I'm glad for it. I've no need for this carry on while I'm trying to focus on Sasha. But Scarlett won't let up about the bleeding dog.

"Was she wearing a pink collar?" she persists. "With a crown on it?"

This time, I do meet her gaze in the mirror. I don't like that she knows that.

"What's it to you?" I ask.

"I thought so," she answers smugly. "It is princess. I know who owns this dog, and it isn't Donny."

"I own the dog," I growl. "She's mine. And Sasha's. She's ours."

Scarlett just shrugs. "Well that may be the case, but I know who owned her before."

I open my mouth to argue when Rory taps me on the shoulder. He gives me a look, and it conveys everything I need to know. This could be important. Whoever owned that dog might be the same person that's been leaking information to the feds.

"I'd love to hear all about that," Rory tells her as he turns around in his seat. "Maybe ye just might be useful after all."

Chapter Thirty-Eight

Sasha

"We've got company," the man driving the car observes.

His eyes keep flicking to the rearview mirror, and a seed of hope blooms inside of me.

Ronan.

It has to be him. I have to believe that Ronan has come for us. That he isn't going to let me die like this. Let our baby die.

The man beside me picks up his phone and makes a call, muttering a quick string of indecipherable words. He's short-tempered, and the voice on the other end of the line sounds even more so. There's a tiny farmhouse up ahead, which I suspect is where they're taking me. There's only one dirt road out of here, and we're on it.

Which means that whoever is behind us has got us trapped.

The men in the front seat speak in rapid fire Russian while I try to crane my neck and get a look at the car behind us. It's too dusty though, and the minute I turn, the man beside me grabs me by the hair and yanks my head back around.

He yells something into my face, which I don't understand, but I get his meaning clear enough. I curl into myself and mentally try to prepare for whatever is about to happen. Up ahead, the windows on the farm house are open, and the barrels of two rifles are poking out.

The driver guns the engine without warning and sends us careening around the corner of the house and towards the back. The car has barely come to a stop when someone's yanking me out and dragging me inside.

I don't resist, but it still doesn't stop him from hurling me onto the floor once we're inside. I crawl under a table and not a moment too soon.

Another spurt of gunfire erupts around us, tearing through the glass and walls of the farmhouse. I can't see into the living room, but I know there are at least three other men in there. In addition to the three who brought me here that makes six. If Ronan is outside, I have to wonder what kind of backup he has.

As I'm questioning it, something thuds on the back porch where we just entered, followed by a crash of shards from the window above the sink. Something wizzes over the table where I'm hiding and hits one of the men in the head. It all happens so fast that during the time it takes me to blink, he's on the floor with his face half gone.

My hand flies to my mouth and I have to fight the urge to retch. Jesus. How many times have I been in situations like this now? This is exactly why I didn't want this life. I don't know how I seem to have forgotten that in my time with Ronan. Now I have a baby to think about too. And no way do I want my kid growing up around this kind of shit.

Another bullet flies through the window and takes out a different guy. His body makes an awful sound as it hits the floor and I can't bring myself to look at it. I close my eyes and count to ten, and in that ten seconds there's another thud.

And then someone is grabbing me, dragging me out from beneath the table and holding my body in front of his. He's yelling something out in Russian when the back door flies open.

There's still gunfire coming from the front, but my eyes are focused on the formidable figure standing in the doorway. Chocolate brown eyes meet mine, and my lungs fill with some much needed air. It doesn't matter what else is happening around me, the one thing I know for certain is everything's okay now. He's here, and I'll be okay. Because Ronan always saves me.

He says something in Russian to the man holding me, to which my captor replies. I'm surprised at Ronan's grasp on the language, though I shouldn't be. He never does anything half-assed, this man. Ronan's gaze meets mine as he raises his gun, and I know he's silently telling me not to be afraid.

I should be. I should be feeling something. But I'm frozen. Numb. In shock, I think. The man behind me raises his knife to my throat.

Ronan moves forward on instinct, but pauses when the blade digs into my skin.

"Andrei."

The way Ronan says his name is a threat all its own. His voice is deadly and calm. His body is too. This is what he was trained for. But even I can't miss the warring rage and fear in his dark eyes. If there was ever a question about how he felt for me, it's unmistakable right now.

"You have such a pretty little whore my friend." Andrei drags the tip of the knife down my neck. "Such a shame I could not spend more time with her. This skin, I have a feeling it would look so lovely flayed wide open."

Ronan speaks to him in Russian again. His voice has lost the calm resolve he displayed only moments ago. The rage is taking over. Turning him. And I know it's only a matter of time before he goes ballistic like he did with Blaine. Only this time, the guy behind me has at least one knife, and I suspect by the sharp object digging into my back, possibly two. He's using me as a shield and I have no idea how Ronan's going to disarm him.

Right about now I'm really wishing that I'd asked Mack to teach me some of that crazy shit she's always doing to defend herself.

"Shall I take her for a little test drive?" Andrei asks. "Just a few slices. You know they say that all blood is the same color once it meets oxygen, but I don't think that's true. So many shades of crimson. You would agree with me, yes?"

Ronan lunges forward, and the man drags me back further, cutting off my air supply as his arm snakes around my neck. He turns the knife in Ronan's direction and waves it back and forth in a disapproving gesture.

"C'mon, my friend. You must know better than this by now. I've heard so many tales about you. The great Reaper of Boston. Men quake in his presence I am told. And yet here you are, completely helpless as I hold your treasure in my arms."

"She is mine," Ronan snarls.

His eyes are moving over every possible angle, searching for weaknesses and assessing the situation. I can literally see him being split in two. He's fighting the urge to be the man he was created to be and the man who I've slowly gotten to know. The cold blooded killer in him would take the shot without fear of hitting me. But the man who has laid beside me in bed, fought off his demons in my presence, and spent every moment he could inside of me is holding back.

Before he can come to any sort of a decision, the knife in Andrei's hand slices down my chest in a sharp shock of pain. My mouth opens and the faintest sound spills from my lips as I glance down to see blood dripping from the long gash.

Ronan's lunging towards us again, but Andrei was prepared for this. The sharp object has disappeared from my back. And before I have time to scream or warn him, the second knife is sailing through the air and into Ronan's stomach.

A shot goes off, and I have no idea where it came from. But the heavy weight around me falls away, and I turn around to check. That's when I see Scarlett standing there, wielding a gun in one hand and a knife in the other. She's completely unhinged, her eyes dark and filled with a thirst for bloodlust. I know because I've seen that same look on Ronan's face many times before.

Andrei is lying on the floor, bleeding from the leg. Scarlett moves closer and stares down at him with a smile on her face that scares me a little. But the reason is stamped in her eyes for all to see. This is the man who hurt her too.

She kneels beside him, digging the tip of her knife into his cheek and dragging it over his face.

"You're not the only one who likes to play with knives." Her eyes flick down to his leg wound. "But I guess you bleed red just like everyone else."

It's obvious what she's going to do. What she wants to do. And I can't handle watching it. I spin back around and run towards Ronan, who is leaning against the wall for support. His eyes are glued to the scene before him, and the man I thought could never be shocked finally is. His face is awash with bewilderment as he watches Scarlett carve up the man on the floor behind me. He's clutching at his wound, and I'm afraid to get a good look at it. Because I don't want to see. I don't want to see Ronan hurt, or worse. I can't handle that.

I whisper his name, and his attention moves to me, some of the haziness disappearing from his eyes. Tears are leaking down my face, and I'm sniffling. I just keep repeating his name, staring at his blood soaked shirt. Fingers graze my cheek, and then I hear the sweetest sound in the world. His voice.

"Shhh," he whispers. "It's alright. I've got you."

And just like that, I forget everything else for a second. He pulls me closer and kisses my forehead, untangling the mess of hair around my face.

"Sasha."

My name sounds like a revelation on his lips. His palm moves to the cut on my chest and he smears some of the blood onto his skin, which serves to strengthen his resolve. He kisses me twice more before pulling away. I grab onto the lapels of his suit because I know what he's doing. I don't want him to go kill that man Scarlett's hurting. I don't want him to go anywhere.

"Ronan."

My hand is wet, and when I look down, it's covered in his blood. It's getting worse. And it's too much.

"We need to go."

I can't lose him. Not now. Not ever.

"I have business with Andrei," he argues.

His words are firm, but his body is weak. Fortitude isn't going to win out this time. He wants to kill the man who hurt me. And maybe a part of me wants that too. But right now, his bleeding wound takes precedence.

"Ronan, I need you," I tell him. "Our baby needs you. Okay? That's all that matters. And if we don't get you into the car right this minute…"

"She's right," a voice interrupts from behind me.

I turn to find Rory standing there, his eyes fixed on Ronan's blood soaked shirt.

"Get in the car, Fitz. I'll finish off Andrei."

Ronan shakes his head, stubborn as ever. "He's mine. I'll be the one to finish him."

All of our eyes move to the man in question, who Scarlett has done quite a number on already. His face and arms and chest are all covered in cuts now, and she's holding the knife to his throat.

"I'm going to finish him," she announces.

Rory shakes his head and yanks her up to her feet without an ounce of finesse. She tries to shove him away, but he holds her steady and kicks Andrei in the face when he moans.

"I won't allow ye to have that on your conscience," he says to her. "No matter how tough you think ye are Scarlett. I will not abide by it."

His voice is hard. Harder than I've ever known it to be. And Scarlett is looking up at him with glassy eyes. I don't know what's going on between these two, but Rory's words affect her. She listens to him, her shoulders falling in defeat. Then she glances back at Ronan, and she gives him a little nod.

"He's all yours."

"I'll put him in the boot," Rory offers, as if this is totally normal. "You'll have all the time ye like with him later. Just get your arse in the car."

Ronan tries to take a step towards the stairs, but his balance is off and he has to cling to the wall. I wrap an arm around his waist and turn back towards Rory.

"I'll need help getting him in the car."

Rory nods, and then he's bolting over to help, but Ronan's still staring at Andrei.

"Ronan." I grab his face and pull his attention back to me. "You can deal with it later, okay? Let's get in the car."

"He tried to hurt you," he says again. "Ye're mine."

"I am," I agree. "And I need you to stick around. For a really long time, okay? Because I can't do this without you."

I try to get him to move forward, but he stops us. I think he's going to argue again, but instead he kisses me. It's rough and possessive. When his lips fall away, his face is as earnest as I've ever seen it.

"I'm not going anywhere," he says. "Because I love you, Sasha."

My eyes clog up with tears, and I'm nodding like crazy because I'm too choked up to speak. Finally, I get myself under control enough to tell him what I've been dying to for the last three years.

"I love you too, Ronan. I think I always have."

Chapter Thirty-Nine

Sasha

Ronan's passed out in the backseat, his head in my lap. Scarlett and I are both applying pressure to the wound while Daisy nudges at his leg, whining in fear.

That fear is spreading through me like toxic sludge, darkening my world that was only just beginning to get bright again.

"You have to hurry," I yell at Rory for the tenth time, although I know he can't drive any faster.

"He's going to be okay, Sash," he answers. "He's survived much worse."

"I don't care," I snap at him. "Where the hell are you taking us? It's been too long. He's bleeding too much..."

"We can't go back to Boston just yet," Rory says. "In case it wasn't clear, we've got mad heat on us right now."

"I don't care about that..." I protest.

"Sasha, we have a friend out here," he explains. "He'll take care of Ronan."

I want to believe him, but when I glance down at Ronan's pale face, I don't know if I can. This is too big to put my faith in someone else. This man resting on my lap is my whole world. My whole life. The sun rises and sets with him. And I know he's strong. He's stronger than anyone I know. But just because he's survived so many horrors in his lifetime, doesn't mean he's going to survive this one too.

"It's too much." I shake my head. "He's been through too much. Eventually, your body can't handle it."

"Sasha." Scarlett grabs my hand and gives it a little squeeze. "Just take a deep breath. It's going to be okay. He doesn't want to leave you. He won't leave you."

"I'm having his baby," I announce.

"I know ye are," Rory answers. "And there's nothing that could stop him from being around for it Sash."

"He told you?" I meet his gaze in the mirror.

"Aye." Rory nods. "He wouldn't shut up about it. How much he needs to protect you. Take care of you. He blames himself for walking on out on you today. For not being there."

I shake my head and trace the lines on his face again. "He just needed some time," I whisper. "That's all."

The tires crunch over gravel, and when I glance out the window again, we're in front of a house. A house in the middle of nowhere.

Rory turns off the engine, and a moment later he's got the back door open. A man walks out of the house and Rory gestures for him to come over.

"Franco," Rory greets him. "He needs help."

Franco glances at Ronan and his lips flatten. He speaks in Russian, and I can't understand what he's saying, but his expression says it all. He doesn't like Ronan.

Another man comes out to join us, and Franco clips out a few words of explanation in their native tongue. The third man glances at Ronan and lifts a brow. I don't know who he is, but somehow I know he's the one in charge. And whatever their beef with Ronan, I don't care. I'm prepared to do whatever it takes.

"Please," I beg. "You have to help him."

The man's eyes examine me, blue as the sky and gloomier than anything I've ever seen. He takes in my expression and my hand clutching at Ronan's shirt, and something shifts in his features. He gives Franco a small nod, and then they're carrying him inside, with me and Scarlett in tow.

"You're going to help him, right?" I ask.

The man with the blue eyes nods. "I will do what I can."

Chapter Forty

Sasha

I don't know who this man is. The one with the blue eyes. But Rory calls him Alexei, and I'm certain he's one of the big fish in the Russian mob. He has to be.

His house is the size of a small castle, and it looks like one too. But it isn't overly luxurious. In fact, it's a little cold, and it reminds me of Ronan's house in that way. Stark. Used for function, but not a home.

He leads us through a maze of halls and directs the men to leave Ronan on the bed. His man Franco is on the phone, and I'm staring at him impatiently, wondering what he's going to do. He seems to understand this, because when he hangs up, he tells me what I need to hear.

"The doctor will be here shortly. In the meantime, I will tend to the wound. You can wait downstairs where Magda will tend to yours."

"I'm not going anywhere," I argue. "He doesn't like people touching him. He needs me here. He won't understand if I'm not here…"

"Sasha." Rory gives my arm a squeeze as he dips his head to meet my gaze. "I will stay here with Ronan. He's not going to wake up right now, because he's lost too much blood. Alexei and Franco know what they're doing, okay. But we need to respect their wishes so that Ronan gets the best treatment. They can't do that if you're here."

My lip trembles and I want to keep arguing. My eyes move to Ronan on the bed, his face soft and relaxed and too pale. The longer I stand here and argue, the longer it's going to take for them to help him. Logically, I know this. But I still don't want to leave him.

I glance at the man with the blue eyes, who is watching me quietly. The one who I know is in charge.

"Promise me you'll take care of him," I demand. "Promise me you'll do everything you can to help him."

His head dips and he gives me a small nod. "You have my word."

My eyes dart back to Ronan once more and then Rory is easing me out the door, directing me to go downstairs. He tells me the housekeeper will help with my cuts, which are the last thing on my mind. I'm barely holding myself together as I stare at the maze of hallways and the door shuts behind me. Locking me out. Keeping me in a void of questions with no answers.

This is the way of the mafia world. They see women as weak. As not being able to handle these types of situations. If it was anyone else, I wouldn't want to see. But it's Ronan. My Ronan.

My troubled, strong, proud man. The man I love beyond all reason. Beyond all limits. It almost knocks me off balance thinking how much I love him in this moment. Tears are tracking down my face as I stumble down the hallway, looking for the way that I came. Maybe I could just wait on the stairs. That way, if he does wake up, I will hear him.

But before I even make it that far, I catch someone peeking at me through another door before she slams it shut. I pause and stand there in confusion. It can't be the housekeeper, because they said she's downstairs. I'm not in the mood to care, but there was something about her face that looked familiar.

Needing the distraction, I walk to the door and knock on it. There isn't a response. But when I turn the knob, it opens without protest. And sitting there on the bed, staring up at me with hazel eyes is the last person I ever expected to see again.

"Talia?" her name leaves my lips in a shocked whisper.

She stares back at me, her face devoid of any expression at all. At first I'm not even certain she recognizes me. This girl is supposed to be dead. She is supposed to be overseas somewhere where she was sold into human slavery and then killed. That's what Mack said. What Mack believes.

And yet, here she is. In the Russian mobster's house. There are a lot of different conclusions I could draw from that. She's probably seen more horrors than I could ever imagine. I wonder if she even remembers her past life. If she even knows what she's doing here. Or how she got here. Which is the question lingering in my mind. What is Alexei doing with her?

"Do you remember me?" I ask her.

"Of course I remember you," she answers. "I'm not brain dead."

Her snappy attitude takes me by surprise. My eyes scan over her body, assessing the situation. She's healthy and well cared for. Dressed in nice clothing and a little thin, but otherwise in good condition. But I never remember her being so hard. Her eyes are different now. They aren't soft like the girl I first met at Slainte. She's looking at me like I've left her with a sour taste in her mouth, and I can't understand why.

"Everyone thinks you're dead," I tell her. "You do know that, right?"

She shrugs.

That's it. There's no emotion there. Nothing. Just a shrug. Like it doesn't matter.

"Do you realize what this has done to Mack?" I ask her. "She's been sick over this whole situation for months. Do you have any idea what she went through to try to get you back?"

This time, a hint of remorse swirls in her pale irises. But it doesn't last long. She looks me dead in the eye and speaks with unwavering conviction.

"I don't want to go back there."

"Okay…" I draw out the word. "But can't you call her? Let her know you're alright?"

"She won't understand," Talia answers. "Mack has never understood. She'll want the girl back that she lost. But I'm not her anymore. I'll never be her again."

"So you're just going to let her think you're dead?" I stare at her in disbelief. "She was your best friend."

Talia doesn't reply. She's got her armor in place, and none of my words are getting through it.

"I'm going to tell her," I say. "She's my friend too. And I can't let her go on thinking that you're dead when you're not. It isn't right."

"Do what you have to," Talia answers.

Her tone is dismissive, and I don't have the energy to keep arguing. She's done with this conversation, and so am I. I edge back towards the door, but before I go, I ask her the only thing that matters.

"Are you okay here? Are you safe?"

Her face softens a fraction, and her voice is sincere. "Yes. Alexei is very good to me. I don't want to leave him."

"Okay," I answer. "Would you like my number though? Just in case?"

She shakes her head.

So I walk out the door.

***

It's been over three hours since the doctor passed me on the stairs.

Magda patched up my wounds as promised and then allowed me to sneak back up here and wait. I haven't heard a peep from Ronan's room, other than the soft murmur of voices and the sound of a heart monitor. It's the only thing keeping me calm, that sound. On occasion, Franco leaves the room to retrieve something or other. And I'm honestly amazed at the medical equipment they have here. He wheeled an IV stand down the hall earlier, along with some other machines I didn't recognize.

It makes me feel a little better, but I still won't relax until they tell me he's okay. Until I can look at his face and see those soft brown eyes staring back at me. The man whose barriers I never thought I could breach. The one who told me he loved me today. The father of my baby.

My head is propped against the wall when the door opens and Rory finally comes out. He reaches down to help me up.

"He's going to be okay, Sash," he says. "You can come and see him now."

"Are you sure?" I ask as I move alongside him. "Are you sure they've done everything they should? What about antibiotics? He could get an infection, or he might need more tests..."

"Sasha." Rory stops and grabs me by the arms to look at me. "That doctor in there is a real surgeon. She works for Alexei, and she knows what she's doing. Ronan has had the very best care. Even better than he'd get at the hospital."

"They have a lot of medical stuff here," I note.

"Aye," he agrees. "As you can imagine, they need it from time to time."

The door opens ahead of us and Alexei, Franco and the doctor filter out of the room. Rory looks at me and gestures for me to go inside.

"I'll give you some privacy," he says.

"Thank you."

I move toward the door frame and hesitate. I'm afraid to look. Afraid of what I'll see. I know they said he's going to be okay, but I'm so anxious I can't help it.

But when I see Ronan lying there in stable condition, my shoulders sag in relief. I walk over and sit beside him on the bed. He opens his eyes to meet mine, and then his hand finds mine beside him.

"Sasha."

The way he says my name is full of reverence. My answer is a jerky nod with big fat tears falling down my face. He gestures for me to lay down beside him and I curl into his side, surrounding myself in his warmth.

"You scared me," I tell him. "I don't like this, Ronan."

"I'm sorry," he answers.

"We're having a baby," I say. "I can't be going through this all the time. I need to know that you're going to come home to me every night. This wondering if you're going to live or die all the time, it's too much."

Ronan nuzzles against my cheek and then kisses my forehead. For someone who has never been shown affection in his life, he's learning how to comfort me rather quickly.

"Sasha, I can't leave the syndicate," he replies. "But I will never leave you either. Ye're everything to me."

"I love you," I tell him. "I love you so frigging much, Ronan. I just don't know how I'm going to do this. I don't know if I can handle it."

He holds me tighter and squeezes, his breath blowing across my face when he whispers his only assurance.

"I'll always come back to ye. Nothing could keep me away."

Then his hand moves over my stomach, and something changes in his features. Where before he was terrified, there's now a flash of pride there.

"And our child too."

I lean in and graze his lips with mine, and his hand tangles in my hair, deepening the kiss. This kiss conveys all the words he can't say aloud. Like how scared he was to lose me too. And how without a shadow of a doubt I am his now. When he breaks away, his eyes are soft and open.

"I haven't any bloody idea how to be a father," he admits. "I'm afraid I'll botch the job beyond repair."

"You won't," I tell him. "I know you won't, Ronan. We'll learn together."

"I don't do well with loud noises," he says quietly. "I worry that when the baby cries..."

His words drift off and his expression takes on a distant look.

"You will adjust," I assure him. "It will be different when it's your own child, Ronan. And we'll figure it out, okay? We'll do whatever we have to."

He nods, but I can tell he's still worried about it. There are admittedly a million things left to figure out. A huge clusterfuck still waiting for us back in Boston with the feds and Slainte and Lachlan's arrest. The informant, the baby, the future. Everything is hanging in the balance right now. And I shouldn't feel calm.

But when I'm here in his arms, and he's alive, and looking at me the way he is right now, all is right with the world.

Chapter Forty-One

Ronan

For the next three days, we remain holed up at Alexei's house. The lad isn't very fond of me after the stunt I pulled before with Mack and the small matter of shooting at his car. But he helped me when I needed it, regardless. I don't have a clue if it's because of the alliance or because of Sasha.

I've noticed he has eyes on us often. Like he's trying to pick us apart, work out what's going on between us. I haven't a clue why. Crow always said this one was funny when it came to women. That he had a soft spot for them. And I've seen him enough times to know it's true. I don't think he's got eyes for Sasha, but I still don't like him looking at her the way he does. I don't like anyone looking at her.

Because she's mine.

I glance at her sleeping form beside mine and wonder how the bleeding hell I ever had the good fortune to cross paths with her. For her to see past my issues and care for me anyway. I haven't worked it all out yet, but the one thing I do know is Sasha is kind and has a good heart. For some reason, she believes there's something in me worth keeping.

I don't take that lightly. Only, I worry I'm going to jack this whole situation arseways if I don't tread carefully. There's still a bit of dread inside of me when I think about having a baby. I've no fecking clue how to care for a baby. But when I look at Sasha and it really settles over me that she's carrying my child, I get a big head over the notion. I fancy the idea that I've claimed her in such a way. That she will never have another but me, and that we might make a family together. The way that Crow said, with that picture he had in his head. I want that with Sasha. Only, I need to sort out all of this other bollocks first.

The benefit of being at Alexei's is that he has a dungeon that could rival my own. He uses it himself from time to time or allows the Russians to do so when the need arises. That very same dungeon is also where Andrei was left to fester until I was in fair enough shape to handle the business that was left undone.

I didn't reap as much enjoyment from the act as I'd hoped. The prick had already contracted some sort of infection by the time I had a go at him and he wasn't as lucid as he should've been. But he did suffer. There were no bones about that.

His death was slow and painful. A standard I set for anyone else who thinks they might touch what's mine. When I finished with him, I sent Andrei back to his men in pieces.

Now there's only the other matter of the feds to contend with.

On cue, there's a rap at the door and then Rory pokes his head in.

"Ye mind?" he asks. "I need a word with you."

I cover Sasha over and then reach down to kiss her cheek right in front of Rory. I don't mind so much, now. I'm not uncomfortable anymore. Worried I'm stuffing it up in front of the lads. The only thing I care about is that they all know she's been claimed.

"I'll be along in a moment," I tell him. "Let me get dressed."

He nods and shuts the door behind him and I dress in the clothes that Alexei provided me. It's no suit, but it'll have to do.

When I open the door Rory is waiting outside, and he gestures down the hall. I walk beside him and into a room where Conor, Michael, Dom and a few of the other lads have joined us as well. Since the shake up with the feds, they've all gone to different safe houses. This being one of them.

"Any word on Crow?" I ask as I take an empty seat.

"The barrister assured me he'll be home for Sunday supper," Dom answers. "They've got nothing but a bloody house of cards. A huff and a puff and we'll blow it right down."

I rock back in my chair with a nod. I suspected as much. This isn't the first time we've had heat on our backs, and it won't be the last.

"And what of the rest of it?"

"Alexei's done his homework," he answers. "They've got nothing. No body, no dice. Some grainy photos of you, and an informant with a past so checkered it won't hold up in court."

He sounds confident, but I still don't like it. I want to tell Sasha it's over. But it won't be over until that witness disappears. A notion I'm not too keen on. I don't like involving women in our business.

"Who is she?" I ask.

"Some junkie whore," Rory answers.

A voice from the door behind us replies.

"Yeah, like me," Scarlett adds. "Nothing more than a whore."

Rory's face pales, and he attempts to backtrack quickly, but it's no use. Scarlett ignores him and comes and sits right down at the table like she has a right to.

"This isn't your business," Dom tells her. "Now you best leave."

She crosses her arms and snaps her gum, shaking her head in refusal. "Nah, I think I'll stay. Because I have something to say on the matter."

The room falls silent, and all of the lads look at each other, wondering who's going to handle her. They all know Rory fancies this girl, so they don't want to step on toes. But he's not saying anything either. So I take it upon myself to sort out this headache.

"Tell us what ye have to say and then be on your way. These meetings are for the lads only."

"Look, all I'm saying is I know this girl. She goes by Shorty on the street. Girl's got a wicked bad asshole for a pimp. He's keeping her son from her to keep her in line."

"Where are ye headed with this?" I ask.

"When I saw her last, she told me that she was getting her son back. That some guy promised he was going to help her. That he'd pay off her pimp if she did what he asked. Set her up with a whole new life."

The room falls silent, and the lads piece together the information Scarlett just tossed us. Donny must have promised to get her son back if she testified as a supposed witness. And then the feds would set her up with a new identity.

"That plan sounds like it requires an awful lot of chips to fall just right," Michael remarks.

"Aye," I agree. "Donny never did think things all the way through."

"She's scared shitless," Scarlett says. "I just thought maybe you don't have to kill her. Maybe you could help her get her son back instead. And send her on her way to somewhere else. I guarantee you won't have any more problems with her if you do."

"Ye can't guarantee something like that," Rory says, the irritation in his voice clear. He knows such a guarantee from Scarlett would likely put her at risk if this plan of hers ever did go south.

"I can and I will," she says. "I know this girl. She's had it rough, okay? She just wants out of this life. She's grasping at whatever life vest will keep her afloat."

The lads all look to me for an answer. Something that would have made me uncomfortable before, but now I take no issue with it. Because it isn't just me that's riding on this working out favorably, but Sasha and my child too. And I need to know that the man who comes home to her at the end of the day is one she can actually stomach to look at. But I also need to ensure her safety.

"We need to speak with this girl," I say. "Then we can sort it out. Dom, you and Scarlett give Alexei the details and he will get us everything we need."

He nods and stands up to do exactly that. Only his phone rings, and he answers it before he goes. The words are few and quiet, but the expression on his face tells me it isn't good news he's just received.

"We've got another problem," he says when he hangs up. "Niall's just had a massive heart attack."

Chapter Forty-Two

Sasha

"**I** don't want you to go," I argue, though I know it's totally unreasonable.

Ronan gives me a frustrated glance. I'm not being fair, but my anxiety is through the roof.

"I have to get this sorted," he says. "They're just going to have a wee chat with me, Sasha. It will be okay."

"But what about their witness?" I ask. "They're going to arrest you."

"The witness is here," Ronan answers me.

I blink at him, not sure I heard him correctly.

"Excuse me?"

"She's downstairs."

My stomach lurches. I don't want to know the details. But I can't stop myself from asking, anyway. I have to know. I have to know if he's telling me what I think he is.

"You mean, as in…"

"Alexei is having a word with her," Ronan explains. "That's all. No harm will come to her so long as she cooperates."

"Right." I blow out a breath and wrap my arms around myself.

Jesus, this world sometimes… it's too much. But I'm in it for good now, like it or not. It still doesn't make it any easier to come to terms with all of these mixed emotions inside of me. I don't want anyone to get hurt. But I also can't allow Ronan to go to prison.

He must be able to see the confliction on my face because he walks over and pulls me against him. His palm flattens over my belly, and my pulse flutters when he examines me with a soft expression.

"I'll do what I have to in order to protect the both of you, Sasha. And that does mean anything. But I want ye to know I'm not a monster. I'm trying to do what's right. I'm trying to believe we can sort this out another way."

"Can I talk to her?" I ask.

He frowns and almost immediately goes to shake his head. "This is mafia business."

"But it isn't just your business anymore," I argue. "This involves me too. I want to know we can trust her. I want to protect you too."

"I don't need ye to protect me," he huffs. "That's my role, Sasha. Make no bones about that, it always will be."

"I get that," I say. "I really do. But just let me talk to her. Let me see for myself. Just so I can be at ease. Otherwise, I'll be going out of my frigging mind wondering."

Ronan quietly considers my words for several moments, his eyes searching mine. He sees the worry on my face. And I know how it is with these guys. They want to take on the burden of protecting us and never let us fret over a thing. But he needs to realize right now I'm not that kind of woman. And he better just get used to it. Because when it comes to Ronan, I'm always going to worry.

And he may not comprehend it just yet, but I think when it comes to him and what we have, I'd do anything in order to protect it too.

"I have to head on," he says. "But Conor can take ye down to speak with her while Alexei is there. I don't want ye speaking with her at any other time. Or getting attached."

"I understand." I reach up and graze his cheek with a kiss which he turns into and meets with his own lips.

When he finally pulls away, he's even more reluctant to go. "Ye make it hard to leave you," he says.

"Good," I answer. "That's the way I want it."

I move to leave, but Ronan reaches out and grabs my arm. "Sasha?"

"Yes?"

"You can tell her we're keeping the dog, too."

***

The girl in the basement isn't what I expected.

At all.

She's young, extremely thin, and can't even be an inch over five feet. Judging from the way her toes are bouncing off the floor, she's scared out of her mind.

She's sitting in a chair with her hands folded in her lap while Alexei stares at her across the table. He isn't speaking right now, only observing. And while I've only known him a short time, I've never seen his gaze so cold as it is right now. This right here is the mobster. The other side of the coin. These guys all have one, but his is admittedly a little scarier than some of the others.

And I don't know whether to thank him or hate him for it. But in the end, my loyalty wins out, because I know he's doing this to protect us. To protect Ronan. And this girl is a threat. Until she proves otherwise, she will need to be treated as such.

Her eyes fly to mine when she sees me standing in the corner of the room. Alexei turns a moment later as though he didn't hear me come in. Conor is at my side, and he makes sure to tell him that Ronan gave me permission before he slips out the door. And then it's just the three of us.

"I wanted to see her myself," I explain to Alexei.

He nods and gestures at an empty seat at the table. I walk across the room and sit down, and the girl never takes her eyes from mine. She's looking at me like I'm the one who holds her fate in her hands, though it couldn't be farther from the truth.

"Hi," I greet her. "I'm Sasha."

"Hi," she whispers.

The room is quiet for a moment, save for the harsh breaths coming from her chest. Her fingers are wrapped around each other so tightly they're almost white. She's so thin that at first glance, one might assume she's a junkie. But her gray eyes are clear and I recognize the expression on her face all too well. That isn't drugs, but stress.

"Look," I begin. "We have a problem, you and I."

"We do?" she swallows, her eyes darting back to Alexei.

I've never been intimidating in my life, but right now, there's something else taking over inside of me. Maybe it's a mother's protective instincts. Maybe it's a love so fierce that it's given me the courage to do what I never could before. Either way, I feel calm and assured with what I'm about to say. And I know now that the choice is hers.

"We do," I answer. "Because you see, it's my boyfriend that you're ratting on. The father of my child."

Her eyes well up with tears, and her body starts to shake.

"We love each other," I tell her. "And we'd do anything to protect what we have. Do you get that?"

"I do," she whispers. "You have no idea just how much I get that..."

"So do you still think Donny is worth all of this?" I ask. "Because let me tell you..."

"He was supposed to help me get my son," she cries. "That's what he said. I'm doing this for my son. That's all. I have nothing against any of you. I just wanted to get my son back."

I glance at Alexei, and he nods. What she's saying is true. And a little bit of my resolve cracks. But then he throws me a bone.

"I have offered to retrieve her son for her. And Crow will send her away with what she needs to start a new life. If she should so choose."

"Right." I blow out a breath.

I look back at the girl, but it's clear she doesn't trust us. She doesn't believe that we'll follow through on what we're promising her. But she can't honestly expect us to be any worse than Donny. I can only imagine what he did to make her agree to this. He had a way of exploiting weaknesses. I'm not surprised in the least he chose to exploit hers too.

"We all have to do things we don't like in this life," I tell her. "I've had to do plenty of it. Make the hard choices. You're going to have to do that too. And if you choose right, then you will live. That's as simple as it can get."

"But how do I know I'll get my son back?" she asks. "I need more than your word to go on..."

"What choice do you have?" I ask her.

A tiny sound of defeat spills from her lips as she shakes her head and tears fall down her cheeks.

"Look, I don't know much for certain in this life, honey," I tell her. "But the one thing I know as sure as the sky is blue is that these guys don't go back on their word. If they say they'll get your son, they will get you your son. And they will walk through hell to do it. But that doesn't come free. Nothing in this life comes free."

She's quiet for a moment, and then her chin straightens and she lifts her head to meet my gaze. The tears have stopped falling, and she's come to a decision. I can only pray it's the right one.

"Okay," she says. "You have my word. If I get my son back, I will disappear. None of you will ever hear from me again."

Relief floods over me because there isn't a single part of me that doubts she's being sincere. Over the years, I've learned to read people pretty well. I've learned how to spot the monsters and the liars lurking just below the surface. This girl is neither of those things.

She's a pawn, like me. Like I was to Blaine and Donny. She did what she had to. But she has no agenda except for getting her son back. And I believe these guys will do the right thing.

"There's just one more matter," I tell her.

"What's that?" she asks.

"My boyfriend and I have grown rather fond of your dog. And well... we're keeping her."

I'm prepared for her to argue, but she doesn't. She just nods, and that's that. Daisy is officially part of the family.

Chapter Forty-Three

Ronan

The shite with the feds ends up taking a lot longer than I'd hoped. They questioned me, but with circumstances being what they were they didn't have enough to arrest me.

The syndicate has a barrister who is used for occasions such as these. He maintains his own connections within the judicial system and he uses them often in exchange for a hefty bonus from Niall. But when the feds get involved it can be a complication. They are used to dealing with mafia now. They know how it works. Witnesses disappear, evidence gets tampered with, things have a way of going wrong before they ever get to trial.

That's why often times they would rather get you to turn on your mates before it ever gets to a courtroom. But they don't understand the ways of the syndicate. They don't understand that the blood oath we swear is real and is for life.

"Fitz," Crow greets me when I walk into Slainte with the barrister in tow. A few of the other lads are here as well, preparing to discuss the future of the syndicate.

"Crow." I nod in his direction.

He shakes the barrister's hand and then we all head down to the basement where we generally meet on such occasions. The room is already set up with drinks when we sit down. Crow takes his place at the head of the table, with me right beside him. He folds his hands over the wood and glances around the room, the expression on his face solemn.

It goes without saying how much Niall means to him. He's like a father to Crow. He's been good to both of us, and I have nothing but respect for the man as well.

"I've been to see Niall," he says. "He's very ill and the docs say it's likely to be a long recovery for him."

"So what now?" Conor asks.

The room is quiet for a pause, and Crow's eyes are glassy when he looks to me. There have been few times I've seen the lad get such emotion in his eyes, so I know the situation is more serious than he's leading us to believe.

"Niall was of a sound mind," he continues. "And though I insisted we wait until he recovered to make any sort of big decisions, he didn't agree. He would like to be at home with his family. He's ready to retire."

Again, the room falls silent. The gravity of the situation sinks in as the lads reach for their glasses and make quiet toasts to Niall and his family. This means things are going to change now, in a big way. Crow will become boss of the MacKenna Syndicate. And he will choose his right hand man.

I'm not in the least surprised when his eyes fall on me a moment later.

"Fitz." He clears his throat. "I'm sure I don't even need to ask ye. But it's my choice, and if I have to choose from any of the lads, I know who I want by my side."

I'm quiet, trying to process what this means for me. He wants me to take on the role of underboss. Run Slainte and all the lads who deal operations through here. It's a heavy role, and I consider it as such.

I don't just have myself to think of anymore. Sasha might not like it. The higher up you move, the more protected you become. But this also means there's the potential for a bigger target on my back.

Crow reads the indecision weighing heavily on me, so he helps me along in his usual way.

"I know ye're going to be a father," he says. "Congratulations, by the way, Fitzy… I didn't know ye had it in you."

Some of the lads laugh, but it doesn't bother me in the way that it used to. I have Sasha, so they can laugh all they like.

"You'll be running the operations here at the club," he says. "No more foot work out on the streets. You said ye wanted more responsibility, Fitz, and this is it. This means less time in the basement. More time for you to spend with your family, which I'm sure Sasha will be happy with."

He leans back in his chair and gives me a moment to think about it. "So, what do ye say? I really can't do without you."

Crow has always been there for me. Has always had my best interests in mind. Even though his focus is keeping the syndicate afloat and running, his lads never fall by the wayside. I told him I wanted to do other things. Take on more responsibility. And this is my opportunity to do so. To prove to Sasha I can be the man she needs. The man our child needs.

"Aye." I give him my answer with a nod.

A smile cracks across his face and he slaps me on the back.

"Grand," he says. "That's just grand, Fitzy. We'll swear you in this evening."

"What about Sasha?" I ask.

Crow makes a gesture to Conor who scrambles out the door to retrieve the barrister who's still waiting outside. He comes and takes a place at the table, and we get down to business.

"Sasha." Crow looks to him. "What do we need to do to keep her safe?"

"At this stage," he says. "It's best she stays wherever she is. Once all of this has blown over, she can come back. But right now they can't use her against you if they don't know where she is."

I nod, because I suspected as much. But his next words catch me off guard.

"I'd also recommend you two get married, sooner rather than later," he says. "So for future situations such as these, you have spousal privilege to fall back on."

Crow looks to me and smirks. "Told ye to make an honest woman of her, Fitz."

I shrug, but even I can't hide the smile on my face this time. All of the lads are looking at me like I've gone mad. I doubt they've ever seen me smile before.

After the meeting wraps up, they filter out of the room and I stay behind with Crow. He probably suspects I want to speak with him in private. I do, but it's not about the matter at hand like he thinks.

He pours us both another drink and then gives me his attention.

"I need a baby," I tell him.

He's silent for a long while, tipping back the glass in his hand and downing the liquor inside it. "I'm not sure I heard ye correctly," he says. "In fact, I'm sure I didn't."

"For practice," I explain.

Now he's looking at me like I've gone mad as well.

"Don't tell me you couldn't do with some too," I argue. "When's the last time you were even around a wee baby?"

He shrugs. "I haven't a clue, Fitz."

"Aye." I nod. "So find us a baby."

Chapter Forty-Four

Sasha

A month has passed since I've been holed up at Alexei's. And I'm not at all happy with it, but I know that Ronan is keeping me safe until everything blows over. I haven't been able to see him as much since Alexei's house is so far out of the city and he's taken on the new role of Underboss.

He assured me that the extra hours aren't going to last forever, but just during the transition. He also assured me that this new role is going to be better for us. And while I was hesitant at first to know he was becoming even more deeply embedded into the syndicate, now I'm inclined to agree.

This change means he won't be out on the streets, putting himself at risk every day. He'll be handling business in the club and the men who work beneath him. And he won't be spending so much time in the basement which is what I really care about.

I know who Ronan is and I'm not going to ask him to change. I wouldn't want him to change. But I want him to know something besides violence. Besides blood. I want him to know what it's like to have a different sort of family. One besides the mafia.

Already, I see the differences in him. His priorities have changed. And when he shows up here in the middle of the night, his face tired and drawn, he's doing it for me. He could go home. But he told me once, in a sleepy murmur, that his home is here with me. Wherever I am that's where he'll be too.

The simplicity of his statement was so honest that he didn't understand how much those words could ever mean to me.

When I wake up this morning and find him with his leg tossed over me, keeping me in place, I smile. He never sleeps in, but it's past ten already, and here he is, still out like a light. I roll into him and graze his throat with my lips.

He groans and then his sleepy brown eyes flutter open. He's still barely coherent, but already he's kissing me back, grinding his hips into me. Ronan always takes me in the morning. And often when he gets home at night too, regardless of how tired he is. Sometimes, we even find each other in the middle of the night, in a dead sleep. Our bodies are bringing us together before our minds ever catch up to it.

This morning though, there's another change in him as he flips me over and moves inside of me. He's no longer rushed or out of control, but slow and gentle. His eyes are on mine, soft and filled with possession.

When I convulse around him, he ceases all movement. His breath is halted, his biceps and neck corded and taut. He's nervous for some reason. Which he hasn't been for a while now. But one thing I've learned with Ronan is that he usually takes a while to process things, and then they come up later unexpectedly.

"What is it?" I reach up and touch his face. He leans into my hand and closes his eyes.

"Sasha…" his voice cracks.

And then he's fucking me again. It's hard and fast now. His face is buried in my neck, and I'm cupping the back of his head, holding him against me. I don't know what's going on with him, but I also know not to push him. He'll tell me when he's ready.

And as it turns out, that's right after he releases himself on a long, painful groan inside of me. I'm still filled with him, kissing his neck when he blurts out what's on his mind.

"Would ye have me as your husband?"

My hands stop moving, my breath sputters, and I stare up at him in shock.

"Are you…" I croak. "Are you asking me to marry you?"

"Aye," he says carefully.

His brows are scrunched together, and he isn't blinking. At all. He's so worried I'm going to say no that he keeps looking for tells. He doesn't need them because I put him out of his misery quickly and without hesitation.

"Yes, Ronan."

"Yes?" he questions. "You will?"

I nod. But he still doesn't look convinced, so I kiss him to seal the deal. He gets so into it that he seems to forget his disbelief, which is exactly what I intended. And that's that.

He collapses beside me and pulls me into the crook of his arm. I nuzzle into him and breathe in his scent, my eyes fluttering shut in the safe haven he provides.

"Sasha?"

"Hmm?" I murmur sleepily against him.

"I don't know how I ever had the good fortune to find you."

***

When I wake up again, Ronan is gone. I suspect he probably had business in the city since that's usually where he goes. But then I hear a noise coming from down the hall. I swear I might be going crazy because it sounds like a baby.

I pad down the hall, following the sound of gibberish that's coming through a cracked door. And when I open it, I find the last thing I ever thought I'd see in my entire life.

Ronan and Lachlan are both hunched over a table, staring at the baby on top of it like they're trying to work out a puzzle of some sort. Alexei is supervising from the side as is Daisy from down below.

"No, see these little flips go like so," Ronan says as he points at the diaper on the table.

"I don't think they do, Fitz," Crow argues. "They don't stay like that."

"Maybe you could tape them," Alexei offers.

I clear my throat from the door, and all three of them look at me like deer in the headlights. Ronan's cheeks flush, and so do Lachlan's. Something I never in a million years thought he was capable of. I just caught the boss and the underboss of the Irish mob blushing over a baby.

"Um, guys..." I point at the half naked little boy laying on the center of the table. "You might want to do something about that before..."

A stream of pee flies up into the air and hits Lachlan on the arm. He stares down at it with a bewildered expression and then him and Ronan are scrambling to put the diaper on.

"Get me the tape," Ronan yells out to Alexei like it's a state of emergency.

"Do you want some help?" I ask them.

"No," both of them say together. And then Ronan adds, "we need to sort this out on our own."

I stifle a smile and slip quietly out the door. Although I'd very much like to stay and witness the rest of the stooges in all their glory, I have a feeling Ronan is attempting to take this very seriously. He's nervous about being a father. And the fact that he's practicing with Lachlan is pretty much testament to that.

Three hours later, I find him passed out in a chair downstairs with Daisy bundled up in his arms. Her head is lolled to the side, her tongue hanging out of her mouth while she snores against his chest. I retrieve my phone from my pocket and snap a photo of the moment before he can wake.

And when I stare at the screen with a huge stupid smile on my face, this is how I know he's going to be a good father.

Chapter Forty-Five

Sasha

After what seemed like an eternity, Ronan has finally given us the all clear to go home. I'm nervous for a whole heap of reasons and I can't even really figure out what they all are.

Mack still doesn't know about Talia. And even though I hardly saw her during my time at Alexei's, I know she's there. And I don't want to lie to her about it. Lachlan hasn't told her yet either, but at some point, one of us will need to.

I'm quickly learning that the syndicate has a lot more secrets than they'd like anyone to believe. Some of those work out to our advantage. Although, I'd never wish ill on Niall, in a way I'm grateful he retired. Because it left the burden of punishment for Ronan's betrayal up to Lachlan. And it's safe to say that it's pretty much been swept under the rug.

But there's also the small matter of dealing with the feds. Although Ronan assured me that it's all been handled, they still need to interview me about what happened at that safe house. So the day we get back to Boston that's where I spend the majority of the afternoon with my syndicate appointed lawyer at my side.

They wouldn't let Ronan come into the interview with me, but it wasn't as bad as I thought. The lawyer handled almost everything, just as Ronan said he would. Since there isn't enough evidence to indict Ronan or I with anything, we are officially free to begin our life together.

We've decided to have a small ceremony at Slainte just like Mack and Lachlan did. It's strange that the place I thought I'd never want to see again is where I'll be reciting my vows. But now that Ronan's in charge there, I couldn't imagine wanting to be anywhere else. We'll be surrounded by our friends and family. Which is exactly what the syndicate is. A family.

The only person who won't be there is Emily. When I told her I was marrying Ronan, she didn't have much to say about it. I'm honestly okay with that. Em is living her life, and I'm living mine. She might not understand my choices, but I've come to terms with them, and that's all that really matters.

Ronan is my life. My breath. My sole reason for existing sometimes. I know it sounds insane, but it's how I feel. We were put on this earth to find each other. And when he looks at me with those dark brown eyes like he's doing right now, I know what we have is one of a kind. A supernova. A love so rare, so unparalleled, it shines brighter than any other in existence.

He wraps his arm around me protectively and bundles me into the car, going so far as to reach down and buckle me in.

I'm smiling up at him, and when he catches me, his fingers graze my jaw and he kisses me. I grab his head and kiss him back, getting really into it before he pulls away.

"Sasha?"

"Hmm?"

"We have to go see about this baby," he says.

"Oh." I glance at his watch and check the time. "Right."

Ronan shuts the door and walks around to the driver's seat. He was relieved for all of two seconds upon leaving the interview, and now he's nervous all over again. But I am too. We're having our first scan today.

I've already got a little bump. Time is slipping away from me, and there's still so much to do. I have to get everything for a nursery and start doing some reading. Mack's called me about twenty times freaking out because she read that her feet are going to get huge and never return to normal. Then she started telling me about the uterus stretching to the size of a watermelon. That's when I told her to stop calling me.

But now I'm all panicky and trying to stay calm for Ronan's sake. I keep thinking about all the things Mack said and how she joked we might have to join the circus after. All I can picture is me morphing into something completely unrecognizable. Already, I feel huge and I'm paranoid Ronan's going to think so too.

Logically, I know I'm worrying over nothing. When he sees me naked, he's all over me. Even more so than usual. He hasn't said so, but I think he likes the sight of me pregnant with his baby. He tells everyone when we see them. He might as well be walking around with a banner that proclaims he got me pregnant.

He pulls into the parking lot of the doctor's office and cuts the engine. But before he can get out, I reach over and take his hand in mine.

"I'm nervous," I tell him. "I know you are too."

My hand trembles, and my voice is hoarse when I speak. "I've been trying to stay strong, because I know this whole thing really freaks you out. But I'm freaked out too, Ronan."

He frowns, and then pulls away from me, stepping out of the car. The dam almost breaks loose right then when I think he's going to remind me that we have a schedule to keep. But instead, he walks around to my side and pulls me out of the car.

He wraps his arms around me and kisses my face. I'm shaking with nerves and he's completely cool and calm now. I didn't expect that. Since we found out and his first reaction, I thought I would have to tread lightly the whole pregnancy. Give him information in little bits and never tell him any of my fears.

But right now, this man holding me isn't the same one who walked out on me that day. This man is my protector. Rock-solid and cool-headed and exactly what I need in this moment.

"Sasha." He murmurs between kisses. "Ye don't need to handle me with kid gloves. It's my job to care for and protect you. Always. If ye're nervous, I want ye to tell me so. I might not have the right words, but I'll try."

I shake my head and a few tears leak out of my eyes.

"I know," I tell him. "I should have just told you. I've just been worried that I'm going to freak you out if I say anything."

"I'm already freaked out," he admits. "But I'm not going anywhere. I wouldn't ever have any notion to. The only place I want to be is here with you. And I don't think ye have any reason to worry. Ye're going to do a grand job of this, I've no doubts about that."

"But Mack said we're going to look like circus freaks," I sob.

Ronan frowns again and shakes his head. "That isn't possible, Sasha. Ye're the most beautiful woman I've ever had the good fortune of seeing. That isn't going to change. No matter how many babies I put inside of you."

"Then I'm going to be a bad mother," I whine.

"Sasha," Ronan's voice grows stern. "Ye're stalling now."

"So what?" I argue. "I don't want to go inside. I think I'm going to have a heart attack. Feel it. It's going crazy in there."

I'm not lying about that. I'm right in the middle of a panic attack. I don't know why, only that I'm so frigging nervous.

Ronan leans down and cups my face in his hands. "Do the counting thing you do," he says. "I'll help if you want."

"You know about that?" I blink up at him as I clutch at my chest.

"Aye," he answers. "I know everything there is to know about you."

I'm still focusing on that little tidbit when he grabs my hand and tilts my chin up. "How does it go, exactly? Five things, right?"

"Right," I answer.

I close my eyes and take a deep breath, the scent of Ronan calming me a little.

"Roasted pine nuts and malt liquor," I whisper. "That's you."

Another breath. I open my eyes and meet his, soft and steady and sure.

"Dark chocolate."

I take another breath, and he kisses me again. When he pulls away, I can still taste him on my tongue. "Mint."

"Two more," he encourages.

My breathing has calmed already, and I feel better, but I like that he's doing this with me. So I continue. The sounds of Boston are all around us. The cars and the people and the usual noise. But the only thing that resonates as I press my face against his chest is him. "Heartbeat."

Ronan takes our connected hands and moves them both over my belly, and he finishes the last one for me.

"Our baby."

Chapter Forty-Six

Ronan

Over the course of my life, I think I've been in a doctor's office only once. When I was still a young lad and Crow's mammy forced me to go.

I don't like these places. They remind me of the dungeon in the basement at Slainte. The one where I handle the clients.

That thought is only confirmed when I spot the table they want to put Sasha up on. I reach out and grab her arm to stop her, but then I remember how out of sorts she was in the parking lot. She doesn't need my worries added to hers.

When she glances back at me in question, I help her up on the table even though everything inside of me is screaming not to. Then I stand right beside her, so if the technician tries anything funny, she'll have to contend with me.

The nurse goes over some questions with Sasha, all of which I listen to with the utmost attention. I feel as though I should know these things. Or that I should have asked her myself, maybe. I make a mental note to ask her more about them later.

They check a whole load of things I never thought to worry about before. Now I find myself wondering if she's eating enough. Or carrying heavy things when I'm not around. I know she's been taking baths. She could slip if I'm not there. Or burn herself when she's cooking. I'm in the middle of sorting out a round the clock security detail when the technician comes in.

She instructs Sasha to lay back and smears some sort of goopy stuff onto her belly. It's already round and I have a hard time looking away whenever I see it. I like knowing that my baby is inside of her. That I was the one who did that to her. I can't imagine ever liking it with anyone else.

But I want to see what Sasha and I made together. I'm staring at the screen impatiently when Sasha reaches for my hand. Her eyes are panicky again, and I haven't a clue how to comfort her. But I try, just as I promised I would.

I lean down and kiss her on the cheek which she seems to like. I do that a lot now. The technician smiles at us, but I don't care. Because Sasha is mine. And I'll do what I like with her.

A noise comes on over the speakers, and both of us move our attention back to the screen as the wand glides over her belly.

I see it. I see my baby. It's just a wee fuzzy spot on the screen as the technician points out. But it's there. And then there's the heartbeat. Strong, like I knew it would be.

The technician starts to speak, and Sasha does too.

"Shh..." I tell them.

Sasha blinks up at me and laughs. "Did you just shush me?"

I clear my throat and my cheeks burn when I realize I did. "I just wanted to listen for a moment longer."

"You can listen as long as you like," the technician says.

So I do. I listen and take it all in. Memorizing every detail on the screen. When I finally look away, Sasha is smiling up at me. She doesn't seem nervous anymore, and I'm glad.

"Okay," I tell the technician.

She points out a few things on the photo and checks everything over. She says that she can't yet tell if it's a boy or a girl, but it makes no difference. Sasha has it in her head that she doesn't want to know, and I agreed that was fine.

I know it's going to be a boy anyhow. It has to be. Because I haven't a bloody clue what to do with a girl.

She wraps up the session and slips out of the room, allowing Sasha a moment to get herself back together. But before she can, I lean down and kiss her. She's the most beautiful woman I've ever seen. It can't be helped, especially right here and now.

When I pull away, she's breathless and flustered. And I like that too.

"Can we go home now?" she asks. "And stay there... for like a week."

"Aye," I tell her. "Let's get you home."

Chapter Forty-Seven

Sasha

When I said that I wanted Ronan to stay home with me, I didn't really think he'd be able to. But he's been here for four days, and he's now officially driving me nuts.

Apparently he took everything that was mentioned at the doctor's appointment as potential red flags. He's been watching my every movement. Helping me downstairs. Refusing to let me cook. Telling Daisy she's not allowed to sit near my belly anymore. I drew the line when he tried to install safety grab bars all over the bathroom, citing the potential slip risks.

"Ronan."

"Aye?" he glances away from his book, his eyes scanning over me like something might be wrong.

"Don't you have to go back to work?"

He blinks at me. And then frowns. "Do ye not want me here with you?"

"Of course I do," I answer him. "But I also want things to be normal. I'd rather you got into the routine of running the club now so when I really need you later on, you can be here."

"I have it all sorted," he says. "I can be here now."

"Okay, but…" I blow out a breath. "You need to chill a little, alright?"

"I don't understand," he answers.

And I know he really doesn't.

"I'm okay. The baby's okay. I know I had a little freak out at the doctor's office. But I'm good now. I don't want you to be so worried about everything, alright? It makes me anxious when you do that."

"But I love you," is his reply.

And I smile, because… well, Ronan.

I crawl across the sofa and sit down in his lap, wrapping my arms around his neck and kissing him.

"I love you too, Ronan," I murmur against him. "You're lucky you're adorable. Because sometimes you drive me crazy."

"Now ye understand how I feel," he says, cupping my ass in his hands. "I worry about ye all the bleeding time, Sasha. All the time. I don't know how to make it stop."

"That's love," I answer. "Wait until you meet our baby. It's only going to get worse."

He kisses me deep and hard and starts pawing at my body beneath my clothes. And then he's carrying me down the hall to the bedroom, discarding them along the way. While it took me months to get him naked the first time, now he doesn't want it any other way. He likes to feel his skin against mine. And I do too.

He makes love to me. It's still feverish, but gentle too. Even after all this time, it still feels like the first time. He comes inside of me and stays there, kissing all over my face.

"This time next week," he says. "Ye're finally going to be my wife."

***

During the week before our wedding, I spend a lot of time picking out things for the nursery. Ronan goes along wherever I do and never complains. He even puts everything together too.

It shouldn't surprise me, but he's very handy at that type of stuff as well. He always reads the instructions three times over before he begins, but once he's done that he whips all the pieces into shape in no time at all.

I like to watch him do these things. Such simple things. But it's part of building a life together. Piece by piece.

When I think about marrying him in only five short days, it still feels like a dream. Our life is nowhere near perfect. I'm marrying into the mafia. This world can be dark and chaotic and full of the unknown. But the one thing I know for certain is that with Ronan at my side, we can navigate it together.

I don't want our pasts to dictate our future. I want to wash away the bad and replace it with good. Which is why I've been working on something for him, whenever I can find the time.

Ronan's life has been filled with evil and torment and pain. He has a dark side, but there's so much good in him too.

I want to remind him of that. I want him to know that he isn't only what his childhood created him to be. So I've drawn something for him. A man with angel's wings. Wings that I hope will spread the length of his back and cover his old tattoos. The codes that were engraved on him when he had no choice in the matter.

It came to me in a dream one night while I lay at his side. And I haven't been able to stop thinking about it since. But now that I've finished, and I'm getting ready to unveil it, I feel sick.

I don't know if he's going to like it. I don't know if he'd even be open to getting another tattoo. And I certainly don't want him to think that I want to change him. Or that I don't accept him for who he is. That isn't the case at all.

All of these thoughts are going through my mind when he looks up at me from his place on the couch. He's reading, and I'm watching TV. Which I insisted we buy. Ronan didn't deny me. And more and more, I catch him watching the true crime shows with me. I think they fascinate him.

But right now, he's looking at me. Like he knows something is up. Which is weird because I used to think he wasn't perceptive at all. But really, Ronan is more perceptive than anybody would ever know. He just doesn't let onto it.

"All good?" His eyes skim over my belly. "Are ye not feeling well?"

"I'm okay," I tell him. "Just nervous."

He closes the book in his hands and gives me his full attention.

"How can I make it better?" he asks, with such sincerity in his eyes I can't help but smile at this handsome man. My soon to be husband. My rock, and my life.

"I love you," I blurt. "You know that, right?"

"Aye," he answers. "I do."

"And I don't want you to change. Ever. Unless you want to, I mean. I just..."

My words fall away and I get that panicky feeling in my chest again. Ronan reaches out and pulls me closer, his eyes meeting mine.

"Tell me anything, Sasha," he says. "Ye have no need to be worried."

"I made you something," I admit. "But I'm not sure you're going to like it."

His thumb skates over the back of my hand, and just that small gesture has a way of anchoring me to him and keeping the panic at bay.

"Show me," he insists.

I get up and walk to the cabinet, pulling out the file folder that has the drawing inside. I'm chewing on my lip as I thrust it into his hands.

"It's just an idea," I tell him. "You don't have to do it. But I thought if you wanted to cover up your tattoos…"

Ronan opens the file and stares down at the drawing. For a really long time. The room is entirely too quiet. And I'm sure he's going to hate it.

"This was really stupid." I try to take the folder back, but he keeps hold of it, his eyes taking in every detail the way they always do.

"I like it," he says.

That's it. Simple and to the point. And just so Ronan. But I need more.

"You do? Really?"

"Aye," he answers gruffly. "You drew it for me. So I like it. I fancy all of your drawings. But this one is mine."

A blush creeps over my cheeks and I wring my hands together. I sometimes forget that Ronan was watching me when I didn't know it. That he's probably seen a lot of things I wouldn't normally have shown anyone. Like my drawings. My journal. My underwear.

"I'll get it done tomorrow," he says, interrupting my thoughts.

"Tomorrow?" I question. "But you'll need to make an appointment. Find the right artist…"

"The syndicate has a lad who does them," he says. "I'll have him come tomorrow."

"Oh."

"It's settled then." He reaches for my hand and pulls me into his lap.

He kisses my face and nuzzles into my neck. His words are quiet and soft and betraying a rare emotion when he whispers into my ear.

"Thank you, love."

Chapter Forty-Eight

Sasha

"**I**'m as big as a frigging house," Mack whines as she stares at herself in the mirror. "Are you sure you want me to walk with you out there? Nobody will be looking at you when you have me thundering down the aisle beside you."

I laugh at her, and it turns out to be just what I need at the moment. I'm a nervous wreck.

"Mack, you look beautiful," I assure her. "And I've got nobody else to walk out there with me. I really need you."

"Oh fine." She pouts. "You're gonna play that card, huh?"

"I am."

She turns to me and starts fussing over my dress. A white floor length, empire waist ensemble with a touch of gold trim. It's not what I imagined myself getting married in. But when I was looking at dresses, Ronan admitted his favorite color on me was white.

He likes to think of me as pure and good. The light to his darkness. I'm definitely no angel, but he's not the devil he thinks he is either. So for him, I wear white.

I hadn't planned on doing anything in the traditional way. I mean, I'm getting married in a strip club. Run by the mafia. There's pretty much nothing traditional about that. But it turns out, Ronan's very traditional in some aspects.

He wanted to see me walk down the aisle. He wanted to show the world that I'm his. I couldn't deny him.

So even though I'm a bit panicky at the prospect of having everyone's eyes on me, I know it will all go away the moment I see his. Standing there, waiting for me.

The music starts, and I grab Mack's arms in a vice grip.

"It's okay, Sash," she says. "Just breathe."

I do. I take a deep breath and close my eyes.

"There's nobody out there but Ronan, okay. Just focus on him."

"Okay." I nod and she guides me out the door.

I'm shaking like a leaf, and my stomach flips when I see the room full of faces. They are all staring at me.

Mack squeezes my hand in hers and gives me a much needed support.

"Look at Ronan," she whispers.

I do. I find his eyes at the end of the aisle. Soft and brown and focused only on me. He's anxious too. Impatient. This was all his idea, but now it's clear he just wants me there next to him. He doesn't like to have me out of arm's reach, especially around this many people. It's just his way of protecting me.

I steel myself with several more deep breaths and take a step. And then another. And my eyes never leave Ronan's. He's the most handsome man I've ever seen. Right now, in his suit, he's even more so. It's the same suit he always wears. But today it's different. Today he looks like my husband.

Mack hands me off to Ronan at the end of the aisle, and he takes my hands in his. Almost immediately, my shaking stops, and everything else falls away. It's only us now, and the sound of Rory's voice as he performs the ceremony.

I recite the vows that were crafted for members of the syndicate. They are by no means normal. They speak of family, honor, and blood. Loyalty and protecting one another at all costs.

They couldn't be more perfect if I'd written them myself.

I will always protect Ronan, just as I know he will always protect me.

When Rory moves onto the blood rite, he hands me the ceremonial blade first. Ronan and I both knew we wouldn't be able to cut each other, which was tradition, so we opted to do it ourselves. The only other option was having Rory perform the ritual, however I had a feeling Ronan might very well murder him if he cut me.

So with Ronan's eyes on mine, while Rory recites the words that bind our souls together for eternity, I take the blade to my finger and then hand it off to Ronan. He does the same, and then our hands are bound together with a piece of ribbon.

"My *anam cara*," we both repeat together.

They are the same words carved into our wedding rings in Ogham script. The words that mean, quite simply, his soul is mated to mine.

The ritual is more powerful than I expected it to be. Raw energy pulses between us, our souls and our love binding us as one. There are tears in my eyes when we exchange the rings. I've never felt more emotional in my life. The love that I have for this man overwhelms me. That love is reflected in Ronan's eyes.

And finally come the words that seal our fates.

My life, my love, my breath.

May we always have each other, in this life and the next.

Rory hands us a cup which we both drink from, and then he proclaims the words that make it official.

We are now husband and wife.

Ronan kisses me, in front of everyone, and he doesn't hold back. When he finally pulls away at Rory's insistence, I'm laughing and a little off kilter.

We both walk to the alter and perform the last and final step of the ceremony. The lighting of the candle.

And then he promptly bundles me up into his arms and carries me to the back office which he insists is custom as well. I'm pretty sure he's making that part up, but I go with it, because… Ronan.

Always Ronan.

Epilogue

Sasha

I'm still half asleep when the creaking of the rocking chair down the hall rouses me.

I glance at the clock and realize that I must have slept through her cries. I'm not in the least surprised that Ronan didn't.

He once told me he worried he wouldn't do well with her cries. He was right. Because every time he hears them, he's the first to her side. She's got him wrapped around her little finger.

I untangle my hair from my face and pad down the hall, peeking in to find Ronan in the rocking chair. Saoirse is bundled in his arms, sucking from the bottle in his hand.

He picked the name. A play on my own. I love it. I love everything about my baby girl. And my husband. And the sight of the two of them together right now, even in my sleep deprived state, still steals my breath away.

He leans down and kisses her forehead with the gentlest of touches, and then his eyes meet mine across the room. Even after all this time, he still makes me feel like I'm on a rollercoaster when he looks at me like that. My whole world is off kilter, and yet it's never been more perfect. Saoirse starts to fuss, and he sets the bottle aside and rubs her back, soothing her almost immediately.

I'm not going to lie and say that I have the same effect on her. I don't. But that's just Ronan. He is the balm to both of our troubles. Our calm in the storm. Whenever she's upset, all he has to do is hold her, and she's okay. I know the feeling well.

And Ronan certainly doesn't mind. He likes that he can calm her. Being a parent has changed him so much. Made him see the emotions he is capable of. He's the proudest father I've ever had the fortune to know. The fact that he's my husband and the father of my child is proof that lightning really can strike twice. I don't know how I ever got so lucky.

When Saoirse is asleep, he bundles her into the crib and then comes back to me. His hand grazes over my cheek, strong and warm.

"Ye should be sleeping," he says. "I didn't want to wake you."

"You didn't," I tell him.

He kisses me and leads me back down the hall to our bedroom. We're both exhausted. But I've never been happier when he falls in beside me and then rolls me beneath his solid frame.

He kisses my neck and gropes around under my nightgown as I tug his briefs down and free his cock. We can barely keep our eyes open, but we can't seem to keep our hands off each other either. That's one thing that hasn't changed.

He's moving inside of me while I clutch at his back and he kisses me all over. It doesn't last. We never do. But these few brief stolen minutes that we get to connect like this are everything to me.

When we both finish, he stays inside of me for a while until his breathing calms. I stroke his back and he's nearly asleep when I whisper in his ear.

"I need to get back on the pill," I tell him. "Before I end up like Mack."

She's already pregnant again with her second. A fact that she never lets Lachlan forget.

"What's wrong with that?" Ronan murmurs sleepily. "We make a good baby."

"We do," I agree. "But I want to enjoy this one for a while longer before another comes along."

Ronan falls onto his side and his fingers stroke over my face. "Okay, love."

And that's that. Things are pretty much always this easy with Ronan. He doesn't argue with me unless it's about my safety.

We just are. We exist in our own little bubble, with the exception of Lachlan and Mack who we see often.

The syndicate is running smoother than it ever has. Ronan manages the club as efficiently as he does everything. And then he comes home to me. Always.

Whatever fears I had, whatever concerns… they don't exist anymore. I don't know if it will always be this way. But what I do know, is that Ronan and I will fight to protect what we have.

And God help anyone who ever tries to take that away.

***

THE END.

Thank you so much for reading REAPER. If you enjoyed it, please consider leaving an honest review on Amazon or Goodreads. You can keep an eye out for my other book releases by following me on social media. All of my links can be found on azavarelli.com

Acknowledgments

Where do I even begin? I have been blessed with the good fortune of having so many people to thank that you might just want to buckle up for this.

Dani Kermon, my friend and confidante. You're always there when I need you and helped me through many of my bad days during the last few months. Words can't express how much that means to me, always.

Melissa Crump. My superstar PA/Admin/BookBestie/ and most importantly my friend. I don't know what I'd do without you. Like seriously, I think someone might turn me into the lost and found. Counting down the days until BIBC 2017 when I can finally meet you!

My street team, The Dark Rebels. You guys are true rockstars, out there promoting my work and being there to support me. I am awed by all that you do for me.

A. Zavarelli's fan group. The place where shenanigans abound and there's always a plethora of men in kilts. You ladies keep me sane. And happy. Thank you for your friendship.

Amy Halter. Beta reader extraordinaire and the woman who inspired nurse Amy~ you are a legend. Never tone it down for anyone ;)

And a special mention to Kristina Lindsey (Chicago 2017 we will make it happen!), Tanaka Kangara, Candace Shuford Kauffmen, Lisa Lajcarov (#weirdosforlife), Agnese Maria Kohn, Belinda Visser, Victoria Stolte, Claudia Bost, and Louise Brodie.

There are a million more, but I'm going to check myself there. This book community is the craziest and best thing to ever happen to me, and I'm so happy to call all of you my friends.

Ciao!

Works by A. Zavarelli

Echo: A Bleeding Hearts Novel Volume One

Stutter: A Bleeding Hearts Novel Volume Two

CROW: Boston Underworld #1

Falling into Temptation

Falling into Exposure

Falling into Surrender

Falling Series Boxed Set

An Escort for Christmas

One Last Gift

Made in the USA
Columbia, SC
03 April 2018